D0742982

Bone
Dance

A Collection
of Musical Mysteries
by the Ladies' Killing Circle

edited by
Sue Pike and
Joan Boswell

RENDEZVOUS
PRESS

Cover art: Christopher Chuckry

LE CONSEIL DES ARTS DU CANADA DEPUIS 1957 | THE CANADA COUNCIL FOR THE ARTS SINCE 1957

We acknowledge the support of the Canada Council for the Arts for our publishing program. We acknowledge the support of the Government of Ontario through the Ontario Media Development Corporation's Ontario Book Initiative.

Napoleon Publishing/RendezVous Press
Toronto, Ontario, Canada

Printed in Canada

07 06 05 04 03   5 4 3 2 1

National Library of Canada Cataloguing in Publication

Bone dance : a collection of musical mysteries / the Ladies' Killing Circle ; edited by Joan Boswell and Sue Pike.

ISBN 1-894917-05-7

1. Detective and mystery stories, Canadian (English). 2. Canadian fiction (English)--21st century. 3. Canadian fiction (English)--Women authors. I. Boswell, Joan, date- II. Pike, Sue, date- III. Ladies' Killing Circle

PS8323.D4B66 2003   C813'.08720806   C2003-903478-X

In memory of Audrey

LADIES' KILLING CIRCLE

Also available by the
Ladies' Killing Circle:

Fit to Die
(RendezVous Press, 2001)
Menopause is Murder
(General Store Publishing, 1999)
Cottage Country Killers
(General Store Publishing, 1997)
The Ladies' Killing Circle
(General Store Publishing, 1995)

Table of Contents

Unchained Melody

More fortissimo. Lift your voice higher.
Your singing is terrible, where is your fire?
Fill up your lungs. You'll never get it right.
Practice, more practice, if it takes all the night!
You push me too hard, she gasped, in despair.
You sit there so smug, relaxed in a chair.
But you will get yours, rang out in her head,
And she forced a high C as she thought of him dead.
Well, her sharp note rose high, vibrating the room,
And the acoustic ceiling started to boom,
And the chandelier fell with that lethal note
And his tirade was stopped by a shard in the throat.

Joy Hewitt Mann's *work has appeared in hundreds of publications internationally. She has won the Leacock Award for poetry and the Acorn-Rukeyser Award. Boheme Press, Toronto, published her short story collection,* Clinging to Water, *in 2000. Boheme will publish her first full-length poetry collection,* Bone on Bone, *and her first novel,* Lacrima Christi, *in 2003. She is working on her next novel,* Los Penitentes.

Knocking on Heaven's Door

Cecilia Kennedy

Who set fire to Glen Wylie's barn? That question brought my boss, Sergeant Carr, to the hospital the night my son was born. He tracked me down at the display case of healthy newborns, where I looked past to the glass room marked INTENSIVE CARE: NO ADMITTANCE. No infant visible, just four white uniforms pulling lights and tubes and equipment toward a tiny hidden table.

Though I'd been on duty that night, I didn't see the big timbers of Wylie's barn collapse. Didn't even hear about it for hours, because I was holding April's hand in the nightmare light of the delivery room. This baby had showed up weeks ahead of schedule, a frantic arrival nothing like the gentle fiction we'd been prepared for in that birthing class. And then Intensive Care had kidnapped the baby.

So my mind was elsewhere when Carr fired off a rapid, "Hey, Tony, congratulations," and scanned the lineup for a baby with the Aardehuis label. When he didn't see one, he skipped straight to quizzing me about Glen Wylie and the likelihood that he might have torched his own barn.

"Fire guys say it was arson. Nothing clever about it: good old gasoline. You think he might a done it? Place is insured to the max."

*   *   *

My sergeant is a round-the-clock kind of cop. Neither sleet nor snow nor the birth of babies matter when he has a problem to solve. I could be like that too, but, though still wearing my OPP constable's uniform, that night my mind was down the hall, where April lay in the recovery room. Alone, because she'd sent me to find out what was happening to our son. I watched that glass room for the emergence of some oracle, a good word I could bring her. In my pocket a list of people to call with the news. Except I didn't know what the news might be.

Still, it was a relief to look away from that bright room and focus on something as uncomplicated as Sergeant Carr and a sixtyish farmer with a rep for thrift, perfectionism and bad temper.

Glen Wylie. The name meant loner. Pristine fence lines. Prize winning Aberdeen Angus herd. A wife who'd left years back, a son and daughter not seen in years. The burned barn yearly painted.

"Wylie wouldn't do it," I said, as the curtains on the glass room snapped shut. "That place was his life's work. Did they get the livestock out?"

"Barbecued," said Carr.

"Then for sure it wasn't him."

Odd how the brain can work on more than one plane: asking what they were doing with that small new person I'd caught the barest glimpse of before they'd abducted him. Simultaneously certain Glen Wylie wouldn't burn a barn with livestock in it. Memory serving up a 4H show ring from years past, Glen Jr. taking second with a young bull; later, in the calf pens, kicked hard with his father's steel-toed boot because he'd

3

forgotten to keep the water topped up. That man let nothing trouble his animals.

But what the hell were they doing behind those drapes?

"What day is it?" I asked.

Carr gave me an odd look, but hey, a lot had happened in the last few hours.

"One in the morning, Sunday. They figure the fire started about ten o'clock last night." He looked cute for a split second and said, "That was Saturday."

"Who called it in?"

"Neighbour saw the smoke around half past. Volunteer firemen got there pretty quick, but there wasn't much left when Wylie came home. Says he was at the Legion."

"He was. As a matter of fact, I had a run-in with him downtown. Must have been on his way to the Hall. Tried to drive through the intersection closed for that Busker Festival I was working. Bashed his truck into a hot dog stand and took some convincing to pay the damage. But there's his alibi."

"Or his cover," said the sergeant, who liked to harvest my brain for useful local knowledge so he could ignore it. "But thanks." Then he paused to look through the glass at the sound and healthy newborns in the foreground. "Which one's yours?"

"Past there in the next room."

"Just cleaning him up, eh? Shouldn't you be with the little woman?"

If this turned out all right, I'd smile, telling my independent April she'd been called my little woman. For now I let it pass, let Carr say, "Well, congratulations on the boy. What's his name?"

* * *

The boy. The boy had no name. So far, he was just a blue-faced wiggle of weak complaint who'd panicked the doctor with his feeble breathing. Six pounds, four. Six pounds of person struggling for breath. April waiting for a word. Me standing here stuck in a moment, waiting for the future to show its face.

How had it come to this?

Foolish question. It had come by means of falling in love with April. Small, dark-haired April, fresh as the whole season of spring. Falling into bed more than once. In spite of all precautions, lying beside her one early morning to take in the news that she was pregnant. Thoughts tangling in my mind like coloured electrical wires in a switch box. How had the methods of two well-educated, intelligent people failed? And we weren't married. Or even close to it, as far as I could tell. Did she want it? The black-wire thought that she might have plotted it.

Then the last strand: this would make me a father. I hung on to that one, turning the idea left and right, and found it hot and frightening to hold, but also tingling with current.

What I said to the still, waiting warmth of woman in the bend of my arm was, "Should we get married?"

And though she said no, not because of this, it appeared I'd said the right thing, jumped a host of fears to land where she felt comfortable.

"What's his name?" Carr had asked. It seemed wrong to be so unprepared with an answer. For months we'd played name-the-baby like it was the best game in town.

"Thomas?"

"Too plain."

"Vladimir?"

"If you're going ethnic, it ought to be Dutch." Then I'd start rhyming off the names of distant cousins: Wisse, Annemieke, Ysbrandt, Laurens...

5

"Hey, this kid's half Irish. Seamus, Siobhan, Kieran, Aidan..."

"What's the last name going to be then?"

"Both," she'd said, decisively. "O'Connor Aardehuis."

"It'll end up being Aardehuis every day, just because it comes last," I told the feminist free thinker but, like always, she surprised me.

"Better that way. Better for a kid to have the father's name. The world hasn't changed that much." She smiled. "Poor thing'll pay for it by having it mangled all the time."

Just seven hours ago, we'd still been kicking names around, thinking we had three weeks to get serious. But all along, I thought there was one name she really wanted and just hadn't put on the table.

She'd met me downtown where I was working extra duty at The Armagh Thanksgiving Busker Festival. A brain wave of the Downtown Business Association, the party shut the main street of our little town to cars so pedestrians could saunter around spending money and enjoying an imported selection of street musicians, jugglers and fire eaters.

Watching the crowds mill across King Street, I had to admit it was looking like a success. The weather had cooperated with a crisp-as-apples October day. The hours stretched with that long weekend feeling. Every twenty minutes, the shuttle bus from the parking lot at the high school discharged a new crew of saunterers. They wandered happily between the apple sellers and craft vendors, pausing to watch the buskers perform.

"I've been thinking about Benjamin," April said as we walked away toward the war memorial square, where the main show took place. Sometimes it seemed that, as the rest of her grew, her face narrowed, got more intense and focussed. Sometimes I missed the other look, the soft, unworried, ready-to-laugh face I'd fallen in love with.

"I love the way you move like that," I teased. "Forward and sideways at the same time."

"Go to hell, Tony," she said. "How would you like to drive your cruiser with loose wheels?"

But she refused to be derailed. "So how about Benjamin?"

"Ben. Benny. Benjy?"

"Okay, okay, you don't like it."

"I just think a boy's name should be short. Two syllables max."

"But girls can be fancy? Okay, then. Isabel, Imogene, Edwina."

"How about something known to civilized man. Like Emily." For days, I'd been pushing Emily.

She didn't answer, because that was when Glen Wylie's pickup truck came down the side street, saw the green light but not the ROAD CLOSED sign, and bashed into the side of a hot dog stand. By the time I got there, Glen was out of the truck, face to face with Peter Walker, the guy who'd sat beside me in Grade Ten typing, new owner of the greasy spoon on Main Street. Trying to pick up a few extra bucks on the tourists, Pete had brought his business out into the road, and now half his ketchup packets and weiners lay on the pavement.

But it was Wylie cursing. Goddamn road closing. Goddamn clowns from out of town. Goddamn cart blocking the road for a man on his way to his beer and four hours of cribbage like every Saturday night.

Under the tractor cap, Wylie's face reddened with high blood pressure and rage. I knew Pete had a temper and took no crap from anyone, and he glared right back. "What about my stuff?" he demanded. "A hundred bucks of supplies ruined here. Never mind what I could have made."

"Never would 'a happened if you stayed on the sidewalk where you belong. What about this dent in my truck? Who's paying for that?"

It took ten minutes to convince Wylie that he was looking at a failing-to-stop ticket from me if he didn't settle Pete Walker with a couple of bills. By then he'd insulted pretty well everyone there: me (bloody cops), the parents of the kids who got too close to look at the dented fender (get them brats off there before I whack 'em where it hurts) and the buskers who took a break from their juggling and unicycling to watch the fuss (grow up and get a real job).

"Hippies and sluts, that's what you are," the last directed at the only woman on the circuit, a skinny redhead who called herself Circus Daisy.

Daisy just stared at Glen like she was collecting eccentric specimens of rural life, then hopped on her unicycle and rode away, flipping the backside of her skimpy skirt at the old crank. The crowd laughed, and finally he handed over the cash, climbed into his truck and drove off toward the Legion.

The buskers had turned out to be an odd bunch, not the tame kids in clown suits I'd expected. A young fire eater with singed eyebrows and the show name of Flame Sucker Bob told me Armagh was the last big busking party before winter drove them south. Young and mostly male, they wore the signs of life on a hard road: burnt skin, tattoos, flamboyant costumes fraying at the seams. A squinting sarcasm lurked under the patter tossed out with multicoloured balls and disappearing scarves of silk, and a cop's instinct said these were people to watch, people who travelled on the edge with nothing to lose.

I could tell by the way she perked up and listened that April's instinct was different.

A juggler with huge plaid pants jumped onto a pair of

stilts. The tall sticks clumped the edge of the crowd with a few fake almost-falls as he grinned fifteen feet above.

"Any Americans with us today?" When someone shyly raised a hand, he formed a mock gun hand aimed straight on, bellowed, "POW!" Grinned again and said, "Just wanted to make you feel at home."

Then a contrite pout and, "Oops. Don't worry folks, this is family entertainment..."

Flame Sucker Bob came next, dipping the head of his sticks into fuel, setting them ablaze, talking all the while about fire and ashes, sounding now like a crazy circuit preacher (fire, the purifying fire of cleansing and retribution...) then, between mouthfuls of flame, yapping out of the side of his mouth (have to do this 'cuz I say so many bad words).

Then Circus Daisy jumped onto a six-foot unicycle.

"Oh! I'm showing my knickers," she said with mock modesty, smoothing her short skirt over matching pink satin panties as she circled the monument to our glorious dead, talking as she went.

"Well, here we are in beautiful Armagh, Ontario, the first annual beautiful Armagh Busker Festival. Beautiful Armagh, home of good solid family folk, a no-skeleton town with a public library, a post office and four traffic lights." Her tone cycled right down the wire between upbeat and sneering, and her smile never showed her teeth.

"Five traffic lights," piped up one of the kids.

"Oh my! This is progress," she teased, "MacNeill's Hardware, the IGA, a cute little diner called Sam's, and the handsome OPP."

Something odd in that speech. But as she wheeled past, she leaned over and lifted off my Stetson, distracting and setting April laughing, everyone else watching to see how the cop would react. Just waited patiently while she lifted a tweed cap, then a few ball caps, juggled the lot and finally returned them neatly to their rightful wearers.

Had I seen her before somewhere? On the streets of Ottawa? Or Montreal? You're a little too old for this, I thought. That red hair came out of a can, and though she was lithe and smooth, wrinkles etched the corners of her eyes.

She was good though, as she cycled around, dropping balloon animals into little laps, juggled balls and eggs and finally knives. An acrobat too. And persuasive. She got two men to squat down and persuaded another onto their backs, making a platform for her to put down a special mounting block, where she placed an upturned pail and balanced herself on one foot on top of the whole mess, twirling flaming sticks above her head.

The third guy, volunteered by his children, was reluctant, but she talked him into position with a relentless barrage of gentle mockery. "Come on my man, not afraid of a little thing like death, are we? I'm not afraid of death. Who here's afraid to die?" she asked the crowd, without pausing for an answer. "If I die, you'll find me up there for sure at heaven's gate, busking away for St. Peter, and how could he refuse an entertaining girl like me?"

Spinning the fire five feet up, she started a Bob Dylan rasp of "Knocking on Heaven's Door" with a special smile for me when she got to the line about a lawman can't ever be free.

That was when I saw the half smile on April's face. I could tell she was thinking hard, and that next thing she'd have some theory about what she was seeing, the patter, the attitude or maybe a metaphor of busking as the performance art of life, because we're all banging for attention at some gate. But I never found out what it was, because the next moment her hand on my arm turned into a vice, and she said, "My water just broke."

*   *   *

"He's going to be okay." I told her. They'd moved her from recovery to a regular room. "His breathing has stabilized; so has his heart rate. But they're keeping him under observation."

Her hand in mine seemed smaller than ever.

"Intensive Care?"

"Yes."

"So they've got to still be worried."

"He said it was just precautionary. If everything stays the same, they'll move him out soon. Maybe even tomorrow."

After that we just sat quiet for awhile. She looked exhausted but wide awake, like she'd just climbed a mountain and needed to take in the view.

"I hardly got a look at him, Tony. Just that he's got dark hair."

"Oh, he's handsome," I assured her. "He'll have your hair, I bet, and dark eyes and from me..."

"Don't tell me he's got that nose of yours."

"'Fraid so."

"Poor thing." Finally, a smile. "Maybe you should make those phone calls."

"Okay," I said, "but they'll be asking his name."

"I've got an idea about that..."

"Thought so."

"...but it can wait till morning."

It was three a.m. before I got home and fell into bed, where I didn't really sleep. Just tossed from thought to thought in the tangled sheets of a long, eventful day. Baby boy Aardehuis bumping up against a busker yelling above my head: "Are you afraid of death?" Which changed in the half sleep to birth. Are you afraid of birth? Carr and his "congratulations on the boy." The boy I'd last seen curled in sleep just like his mother, small red face peeking out from under cover.

Then for a long time I thought about kids and how you care for them, and because of Glen Wylie's barn, remembered how some people didn't.

A long ago summer Sunday afternoon at the little man-made beach where all the farmer tans displayed themselves on the St. Lawrence shore. Mothers sitting in a huddle of folding chairs gossiping and shaking sand out of towels. Playing in the water with Glen Jr. and the sister who might have been ten or eleven, older than us for sure. Barbara? Brenda? No, it was Bonnie. A pretty girl with long loose hair and a smile she hid behind her hand because of a dead grey tooth. Back then, I'd thought Glen's dad was a great guy, full of laughs, much preferable to my own father who, to my deep mortification, clumped along the beach in wooden shoes. I was trying to pitch Glen Jr. into the water from my shoulders when Mr. Wylie took over and gave every kid who wanted one a glorious toss into the waves that seemed to fly forever.

Then Bonnie, next in line, laughing, jumping up and down, turned a cart wheel in the water out of pure bubbling excitement. Somehow a long arm flung out wrong sent a splash up into her father's face, or maybe she hit him, and I'll never forget how he turned in an instant from laughter to rage. From father to monster, bending over the cringing girl with a look I didn't see again until it was on the face of a guy outside a bar in Port Rose, my first posting. A guy smashing his wife's teeth with a bottle of ale.

The scariest thing was how Bonnie knew right away that

she had to run. She was used to this.

Hard to say how many of the other bits of memory came from that one afternoon. My mother rubbing lotion on Bonnie's legs, frowning at the scabs, two parallel brown stripes on her calf. The pale and shrunken Mrs. Wylie looking away.

I remember the car ride home because I broke one of those unwritten but understood family rules, which in our case was don't talk about how you feel. But I needed to ease the shock of that moment in the water when a nice man had terrified me, so I circled the problem, talking out of the back seat to the backs of my parents' heads saying: "Glen's dad gave us lots of throws. He was fun. He got real mad at Bonnie. She must have hit him."

My mother broke a rule too: no talking about the neighbours. Maybe it didn't count because she said it in Dutch, just looking straight ahead as if daring my father to disagree. "*Er moet iets gedaan worden,*" she said, "*Voor dat iemand in het ziekenhuis beland.*" I understood enough: something had to be done. Before someone ended up in the hospital.

"Such a man should never have children," Dad said.

Now, twenty years later, I wondered what my mother had done. Maybe called the Children's Aid, maybe then, or after the wife took off. Was that why Glen and Bonnie, with her neglected teeth, were removed the same year Wylie built his third extension on the barn?

Hard to sympathize with a man like that. The most I could do was feel bad for his cows, dying in the biggest bonfire of the year. A barn fire is fast and frightening; a sight both terrible and beautiful, and I was almost sorry I'd missed it. It reminded me of the flames in the square last night, twirling above the head of Flame Sucker Bob. You could acquire an appetite for fire. Any chance he might have hankered after a bigger blaze?

Then I came wide awake, remembering Pete Walker facing Glen Wylie across a litter of spilled food. Fifteen years ago at Armagh Collegiate, Pete Walker's nickname had been Pyro Pete. Earned with an outhouse and a chicken coop and finally a drive shed up in flames. That had got him caught and probation.

But all that was in the past. Wasn't it? Pete was my age now, a thirty-one year old dad, starting his own business, working hard. Pyro Pete was history. Wasn't he?

At six-thirty, I gave up pretending to sleep and hit the phone. My staid Dutch mother and her quiet happiness. Eamon O'Connor, April's excitable Irish dad, who ran through forty-nine ways he'd get here from New Brunswick by the end of the day. My brother Mike.

Everyone wanted the play-by-play, weight and a name. They got a Reader's Digest summary, six-pounds-four, and "April's got something up her sleeve."

"She would," said Howard MacNeill, the last call and my oldest friend. Howard owns the hardware store, runs every other organization in town and just became a Volunteer Fireman. "You hear about Wylie's barn?" he said.

"Yes."

Long silence.

"What is it, Howard?"

"John Kozak was downtown at that busker thing last night," he said, naming another fireman. "At the scene, he mentioned Pete Walker had a dust-up with Wylie."

"Shit."

"Yeah. Nobody said anything, but you could tell they were thinking."

It took no trouble at all to imagine those big guys carefully avoiding eye contact, everyone of them thinking of fires long ago. Thinking maybe Pyro Pete was back. Also thinking he'd shown no signs for years, and now half of them played pickup hockey with him. They'd look away so they wouldn't be seen thinking that a guy they liked might have put a match to a barn and a herd of cows.

"Did Carr twig?"

"I don't think so."

"Thanks for the heads up."

Too early for the hospital, but I wanted to get moving, wanted to see April and the baby, so I drove slowly and took a detour past Wylie's farm, all the way wondering what to do about the possible return of Pyro Pete. If Kozak had kept his mouth shut, it might have been possible to do a little quiet checking on my own, see where Pete had been last night, hopefully keep that history where it belonged, back in time. But the whole Volunteer Fire Department was already on that page. Was it better for Pete if Sergeant Carr knew the whole story, and we proved he was in the clear?

"Glendale's Aberdeen Angus" said the sign by the farm gate, but it leaned askew, as if it had been clipped by the fire trucks.

There was a cruiser parked near the smouldering ruin, and Sergeant Carr stood beside the farmer, two hunched figures, hands deep in their pockets, staring at the wreck. I joined them in the viewing, and in the frosted morning our breath showed up white against the charred timbers and blackened concrete.

"Fifteen of the best," said Wylie. "Brucedale's Jennie, Maryann, Kathleen, Emily..." His face had the caved in look of a man about to cry, and there was a singsong to his voice, like he was reciting the names of lost relatives. But I couldn't help but be pissed off that he'd used Emily to name a cow.

Sergeant Carr said, "The only thing I found this morning was this bit of rag ripped on the gate down there." He held up a scrap of pale blue denim, jacket weight. "Might have been there an age anyway. Might mean nothing."

"I know who done it," said Wylie, beating me to it. "Ask your boy here. That Pete Walker used to set fires. I knock over his goddamn wiener stand, he comes and burns my barn."

"Huh?" Carr looked lost. I gave a quick summary of the confrontation on main street, also Pete Walker's old fondness for fire setting, emphasizing that all that had happened long ago. "Those guys never lose the taste." Carr turned toward the cruiser with a springy stride. "I'll find out what he was up to last night. If we're lucky, we'll have this put away."

Still early at the hospital, I detoured toward the cafeteria and breakfast. Coming out of Emergency, I bumped into Flame Sucker Bob and Circus Daisy, Bob sporting a big gauze bandage over most of his forearm. Daisy, wearing normal clothes, sweatshirt, jeans, backpack dangling from one shoulder, looked more than ever like someone I ought to know.

"What happened to you?" I asked.

"The show got a little out of hand," the flame sucker grinned. "Occupational hazard."

"Experimental new stunt," said the redhead.

You had to wonder if Bob's new stunt involved strictly performance fire. If he was another guy who would never lose the taste. If he didn't enjoy flames so much, he mightn't once in a while be tempted to set a really big bonfire.

"What time was that?" I asked. "I had to leave the show early."

They grinned at each other, and for the first time Daisy's smile showed a row of perfect teeth. "Just at closing. The grand finale. Good thing he fried himself and not me."

Closing would have been nine, nine thirty. Plenty of time to find a target out of town.

"Then I brought him here, and he spent the night waiting for a doctor."

They did both wear the rumpled, weary look of people who'd spent the night in waiting room chairs. While I wondered who she looked like, Bob asked, "Hey, is there someplace decent to eat this time of day?"

"Cafeteria," I offered.

"No," said the redhead. "Sam's will be open. Let's go down there."

I remembered then, what had jarred last night in her patter; the mention of Sam's. "They changed the name to the Two by Four."

*   *   *

"Eamon," said April. "I'd like to call him Eamon, after my dad."

"Don't you think he needs a few consonants?" Really, I was so pleased to find they'd sprung him from Intensive Care, I could hardly pay attention.

"So put some in the middle." She bit down on her lip, looking tense and shy, a look I hadn't seen before, and I realized she was nervous.

"Amen Aardehuis..."

"Tony!"

"It sounds fine. Really, it's great. I like it, and even if I didn't, I couldn't say no to you. Not after what you went through yesterday."

The bedside phone rang, and instead of a congratulating relative it was Carr, looking for me and sounding pissed off because Pete Walker had been playing pool all night with three guys who would swear to it.

"Too bad," I said, but I was smiling when I hung up.

Then I lifted the small flannel wrapped person out of his plastic case and carried him over to the window for better light. "Eamon Aardehuis. That's your name, kid." Holding him, my hands felt huge. "And if you hate it when you get to high school, you can blame your mother."

"Tony..."

I looked out the window and saw Daisy and Flame Sucker Bob crossing the parking lot. In the cold October breeze, she stopped to pull a denim jacket out of her back pack. A denim jacket with a chunk ripped out of the right arm.

Things don't usually click like that, all at once. That she'd known about Sam's, but not the new name; four traffic lights instead of five. That Circus Daisy was from Armagh, and that was why she looked familiar. That she'd never lost the habit of hiding her teeth. That once she'd had the same grey tooth as Bonnie. That she was Bonnie. That she'd burned her father's barn and the animals he'd cared more for than his children.

I held Eamon up to my face and smelled the newborn smell of his dark hair, felt the heat of his skin next to mine and watched them climb into a beat-up van that would certainly fail a safety check. The thing shook into life, puffing out a dark exhaust.

I thought about unwanted children, holding Eamon, who hadn't exactly been wanted. Not looked for, anyway. I thought about welted legs and a town with an unpaid debt. I thought about a burned barn, and I thought about revenge.

Eamon gave a powerful little wiggle and sneezed. "I feel sorry for the animals," I told him. "But not for him. What do you think? Think we should just let her go?"

He looked up at me with eyes that would likely be as dark as his mother's. Blinked what might have been agreement, might have been telling me what I already knew. The First Annual Thanksgiving Armagh Busker Festival was already over. They'd be moving on, crossing the border, heading south. But there was no need to rush. There's always more time to think than you might guess.

Cecilia Kennedy *lives and writes in Brampton, Ontario. Her Tony Aardehuis stories have appeared in* The Grist Mill *and in* Storyteller, *where she won the Great Canadian Story contest for both 2001 and 2002. She is working on a mystery novel in which Tony finds his first dead body.*

There's No Business Like Show Business

Pat Wilson

From under his lowered eyelids, Lex surveyed the group in front of him. The usual assortment, he thought. A couple of cripples leaning on their crutches, some old bird in a wheelchair, two or three middle-aged women weeping loudly, and a tall, gaunt man who looked like he was at death's door.

Lex felt a tightening in the pit of his stomach. Billy wasn't there! Maintaining his posture of deep prayer, he ran his eyes along the row in front of the platform. Where the hell was Billy? Just as the tightening began to coalesce into a gut-wrenching throb, Lex saw Billy hobbling up the centre aisle, leaning heavily on his crutch and hanging on to the arm of Charlene. Billy's golden curls glowed in the light. His luminous blue eyes were fixed on the cross strung up over the back of the platform, and at each step, he moaned softly as if in deep pain. He was the perfect picture of a suffering child. Hard to believe he was nearly thirteen! Then Lex's gut spasmed. Charlene had that look again! Her eyes, hot with longing, were fixed, not on the cross, but on him. Even from the distance, Lex could see her hips swaying provocatively, straining against the skin-tight fabric of her skirt.

The pair arrived at the front of the platform and jostled their way between two of the women. Lex hoped Charlene wouldn't get sidetracked tonight. It didn't happen often, but when it did, she disrupted the whole flow of his performance. That time in Abilene, she'd taken advantage of being up on the platform, and instead of following the script, had pressed herself against Lex. Fortunately, few realized the lasciviousness of her embrace, but Lex was all too aware of her hand insinuating itself down the front of his white pants. That time, Lex was able to pass off her passionate advances as "loving zeal" inspired by the Holy Spirit.

Lex decided he'd better move fast while the crowd was still hot from his hellfire-and-brimstone-you-better-get-saved sermon. They stood a chance to lift a good offering here, well into the thousands, that is, if Billy and Charlene did what they were supposed to do without any improvisation on their part.

He headed for the middle-aged women first. One tap on their foreheads, and he could count on their going down like felled trees. It was always a good opening act.

"Heal!" Lex bellowed, smacking the flat of his hand against the forehead of the first woman. Right on cue, down she went, to be adroitly caught by Joe and an usher, then discreetly laid out with a small blanket over her legs. Lex proceeded along the row. As each woman went down, the audience shouted "Amen" and "Praise the Lord".

He could feel the growing pulse of excitement in the crowd. They loved it when people were slain in the Spirit. It meant things were going to happen; that this was going to be a holy-hallelujah-one-hell-of-a-meeting; that the Spirit was moving and anything could happen.

Lex took a deep breath, stood in front of Billy, and looked down at him. "My son, what do you want of the Lord?" he asked in a voice dripping with pity. The crowd fell silent.

"If only He would see fit to heal me, poor sinner that I am," Billy said in a clear, childlike voice.

It was Charlene's cue. Lex held his breath.

"My poor son," she cried, with just the right note of motherly concern in her voice. "Crippled since birth and a sweeter soul there never was. Not a mean bone in his poor, crippled body. And he loves the Lord and all of His creation. Yes, he does. Why, I've known him to pray for the little sparrow fallen from its nest, and it would rise up and fly away, healed."

The crowd let out a collective sigh.

Lex drew himself up to his full six foot two inches and threw back his head, well aware that his mane of white hair caught the carefully positioned spotlight so that he seemed to have a glowing halo about his head. He raised his arms and fixed his eyes upon the crowd.

"Do you believe that God loves this little child?" he asked them.

"Yes!"

"Do you believe that God can heal this little sparrow?" he continued.

"Yes!"

"Do you believe that God will make his poor body whole again?" he shouted.

"Yes!"

"Do you believe that God will heal him tonight? If you do, say Amen!"

The crowd was on its feet. He could hear their cries and sobs mingling with the shouts, and on cue, Gloria hit the first bass note on the organ and launched into "Amazing Grace". The crowd sang along, and as the noise and confusion hit a fever pitch, Lex leaned forward, laid his hands on Billy's blonde curls, noting as he did so that it was time for Charlene to get out the Clairol bottle again, and shouted, "Be healed!"

Billy threw his crutch up into the air, narrowly missing Joe, and leapt up onto the platform. "I can walk! I can walk!" he screamed, capering up and down several times. "Oh, thank you, God! I can walk!"

"It's a miracle," screamed Charlene, also leaping up onto the platform. Lex drew back, keeping a wary eye on her. But Charlene had switched fully into her doting mother role. Ignoring Lex, she swept Billy into her arms and turned to the crowd, her eyes streaming.

"My little son! My precious sparrow! He is healed. It's a miracle!"

"It's a miracle!" the crowd roared back.

"It's a miracle!" Lex shouted, moving swiftly down the row in front of the platform, smacking forehead after forehead.

It never failed. In the religious fervour of the moment, down they went like ninepins, joining the ladies on the floor. Usually, one or two of the cripples might even take a few faltering steps before they, too, succumbed to the power of the Spirit. If any seemed to be taking a little longer than necessary to go down, Lex could count on Joe placing a discreet knee behind their legs to tip the balance.

Only the tall, gaunt man at the end of the row remained standing. As Lex reached out his hand, the man lifted his head and looked directly into Lex's eyes. For a split second, Lex thought he was going to be sick as the acid in his gut churned its way into his throat in a burning rush.

The man's eyes were black, depthless and deadly cold.

Lex drew a deep breath, pulled himself together and smacked the man's forehead. "Heal!" he commanded.

The man's skin felt cold and clammy to Lex's touch, and a wave of revulsion shuddered through his body. The man remained standing, his cold eyes fixed on Lex. Mindlessly, Lex pulled back his hand. He could see the look of puzzlement on

Joe's face, but he ignored it and turned away from the man. He wasn't touching that guy again—not for a million bucks.

Sucking in a deep breath, he tried to steady his nerves and get back into the flow. Even as he turned, Lex was still aware of the intense stare of those eyes, burning on the back of his neck.

Thank God he had Loretta to give him a few minutes to compose himself. A spotlight slowly brightened until she was standing revealed to the audience.

Lex paused for a moment to allow the crowd to savour the sight of Loretta, dressed in a flowing blue gown with a dazzling white shawl over her long dark hair. To any lapsed Catholics in the audience, and there were always a few, she looked like the embodiment of their very own Virgin Mary.

Virgin! Lex smiled inwardly as he remembered last night's romp. The woman knew more positions than the Kama Sutra.

To his surprise, Loretta ignored the script and stood, gazing in absolute horror and fear at the tall man, now directly in front of her. She seemed unaware of Lex beside her. Lex swallowed hard against the rising knot of bile in his throat. Why couldn't people just do what they were supposed to? She wasn't even in the right position. She was going to break the mood if she wasn't careful.

With a touch on her arm, Lex re-positioned Loretta under the spotlight with the yellow gel. It bathed her in a golden light, so that she looked as if she were glowing.

He heard the crowd draw in its breath. The symbolism was not lost on the non-Catholics, either.

Out of the corner of his eye, he caught Charlene sidling across the platform towards them. What the hell is going on? Why is she coming over here? He shot her a baleful glance, but she ignored it and continued her slow shuffle until she was standing in the shadows behind Loretta, outside the pool of light from the spotlight.

Slowly, Loretta raised her eyes. He saw her lick her lips tentatively. She seemed to be struggling with herself. The crowd fell silent.

Lex swallowed hard again. He was all too aware of Charlene standing behind them. Anything could go wrong now. The silence began to lengthen.

"Speak to us, my daughter," Lex prompted her. "Give us the Words of Life tonight."

"I have come…" Loretta began. Her voice seemed thin and strained. Lex saw her draw in a deep, ragged breath, straighten her shoulders and look defiantly at the tall man. "I have come with a message tonight," she said in a clear, ringing voice that carried to the last rows in the auditorium.

"A prophecy." "The Lord is speaking to us." "A message from God." Joe started the whispers that flowed through the crowd like a spring brook. Gloria pulled out the tremolo stop and the soft strains of "Lord Speak to Me" filled the air.

He found it hard to concentrate on the script with Charlene so close. Only a year ago, Charlene had been the Voice of Prophecy, but once Lex had seen the possibilities in Loretta, Charlene had been relegated to the role of the Crippled Boy's Mother. At the same time, Loretta had also replaced Charlene in Lex's bed. Lex knew that both decisions still rankled with Charlene.

He sighed inwardly. One day, he'd have to let Charlene go. He could see that writing on the wall. But, right now, he just hoped that no one in the crowd was aware of her.

Loretta slowly raised her arms so that the flowing sleeves of her tunic fell back like wings behind her and raised her face towards the roof of the auditorium. Six hundred or more souls fell silent in breathless anticipation. The only sounds were a few stifled sobs and the soft throb of the organ's bass notes.

"Thus saith the Lord," she began. "I have poured out my blessings on my people…"

"Amen! Hallelujah! Tell it, Sister. Yes, Lord! Praise God." The soft incantations began to rise from the crowd.

"But my people have not heeded my word. They have sinned and sinned mightily…"

"Yes, Lord. Sinned, Lord…"

Loretta's voice rose a notch. "Sinned! Sins of the flesh…fornication, adultery, unclean acts…" She seemed to hesitate for a moment, and Lex could see her eyes flick to the tall man in front of them. "Yes, sin…" she continued.

"Amen, Lord. Yes, God…"

Slowly, Loretta let her arms fall and then, with a swift movement, began to point to various people in the audience, raising first one arm and then the other. As she did so, it seemed to them that bolts of lightning shot out from between her fingers, illuminating them and their dark sins. Lex smiled. The small narrow-beam high intensity flashlights sewn into the skin-toned surgical gloves she wore really did the trick. "I know you and I know your sins. I know what you do in the dark of the night. I know what evil thoughts linger in your mind…"

People screamed and cried as the light flashed on them. Gloria changed the musical accompaniment, dropping into the deep sonorous chords of the Death March, letting the sound echo and reverberate around the room, until every person felt the noise and thunder pounding in his brain.

"I know you and your secret sins. I know what you lust after…" Loretta suddenly whirled and pointed at the man in front of her. "I know your hatreds and your false pieties…"

An expression of exultation lit up the man's face, and he looked, not at Loretta, but beyond her into the shadows at the back of the stage. He spread out his arms and jerked spasmodically, then seemed to fold in on himself until he was just another crumpled heap on the floor in front of the platform. Joe stepped forward, straightened his legs out and folded his arms across his chest.

Lex was impressed. He hadn't thought Loretta had that kind of power. His mind played with the idea of having Loretta do this as part of the act. While not as dramatic as his own laying on of hands, it was pretty effective. He wondered if she could do it again, or if this was just some kind of lucky fluke.

"But I, the Lord your God, forgive you, each and every one of you. I know you are tempted by Satan."

Again, the enthusiasm of the crowd began to rise, "Yes, tempted, Lord. Not our fault… Amen, Sister."

"Thus saith the Lord…" Loretta let her arms fall to her sides. She bowed her head as if in absolute weariness and stood silent in the golden glow of the spotlight.

"Tell us, Sister," the audience begged.

Lex stepped forward. "Sister," he said. "If the Lord has a Word for all of these sinners, then speak it now."

"Yes, speak it!" the crowd shouted.

Loretta raised her head, looked directly out over the watching eyes and held her hands out in a pleading gesture. "Thus saith the Lord. You have sinned by holding back that which belongs to me," she said softly, her voice breaking slightly on the last words. "You have kept back that which I require of you. I have opened the windows of heaven and poured down gifts upon you, and you have used them to satisfy the needs of your flesh rather than the needs of your souls. For what profiteth it a man if he should gain the world, but lose his soul?"

Lex could see that quite a few people were nodding in agreement with her scriptural references. That's what made

Loretta so good…she knew her Bible inside and out. Not surprising, since she was the only child of a tight fundamentalist preacher in a small town on the Prairies. She'd told Lex of the endless hours spent memorizing bible verses, the punishment for any small infraction of her father's rigid rules. No wonder she'd left home as soon as she turned eighteen. If Lex hadn't found her in that truck-stop restaurant, she'd still be pouring coffee for ten-cent tips. Now, she was the Voice of Prophecy in the Salvation Revival, and she was damn good at it, too. Lex permitted himself a small smile. Bet her old man would have an apoplectic fit if he knew what his little girl was up to.

"Thus saith the Lord: bring me your harvest. Hold not back a penny, but be as the widow with her mite, and I, the Lord God Almighty, will pour down blessings until your cup runneth over with them!"

"Bring me your harvest!" Loretta's voice was tearful and full of sorrow. "Bring me your harvest…" she whispered, then fell to her knees and began to pray.

Lex doubted there was even one hard heart that wouldn't be moved at the sight of her beauty and obvious piety. He gave an imperceptible nod to Joe, who began handing the baskets to the ushers. Gloria pulled out the Basso Profundo stop and stomped hard on the swell pedal. "Beneath the Cross of Jesus…" poured forth in a mighty wall of sound. A spotlight began to glow over the suspended cross behind Lex and Loretta.

"God has spoken directly to you. Do what He has commanded of you. Bring Him your harvest," Lex said, his voice intense and commanding. "Empty your pockets, pull out your bankbooks, and give to the Lord of the Harvest what is rightfully His. Leave those nickels and dimes for the beggar on the street, but give to the Lord a silent harvest of your bills and cheques."

To Lex's annoyance, Charlene broke from the script

completely and went to kneel down beside Loretta. Now what? he thought. Although, he had to admit, it looked good, the purity of Loretta next to the obviously shop-worn Charlene. Maybe he'd leave that bit in. The Saint praying with the Sinner. Yeah, he liked it. Gave everybody a good feeling, he could see that. Those in the crowd who were watching the little tableau were nodding and crying happily.

And it seemed to make them all feel generous, too. Lex noted with satisfaction that the offering baskets coming back to the platform were full to overflowing. He'd never seen it this good.

It was time for Gloria to open up all the stops. The auditorium reverberated with the militant strains of "Onward Christian Soldiers", Lex raised his hands in a final blessing, and it was over. Wearily, he made his way to the back of the platform behind the backdrop and slumped into a chair. From his inside pocket, he dug out the mini flask and took a long pull.

It had been a rough night.

He could hear Joe working the floor in front of the platform, helping people back up, giving them a small bible and a handful of tracts and encouraging them before he sent them on their way.

"Uh, Boss, we have a little problem here." Joe's voice at his elbow roused him.

Lex looked up distractedly. "What is it, Joe?"

"That old guy on the end?"

"Yeah. What about him?"

"He's dead."

*   *   *

The auditorium was darkened and cold. Hours had passed

since the body had been removed, and only the white chalk outline and the yellow police tape were left to show that anything amiss had taken place.

Lex longed for a drink, but he was all too aware of the detective's skeptical eyes watching his every move. God, what a mess! he thought. Murder! The worst possible thing that could happen. He slumped back into his seat. He wasn't sure how he was going to pull out of this one. It was the kind of news that made headlines anyway, but by happening at a Revival, it was going to be top tabloid fodder. He rubbed his hands wearily over his face and felt the beginning of stubble on his chin. He'd look like hell on the front pages when the press, already ten deep outside the police cordon in the parking lot, got through with him.

"So, just to tie up a few loose ends, sir, could we just go over the details one more time?" The detective lounged in a seat in the front row.

Lex dragged his attention back to the present. "Certainly, detective. Whatever I can do to help you in this tragic, tragic event."

"Now, about Miss Danvers. Did you know that the deceased was her father?" the detective asked.

They'd already taken Loretta away. Lex still couldn't believe it. "No, no, I had no idea. None at all."

"Did she seem unusually upset tonight?"

Lex hesitated. He pursed his lips as if trying to remember. "Well, she was a little distracted, but I didn't think anything of it." He had a momentary flash of Loretta's strained and white face, her eyes fixed on the man in front of her.

"Did you see the gun in her hand?"

"No. She had palm flashlights. I don't know how she'd hold a gun."

The detective sighed. "It's a very small calibre gun, only good for close range. It is possible to hold it and pull the trigger, even with a palm light."

Lex replayed the scene again. Loretta pointing at the old man and his falling like a sack of potatoes.

"Did you hear the discharge?"

"No. It was hard to see or hear anything. You know, lots of flashing lights and the organ really pounding out the music."

Loretta had shot the old guy in cold blood, straight through the heart. God! Lex shook his head in disbelief.

"Did the deceased say anything to Miss Danvers before the incident?"

"No. He was just there in the front with the others. I never saw him before tonight." Lex suppressed a shudder as he thought of those cold, dead eyes looking into his own.

"Did you know that Miss Danvers possessed a firearm?"

"No." They'd found it in the pocket of Loretta's gown. Loretta had protested that it wasn't hers, that she'd never seen it before, but the fact remained that it was in her possession. Lex wondered what else she'd kept from him.

"Well, I think that wraps it up for now, sir. You'll need to stick around for the next week in case anything else comes up, but for the meantime, you're free to go back to your hotel." The detective closed his book with a small snap and hauled himself up out of the chair. "Please call the station and let us know if you're planning on leaving town for any reason."

Lex waited until the detective closed the door behind him, then blew out the deep breath he hadn't realized he'd been holding and pulled out the flask. He took a long drink, feeling the liquor burn its way down his throat and into his stomach.

From the shadows behind the platform, Charlene sauntered over and sat down next to him. She reached for his flask, took a swallow and said, "Are they gone?"

"Yeah. Helluva thing, isn't it?"

"Well, Lex honey, don't worry, the show will go on. You still got me'n Joe and Gloria."

"Yeah. But it won't be the same without Loretta."

"Sure it will, honey." Lex could feel Charlene's hand on his knee. Somehow, it felt comforting. "We'll just go on as we always have. Only now, I'll use some of Loretta's stuff. Dye my hair black. Spout the Bible. I can do that, honey. You'll see." Her hand moved up his thigh. "It'll be just like it always was. The four of us."

Lex put his hand over hers and squeezed. Good old Charlene. He could always count on her in a pinch. They went back a long ways, he and Charlene, all the way back to their carny days when he was a barker for her Annie Oakley show. Yeah, they'd make out okay. They were survivors, he and Charlene.

*　　*　　*

Charlene heard the musical cue and got ready to take her place on the platform. She gave the black wig one last pat, pulled the white veil up over it and sucked in her stomach.

It felt good to be back in the spotlight again.

And all because of a chance meeting with a bitter old man. He'd come looking for his daughter, acting on a rumour he'd heard from some member of his small-town congregation, but he'd bumped into Charlene first.

Under Charlene's gentle prodding, he finally admitted that he'd brought a gun with him. He told Charlene that his death would be worth the sacrifice if he could save the soul of his only daughter. He would pay the penalty for the great sin of murder, he knew, but he was willing to forego his place in heaven for her.

It didn't take Charlene long to convince him that there was

a better way. He would have heaven and his daughter would have time to repent before she stood before the heavenly throne.

As she said to him, "It's better far for her to rot in prison than to rot in hell." That argument clinched the deal.

When the time came, Charlene had no qualms about shooting the crazy old coot. Slipping the gun into Loretta's pocket was a simple flick of the wrist.

Charlene smoothed the blue fabric over her hips, took a deep breath and stepped forward. "I have come with a message tonight," she began.

When **Pat Wilson** *'s not "on the road" delivering seminars, she's busy writing and is the author of numerous non-fiction books. Her* Living in Excellence *work is a best-selling motivational audio cassette program. She now writes in the "empty nest" she shares in Nova Scotia with her husband Gerald, two cats and a dog.*

In Texas They All Carry Guns

I didn't like the way they sang,
And told it to their face,
The heartaches, and the done-me-wrongs
And the dreadful brooding pace.
I ridiculed their thinning hair
And the non-electric bass
And their oh-so-dull outfits—
They were so sadly out of place.
I screamed at them from the bar stool,
"Country singing isn't hot!"
My heckling killed the audience,
What killed *me* was how they shot.

Joy Hewitt Mann

Don't Cry for Me Argentina

Joan Boswell

Father leaned against the wall of my room. Home in Buenos Aires on a five-day pass from his posting at an army prison in the northern Argentine pampas, he'd insisted on spending his leave closeted in our apartment—unwilling to meet old friends, go out for meals or see a show.

"I only want to be here and spend my time with you and your mother," he said when I suggested we go to a tango competition.

For five days Father never let Mother out of his sight for more than a few minutes. He sat with her on the balcony of our Recollect District apartment, held her hand as they watched television, slumped in a kitchen chair as she prepared meals. He looked ill—gaunt with dark-circled eyes and gray skin; and he acted depressed—quiet and withdrawn.

That he'd come to talk to me while he waited for his ride back to the north seemed like a positive sign.

"We're losing the war. The Generals should have known the British would never give up the Malvinas," he said.

"Will that be a good thing?"

"It'll mean the end of them, of the Generals."

"Father, what's the matter?"

Although his expression remained impassive, he stared at

me with a frightening intensity. "Paula, you've always been a good daughter. I have something important I want you to know. First, you must promise not to tell your mother; she's been sick, and I can't burden her. Also, you must not act until the Generals are gone."

The hunted look in his eyes and the urgency of his words frightened me.

Mother stepped into the room. "Enrico, they're here—it's time to go."

Father enveloped me in a bear hug. "Never forget how much I love you," he said in a normal voice and then whispered, "The tiger—remember when you were a little girl?"

The tiger! What could a tiger have to do with anything?

After he'd gone, Mother prepared two cups of *maté* that we took to the balcony, where we sat amid a jungle of greenery inhaling the spicy fragrance of geraniums.

"Mother, I can understand why he's so thin. It's happened since the army moved him north to the pampas. The heat and humidity must be terrible, and the food's probably rotten. But it isn't just his weight. He's so withdrawn and different than he used to be." I reached over and clasped her arm. "What's wrong with Father?"

"It's his job. Something about it is destroying him." Mother gently laid her hand over mine. "But he refuses to talk about it. He says it's better for me not to know." Tears slipped down her pale, papery cheeks. "I pleaded with him to set up an appointment with Dr. Rodriguez. Even if the doctor didn't think Enrico was sick, and I can't imagine that he wouldn't conclude immediately that he was, he's an old friend and would provide Enrico with a certificate saying he was unfit. If he had that, he could apply for a medical discharge."

"What did Father say?"

"That there was no point seeing Franco Rodriguez because they would never allow him to leave the army: there was no way out."

"When's his next leave?"

"When I asked, he said he wasn't sure and, if he didn't come back, to remember how much he loved us." She sobbed and reached in the pocket of her printed green skirt for one of her embroidered handkerchiefs. "I knew he wanted to say more, but he was afraid."

I wondered if I should bring up his cryptic reference to the tiger, but I didn't think she'd heard his remark, and I decided it wouldn't be helpful to tell her. Reluctantly, I went off to classes at the Catholic University.

During my lectures and long after I should have slept, I puzzled about his reference to tigers, but I couldn't relate tigers to anything important in my childhood.

Thursday morning, we were drinking our usual strong coffee and munching sweet rolls liberally spread with *dulce de leche* when the phone rang. Mother answered.

"Yes. What? It can't be. He was here earlier this week. I don't understand. A prison riot? Shot." She listened, said "Thank you" and replaced the phone on its cradle.

"You heard," she said, her eyes wide and her face slack, as if all the supporting bones had disintegrated.

"Tell me."

"He was shot by a prisoner who grabbed his gun."

She sank down and buried her face in her hands. Then she lifted her head. Instead of tears, her eyes reflected pain and anger.

"How could they phone? When an officer is killed, they always send a senior officer to break the news. This phone call is a slap in the face, an insult, they've told us as if he was no more important than a dog run over in the street."

There was fear and resignation in her voice and in her eyes. "They killed him," she said.

A week later, two days after Father's funeral, Mother and I again sat on the balcony. Mother, who normally rose every minute to deadhead flowers, water wilting plants or tie a tendril escaping from her jungle, did nothing. Instead, she hunched down in her chair with her hands lying quietly in her lap. I toyed with a strand of my hair, repeatedly twisting it around my finger and releasing it.

Looking down at the street below, I noticed a green Ford Falcon, the car the army always drove when they arrested people or picked them up for questioning, cruising slowly while the man in the passenger seat peered through his dark glasses at the apartments. In front of our building, the vehicle glided to a halt.

"Mother." I reached over and grabbed her arm. "Mother, it's the army."

She roused herself, and we watched two uniformed men leave the car. Seconds later, our buzzer sounded. The terror I saw in her eyes must have been reflected in mine.

It wasn't as if we'd committed any crime. In Argentina, the green Falcons had stopped at the homes and offices of thousands of people who, as far as their relatives and friends knew, had never said or done a subversive thing. Many men and women had never been heard from again.

"Thank God he didn't tell us anything," Mother said in a tiny voice.

The buzzer demanded a response. With slow steps, Mother went to the intercom and let them in.

Two uniformed men, eyes blanked by dark glasses, strode into the room. Their aggressive body language and cruel turned-down mouths threatened and intimidated.

"Where are his papers?"

Mother, her thin hands trembling, pointed to the desk in the corner of the living room.

The taller one riffled through Father's meagre store of documents and threw two or three in his briefcase.

"Any more?"

Mother, beyond speech, shook her head; it probably wouldn't have mattered what she said, because they ignored us as they checked drawers and cupboards before they pulled books from shelves in the kitchen and living room.

"Father was an army officer. Why are you doing this?"

The short one, whose body odour repulsed me, stopped and sized me up before he snarled, "Some officer."

"You." He pointed at Mother. "You, come with us."

Helpless to do anything, I grabbed and squeezed her emaciated hand and murmured, "It'll be okay, you'll be back soon."

I was alone.

What should I do? On the one hand, I could go to police headquarters and demand that they release my mother, the widow of a recently deceased army officer. But, like her, I believed they'd deliberately killed my father. Would going to the police make it better or worse for Mother?

On the other hand, if I didn't go and show righteous indignation, would it confirm the army's obvious suspicion that not only were we aware he'd committed a crime but also knew the details? Furthermore, if I didn't insist on being told where they were detaining her, I wouldn't have the smallest chance of locating her, not that they were likely to tell me no matter what I did. The Generals believed in secrecy, rumour and terror.

Who to go to for advice? The answer—no one.

Families who hadn't had a visit from the Ford Falcons pretended nothing was happening.

Families who had often lived in limbo. I thought of my friend Alicia, whose whole family—father, mother and two brothers—had disappeared eight months ago. Alicia had tried every avenue to discover her family's whereabouts but learned nothing. Finally, as a last resort, one Thursday she went to the Plaza de Mayo and joined other women whose loved ones had vanished. Silently, they circled the obelisk in the centre of the square, each one wearing a white headscarf and carrying a placard with the photo and name or names of the disappeared. Las Madres de la Plaza Mayo.

Because my father was in the army, I'd never imagined I'd be in Alicia's position. And it was too soon to say I was; occasionally those taken for questioning did come home. No, for the moment I'd do nothing, I'd wait and keep a vigil for Mother.

Whatever reason they'd murdered my father had to be the same reason that had brought the army to our apartment. And, whatever it was had been terribly important to Father. I didn't have much time—they might come for me at any second. I had to figure out what he'd meant by his cryptic reference to the tiger, and I couldn't wait for the Generals to lose power.

While my mind twisted and turned, searching for clues, I wandered to the living room and began to replace the books on the shelves. As I picked up a photo album, it occurred to me that the snapshots might give me a hint. Perched on the blue plush couch, I opened the book.

The snaps of Mother and Father in the early years before Father lost his business and enlisted in the army broke my heart. Younger than I was now, their optimism and joy jumped off the page. After my birth, the photos continued to reflect a happy life, particularly those taken with my grandparents at the beach and the zoo.

The zoo. The tigers at the zoo—a vague memory of terror. Why? It came to me. I'd been frightened by the intensity of a tiger's gaze and screamed that he wanted to eat me. At night, I'd been afraid to sleep in case the tiger crept in and gobbled me up. My father had bought me a toy tiger, but it hadn't banished my fear, and he'd done something else; what had it been?

No other photographs solved the puzzle. Maybe the box of children's books and toys stashed in my closet would trigger a memory. I scrambled deep in the cupboard and hauled out a cardboard carton bulging with mementos. The removal of the first layer of treasured books reminded me of the evenings when Father had read to me. Tears blurred my eyes.

Cuentos de Hadas de Grimm, how those fairy stories had thrilled me. And *Jorge el Curioso*, that little monkey's curiosity had landed him in such trouble. The sight of *Negrito Sambo*, worn, tattered and circled with an elastic, as if to hold loosened pages inside produced a vivid flashback—this book had helped overcome my fear. I'd loved *Little Black Sambo* because the tigers chased each other round and round the tree until they metamorphosed into butter.

Pure, unadulterated fear. This was what he'd meant. Inside the book I'd find the answer; find the cause of his death.

The door buzzer. A long sustained buzz—the green Falcon had returned.

Frantically, I piled the books in the box with *Negrito Sambo* tucked in the middle. As I shoved the carton in the cupboard I prayed that the elastic wouldn't break; that the officers wouldn't open the book; that they wouldn't be interested in my childhood treasures.

Saying nothing, the same two men pushed past me. I stood irresolute, unsure of where to go or what to do.

In the living room, the two of them once again pawed through the chaos they'd created and tossed more books from the bookcases. Then the shorter one entered my room and the other one went to my parents'.

"Come in here." An order from the short one who smelled of garlic and dirty underwear. He pointed to the shoeboxes of file cards on my desk. "What are those?"

"I'm at the university. It's information for my thesis on nineteenth century immigration."

Because of his reflecting sunglasses, I couldn't see his eyes, but by his little smirk and his theatrical pause before he upended the boxes and watched the cards cascade to the floor, I knew he revelled in his abuse of power. Of course I didn't protest—I didn't want to do or say anything to draw attention to me or my room.

He hauled everything out of my cupboard and dumped clothes, old textbooks and the box of children's toys and books.

I stopped breathing.

If he looked at me, would he know? Was *Little Black Sambo* pulsing on my forehead in neon lights? Could he read my fear in the sweat beading my forehead and running between my shoulder blades?

After a cursory glance at the worn, much-loved books, the Teddy bear with a button replacing an eye and the battered dolls, he ignored my childish keepsakes. I breathed. The taste of bile filled my mouth. I wanted to rush to the bathroom and vomit.

They found nothing.

After they'd gone, I was sick repeatedly and then, weak-kneed and faint, I staggered to my bed, threw myself down and sobbed myself to the verge of hysteria before I rolled over and said, "enough". Time to face up to fear.

I picked up *Little Black Sambo* and slipped the elastic off. The original contents had been removed and replaced with pages cut to fit inside and stapled to the cover. Lists of names and dates penned in my father's meticulous handwriting filled the pages.

Inside the cover he'd folded and secured an envelope addressed to me.

My darling Paula, I am writing this to you and not to your mother because I want to protect her from the shock of discovering what I've done. Please use this information to give a little bit of peace to the families involved.

I will burn in hell for the terrible work I've had to do here in the prison, but by keeping this record I hope to ease the pain for those who do not know.

The women whose names are listed were killed here. The guards raped many of them repeatedly until they were pregnant. The babies were taken and given to military families. I have written the gender and date of birth of each baby underneath its mother's name and I have made as complete a record as I could.

If you are reading this, I am dead but I want you and your mother to remember how much I loved you and how I wish I hadn't joined the army or been stationed to work in the prison.

Your loving father.

My face must have appeared as boneless as my mother's face had when she'd heard about Father's death.

The contents of the letter explained his physical and mental disintegration. And I was as sure as I'd ever been about anything that he'd been killed because another guard or a superior officer suspected what he'd been doing. I thanked God that he hadn't revealed the hiding place to my mother and that I hadn't mentioned his reference to tigers. I prayed that ignorance would protect her.

Terror threatened to immobilize me, but I refused to allow it. I had an obligation to Father, an obligation to pass on to the mothers of the Plaza de Mayo the information he'd given his life to collect.

Today was Tuesday. Where should I hide the book until Thursday? There was no time to waste. The police habitually turned up repeatedly seeking more information or terrorizing you into confessions of wrongdoing.

With the book clutched in my hand, I rushed to the kitchen, tore a strip of aluminum foil from the roll, wrapped the book and sealed the edges with cellophane tape. On the balcony I grabbed Mother's trowel, dug a hole along the side of the largest potted plant, a fig tree, inserted the package and buried it. I detached six or seven leaves from the plant and spread them to cover the disturbed soil.

The buzzer sounded; they had returned.

"Your mother says you have a locker. Show us."

Oh, God. Had they tortured her? Or had it been a routine question? Where was she? How would I locate her?

Apparently, they didn't find anything in the locker, but back in the apartment they continued their search. I was shaking and hoped most people did this, whether they had anything to hide or not. Planted in the middle of the living room, I watched them.

The smelly one strode into my bedroom, where he kicked the file cards into even greater disarray and smiled at the mess. He bent down, picked up *Grimm's Fairy Tales*, thumbed through it and tossed it on the floor. I stared, mesmerized, as he chose two of my favourite dolls, wrenched their heads off, held them upside down and shook them. Finally, he drew a knife from his pocket and faced me as he eviscerated my dear old Teddy. Stuffing leaked out as he tossed the disembowelled bear on the floor.

Finished with the books and toys, he pulled the covers off the bed, slashed the mattress and flipped it on top of the stew of books, toys and file cards. Back in the living room, the two men smashed five of Mother's treasured Royal Doulton figurines, slashed the cushions on the sofa, flipped the chairs and slit the fabric covering the bottoms.

The balcony was next.

All I could think about was the buried aluminum-wrapped package; the grenade with the power to destroy.

Systematically, the smelly officer destroyed Mother's tranquil oasis. He chose randomly; tipping two geraniums out of their jardinieres—leaving three untouched; pulling one climbing vine off the trellis—ignoring the other; upending Mother's basket of gardening tools—passing up the opportunity to smash a shelf stacked with terra cotta pots.

I couldn't avoid thinking about the fig tree; in fact, I could think of nothing else. Resolutely I fixed my gaze on the building opposite and considered how ironic it was that tigers running around a tree had comforted, while buried tigers terrified me. Distracted when he dropped a hanging basket of fuschia on the floor, I turned. Noticing me staring, he tramped in the spilled dirt before he stomped into the living room. The balcony was a shambles; the fig tree untouched.

As I waited with a sense of inevitability for the order to go downtown, I worried about my resistance to pain, my inability to safeguard Father's secret if they tortured me. I visualized electric shocks, fingernails ripped off, sensitive parts of my body burned and wondered how long I'd hold out. Absorbed in my thoughts, I failed for a second or two to take in the smelly one's words.

"We'll be back. Your mother will tell us where to look."

Poor Mother. She couldn't reveal what she didn't know. I was glad for that, but the thought of what they might do to her filled me with horror. The best way to help her was to get the book out of the apartment and to make absolutely sure I passed the notes hidden in *Little Black Sambo* to the right woman.

I'd heard that every Thursday, when the women arrived at the Plaza de Mayo, soldiers with cameras sat in the windows of the Casa Rosada, the pink building at the end of the square housing the offices of the Generals. Also, the gossip was that the Generals' spies had infiltrated the protesters. If a soldier noticed me passing something to one of the women, or if I chose the wrong woman, not only would Father's sacrifice be pointless, but also I'd make the situation much worse for Mother and be in terrible trouble myself.

Every time I thought of Mother I wanted to stop and begin my search, my trek from official to official pleading for news of her or her whereabouts. But I couldn't stop now; I had to deliver the book.

So many names on Father's lists, but to locate a relative in the square I would focus on one or two particularly distinctive ones. I excavated *Little Black Sambo*, chose Alexandria Michielsen and Sharon Browne, two young women whose European ancestors had not come from Italy or Spain, and resolved to find a woman carrying a sign with one of the names.

How to camouflage the book? A Missal wouldn't draw attention. I collected Mother's from her bedside table. It was the perfect size—slightly larger than *Sambo*. After removing the Missal's cover, I slipped father's notes inside and secured the cover with an elastic. Once I'd rewrapped and reburied the parcel I went for a walk and disposed of the tell-tale pages of the Missal in a public waste bin. Back home, because every woman in the square wore one, I made myself a white headscarf.

On Thursday, dressed in nondescript clothes, I hooked a shopping bag containing the Missal and white scarf over my arm and rode the subway to the Plaza. When I arrived, I crossed to the Cathedral and mixed with the throngs of worshippers who flowed in and out throughout the day. Kneeling in a pew, I prayed that the Church would intercede on the people's behalf—a request unlikely to be answered as, so far, the Church had supported the Generals.

Outside, with the white scarf in place, I wandered over to the Plaza and stood with other onlookers as I scrutinized the placards. A woman of my mother's age with dark blonde hair tucked under her white scarf and blue eyes reflecting deep sadness walked past carrying a sign with a graduation picture of a serious, dark-haired girl and underneath, printed in bold, black ink, "Where Is Alexandria Michielsen". I slipped into the slow-flowing stream of women and caught up with her.

With my head bent to prevent the curious from noticing that I was talking—the vigil was done in silence—I said in a low voice, "I have information about your daughter and other young women who've disappeared."

The woman stopped as if I'd shot her.

"Alexandria, you know about Alexandria," she said in a thin high voice.

"I think we should continue to walk," I murmured and, indeed, several soldiers stationed on the edge of the Plaza had glanced our way.

"Yes, yes, of course. Is she alive?"

Impossible to say the terrible words; I remained silent.

"Oh, my God. In my heart I thought she was dead, but unless you know for sure, you have hope."

"Alexandria had a baby, a son."

Her mother clutched my arm and sagged against me. I supported her as well as I could, but our staggering lurching gait was sure to draw the soldiers' attention. Out of the corner of my eye I saw another woman size up the situation and quicken her step to join us. With each of us holding an arm, the Samaritan whispered, "We must keep going."

After we'd made a complete circle of the square, Alexandria's mother thanked the unknown woman, removed her supporting arm and, still clinging to me, walked on.

"What happened to my grandson?"

"He's been adopted."

"How do you know this?"

"I have lists written by my father, who was an army officer himself. They killed him because they suspected he'd made a record. I've hidden the lists of women and their babies inside a Missal. In two hours come into the Cathedral. I'll be on the right in the fourth pew from the front. The Missal will be on the seat next to me."

I stopped whispering as we walked past a phalanx of soldiers.

"Please move the information along quickly. If they pick me up, I don't know how brave I'll be."

"Thank you for doing this."

"Pray for me and for my family." Only God could help my father, but prayer might miraculously protect my mother from the wrath of the Generals.

I gently detached the woman's arm, increased my pace and drew ahead of her. After four more turns around the square I drifted to a street leading away from the plaza. With my white scarf tucked in my shopping bag, I wandered along studying displays in shop windows.

One hundred and twenty minutes later, after I'd visited a dozen stores, bought a pair of gloves, checked at least fifteen times to assure myself no one was following me, I walked to the Cathedral. In the fourth pew, I knelt and prayed for the safety and health of my mother, for the souls of the women and for my father.

Surely he wouldn't go to hell when he'd been brave and put himself in great peril to record the terrible deeds of the Generals' regime. Surely God would forgive anything else he'd had to do.

Alexandria Michielsen's mother slipped into the pew, picked up the Missal, crossed herself and left.

I made my way home, content that I'd done what Father wanted; that he would have been proud of me. Now, I'd begin my search for Mother. Optimistically, I told myself that she might even be waiting when I returned.

As I walked up my street, I saw the green Falcon parked in front of our building.

Since visiting Argentina, the plight of the "disappeared"' has haunted **Joan Boswell**. *A member of the Ladies' Killing Circle, she has had stories in their four previous anthologies as well as in magazines and books in Canada and the U.S. In 2000 she won the $10,000 first prize in the Toronto Sunday Star Short Story contest.*

When the Red, Red Robin

R.J. Harlick

He sucked in his breath at the sound he'd been waiting for, a faint, almost flute-like trill. Perhaps it wasn't a trill at all. But just in case, Harry raised his binoculars. It never hurt to be too prepared. Boy Scout Harry. That's what his buddy, Sam, called him. He even had his notebook handy to check off another species. Fifteen was his count so far this summer.

One more sighting, and he'd tie Sam's record from last summer. Two more and he'd win.

The new bird guide he'd got for his thirteenth birthday said ferns were the preferred habitat of the shy Hermit Thrush. So he focused the lens on some big ferns growing in a small clearing beyond the next line of trees. A long, feathery frond wavered. Harry waited, not quite believing his luck. He knew the wind hadn't moved it, since the breeze seldom got this far into the Mont Orford forest.

A single flute note sounded again, followed by the thrush's familiar spiralling scale. Although Harry was sure it came from behind those ferns, he didn't want to leave his hiding spot for a better view. He might scare his target away. A sighting in flight didn't count. Instead, Harry shifted his position behind the fat spruce so he could focus his binoculars on a gap through the ferns.

If it really were the Hermit Thrush, Sam would turn green. Even eagle-eyed Sam hadn't checked off this species yet.

Harry's pulse quickened at the sight of a brown flash behind the emerald green fronds. He could swear it was the same rusty brown colour as the picture in his guide. If he saw brown spots, he would be golden. Only problem, in order to see the spots, the target had to face him. Trick was how to get the target to turn around without sending it into flight.

But if Harry was anything, he was patient. He'd proven it last summer, when he and Sam were going after the Eastern Bluebird. His buddy had spotted the streak of blue near a flock of male American Goldfinches by one of the Arts Centre studios. But that sighting didn't meet the rules he and Sam had laid down. The target had to be alone, away from buildings and most importantly had to be making its distinctive call.

Sam had read in a book at school that the Eastern Bluebird liked open fields. So for most of that blistering afternoon they'd hidden in the shade of the red pine plantation they called the Telephone Pole Forest, next to Farmer Moineau's cow pasture. Eventually, Sam had given up. But Harry had hung in. Even passed up a boat ride on Lake Memphrémagog in Sam's uncle's new inboard.

Finally, with dinner time fast approaching, his patience had been rewarded with the unique song of guitar-like twangs. Then he'd sighted the telltale blue plumage. Despite his growling stomach, he'd remained hidden in the underbrush watching the Eastern Bluebird preen herself. And that was another rule. Only the female of the species counted.

The ferns moved again. Harry held his breath. He thought he saw a couple of brown spots, but couldn't be sure. He had to get closer to see over the ferns into the hollow where the Hermit Thrush remained hidden. He inched silently forward.

One step. Two steps. Three. A brief flutter stopped him.

As the scale of warbling notes filled the clearing, he slowly brought his binoculars back up to his eyes. He pointed them to where he'd seen the movement, directly into a narrow trench at the edge of the fern patch. He almost chortled out loud when he saw the characteristic brown dot markings against a white background.

Point scored for the good guys. One more, and he'd beat Sam.

But his sighting was almost ruined by the abrupt appearance of the American Robin.

What's going on? Same thing happened last year. Harry had no sooner checked off Eastern Bluebird in his book than out bobbed this red-breasted menace. This time the intruder bobbed again, straight towards the hollow where Harry's present sighting roosted. But, since their rules didn't say how long the target was supposed to be alone, Harry figured this one still counted, like last year.

*   *   *

Halfway back to the Arts Centre residence, Harry decided to go to Sam's place instead. He couldn't wait until music camp next morning to gloat over this new sighting. He wanted to see the look of disgusted envy wash over his friend's freckled face.

He trudged along the tree-shaded lane to the large stone cottage where Sam spent his summers with his aunt and her Russian husband, the director of the Orford Arts Centre, a fussy two-story building whose wrap-around verandah covered more ground than the tiny bungalow where Harry, his mother and kid brother lived in Sherbrooke. But Harry didn't care if Sam's uncle was a "big" name in the music world. His buddy was just a regular guy and treated Harry, the musical prodigy, like one too.

As Harry stomped up the stairs of the verandah, he could hear the strained notes of a violin. Sam's practising, he thought. He banged the brass door knocker. The violin continued screeching. Too bad Sam hadn't inherited any of his uncle's musical genes.

When no one came to the door, Harry followed the sounds of the violin to the back garden, where he didn't find Sam practising. Instead, he whistled under his breath. Next to the roses stood a Baywatch babe with bright blonde hair.

Bummer. If only he were old enough to date.

With her eyes closed in concentration, she dragged the bow back and forth over the strings of the violin. A shame her playing didn't match her looks.

Too shy to interrupt, Harry waited, hoping this prime-time knockout would open her eyes. He glanced back at the empty windows of the cottage and saw no sign of Sam, his aunt or his uncle. Deciding Sam wasn't home, he turned to leave.

At that moment, Sam's uncle came rushing around the side of the building. Harry was always surprised by the man's size. Looked more like an NHL hockey player than a violinist. But Harry knew no self-respecting hockey player would be caught dead in a red lacy shirt like the one Mr. Malinovka was wearing.

"Sorry I am being late, Zoë darling," the maestro shouted in his thick Russian accent. Then he directed his intense gaze at Harry. "What you doing here, boy, pestering my protégée?"

Zoë stopped playing and looked at Harry with the bluest eyes he'd ever seen. "Please, sir," she said, "he wasn't bothering me, only listening to my dreadful music."

"Nonsense, my dear. You playing marvellous. Only need practice." He turned back to Harry. "Now go, boy." He shooed Harry away with his long musician's fingers.

But Harry stood his ground. He'd tangled with Mr. Malinovka before. "I'm looking for Sam, sir. Do you know where he is?"

The maestro glowered. "Looking for silly birds. Better he practise. You too, boy."

As Harry walked away, he turned for one last glimpse of the beautiful Zoë. Her golden head shimmered against the red shirt of the maestro. While one of his thick arms enclosed her bow arm, the other circled around her slim back to grasp her slender hand on the violin's neck.

Old lech, Harry muttered to himself. Above their bowed heads, Harry caught sight of another flash of gold, flitting from branch to leafy branch.

The rare Yellow Warbler. First sighting. Too bad the building ruled it out.

*   *   *

Next morning, in anticipation of wiping the dimples off his buddy's laughing face, Harry crammed his notebook into his cello case. Sixteen sightings, he was going to crow, one more and I beat you.

But he wasn't able to dish out these words, for Sam wasn't in the first class.

So Harry fidgeted through the boring music theory lesson that neither of them liked. He fully expected to see Sam at orchestra practice, the one class his friend really enjoyed, even if he was only a member of the violin section because of his uncle. Sure wasn't because of his musical talent.

But instead of Sam whizzing elastic bands at the timpanist's Jello bum or whatever else Sam had thought up to get a rise from the fat man, Harry found his buddy's chair vacant and the other orchestra members in an uproar.

"What's up?" he asked a fellow cellist, a boy several years older who'd also been at the music school last summer.

"The flautist, Yvette, has gone missing."

The image of the older girl with cinnamon hair and a freckled ski-jump nose popped into his mind. Harry snorted. "Probably run off with some guy."

"Maybe, but don't forget about Chantal last summer. They never did find her."

How could he forget big boobed Chantal with the weird hair? The guitarist had gone missing the day after Harry had finally been rewarded with his magical sighting of the Eastern Bluebird. He started to ask when Yvette was last seen, but was stopped by the conductor raising his baton.

For the next couple of hours the Mont Orford Chamber Orchestra practised its signature piece for the coming festival. Although their rendition of Tchaikovsky's *Rococo Variations* was almost as good as any recording by the Montreal Symphony Orchestra, it was missing a couple of ingredients, the fourth violin and the second flautist.

*   *   *

Curious to know what had happened to his buddy, Harry stopped again at the Malinovka cottage. And since Sam was keen on Yvette, Harry also wanted to see what his friend's reaction would be to her running off.

Harry knocked on the screen door. Mrs. Malinovka clattered towards him in the high-heel shoes he thought dumb, along with her sucky city clothes. After all, this was a summer camp. Everyone else wore Nikes and T-shirts.

She thrust her sourpuss face up to the screen and pursed her lips. "Sam's not here," she said.

But Harry could hear the off-key arpeggios of Sam's practising. "If you don't mind, I'll wait out here until he's finished," he said.

"I told you, he's not here." She started to close the main door.

Harry refused to move, knowing Sam's aunt only wanted to get rid of him. She resented his musical talent even more than the maestro did. "Such a waste," Harry had once overheard her saying. "The son of a nobody cleaning lady." His response had been to play even more brilliantly at the next recital.

"That's Sam playing his violin," he said.

Sam's aunt laughed shrilly. "Ha! That squawking comes from my husband's newest protégée." And slammed the door on Harry's face.

I don't blame the lech, Harry thought as he clambered down the steps. Who'd want to be married to that old bag?

Harry trudged back to his residence.

Not like Sam to miss orchestra practice. Wonder what's up?

He had a half-mind to go look for him, but didn't know where to start. His buddy was like him, only interested in music and birding.

When he reached his small room, Harry wasn't sure what he was going to do for the afternoon. He could practise his cello, but he didn't feel like it. He could study for tomorrow's music theory test, but that was boring. So he decided to go after sighting number seventeen and finally beat Sam. He felt pretty sure he could do it, for he'd already had one sighting of the golden plumage of the Yellow Warbler.

*   *   *

After lunch, Harry looked up the warbler's preferred habitat in his bird book and laughed. This was going to be a breeze. He knew the perfect spot, and it was only a short distance from the Malinovka cottage, which helped to explain yesterday's sighting in their garden. He shoved his binoculars, guide and notebook into his backpack. And, figuring it could be a long, hot afternoon, added a couple of cans of Pepsi and a bag of Doritos.

He headed back along Sam's shady lane. He was almost past the stone building when he realized a cop car was parked beside the verandah.

Uh-oh, he thought, hope Sam's not in trouble. But just in case, he decided to hunker down in the cool shade of a thick maple not far from the car. He'd find out from the cops when they came out.

He watched a large splotch of hot sun creep along the grass towards his bare legs. But before it reached his dirty Nikes, two cops walked out the front door, followed by Sam's aunt. Afraid she might see him, Harry scrambled behind the tree. He heard voices, then footsteps crunching along the walk. A car door slammed, followed by another.

He stepped out from behind the tree and into the glare of Mrs. Malinovka.

"I should have the police arrest you for trespassing," she snarled from the verandah.

The cop car backed out of the drive.

He called out, "Is Sam okay?" But Sam's aunt had already escaped inside, with the door banging behind her.

Harry watched the gleaming car disappear around the corner. He didn't bother to chase them, because he knew their visit had nothing to do with his buddy. Otherwise, Mrs. Malinovka would've marched him right up to the cops, telling them it was Harry's fault her nephew was in trouble, just as she did whenever she caught them up to one of Sam's tricks.

So Harry continued on his quest, figuring Sam was bird watching too and would be home when Harry returned this way.

*　　*　　*

Harry followed a narrow path through the woods to one of the many streams that trickled down Mont Orford. His guide said that the Yellow Warbler preferred mature deciduous forests, particularly along riverbanks. He knew of a perfect spot, off the beaten path with little chance of someone coming along and scaring his target away.

Another hundred metres and he arrived at a break in the hardwood forest, where the stream widened into a deep pool of clear crystal water. Large irregular boulders, some flat, some round, lined one side of the pool; dense thickets the other.

Jumping from stone to stone, with a refreshing soaker or two, Harry crossed over to the thickets. He found a small break in the bushes where he could hide and still get a good view of the other side of the pool. He removed his binoculars, notebook and a can of Pepsi from his pack and sat down to begin what he hoped wouldn't be as long a wait as last year. He couldn't. He had a cello masterclass at five.

A hot breeze stirred the trees. A dragonfly flicked back and forth over the still water. He caught sight of a flutter of movement in some foliage on the opposite bank, but the colours were orange and black, not the gold he was waiting for. He wiped his brow, sipped his Pepsi and tried not to think about how good a swim would be.

He'd finished the Doritos and was starting into his second Pepsi when he saw a brief shimmer of gold further downstream.

It vanished then appeared again a few seconds later, this time closer. He sucked in his breath and held it. And finally let it out in one low whistle, when the female Yellow Warbler landed directly across from him on one of the flat rocks.

I was right, he thought gleefully. Now all she had to do was make her call, and he'd finally beat Sam.

He silently raised his binoculars and focused them on his target. Wow! Too much! This was the best sighting of all. None of the others had revealed so much. He couldn't wait to make Sam turn green.

And when the first tentative notes of the call finally drifted from the rock, he almost peed his pants. Too bad, though, the call didn't go with the looks.

He watched and waited, certain of what would happen next. And sure enough, within fifteen minutes the menace arrived, bobbing along. The American Robin—though he could hardly be called "American"—with his puffed up red breast.

But rather than leaving as he usually did, annoyed at the intrusion, Harry stayed and watched. His eyes almost popped through the lens when he saw what happened next. Way better than health class. He should've stuck around those other times too.

He was surprised, however, by how little time it seemed to take for the action to reach its climax. Before he knew it, he was left panting for air, while the robin calmly sauntered away, his red breast puffed out even further.

Then he noticed another robin, this one a female, peeking through some bushes beyond the rocks where the Yellow Warbler preened. Curious, he watched this new red-breasted menace bob from tree to tree until she stopped behind a large maple not more than a few metres away from his target.

But when he saw the look in her black beady eyes and a

wing that wasn't a wing slowly rising, a sudden chill went down his spine. He was about to discover why his two other sightings had gone missing.

"Zoë, get out of the way!" Harry yelled, bursting from his cover. "Mrs. Malinovka has a gun!"

Zoë dove into the water, Harry after her. The gun exploded.

Feeling like a bull's eye, he clung to the naked girl on the bottom of the transparent pool and waited for another bullet to rip through the water.

Lungs bursting, the two were forced to come up for air. Harry broke through the surface fully expecting to hear another gun explosion. Instead he heard radios. Police were scrambling over the rocks. In their midst stood Sam's aunt, in a red blouse, looking more like a trussed chicken then a bobbing robin. And behind them beamed Sam's freckled face, his fingers raised in victory.

*　　*　　*

Feeling as though they'd been caught with their hands in the cookie jar, Harry and Sam told the police about their bird watching contest. Except instead of the feathered variety, which had become boring, they owned up to spying on girls who played their musical instruments alone in the forest. They targeted only girls whose colouring and instrument sound corresponded to that of an actual bird. Twice, Maestro Malinovka, whose name meant robin in English, had ruined the sightings with his bobbing intrusion.

Next day, Harry led the police to the locations where he'd spied on the Eastern Bluebird, their name for Chantal with the blue streaked hair, and freckled Yvette, the Hermit Thrush. It didn't take the police long to uncover the girls' bodies. Sam's aunt had taken to getting rid of her husband's protégées before he got rid of her.

From his buddy, Harry learned that Sam was the one who'd brought in the police. Turned out Harry hadn't beaten Sam after all. Yesterday, while Harry had been crowing over his sighting of Yvette, his buddy had been less than a hundred metres away. As Sam was leaving, he'd seen his aunt walking in the same area. Later he'd caught sight of her hiding a gun. When he heard Yvette was missing, he went to the police.

Unnerved by their experience, and with a strong warning from the police, both boys ended their contest. In future they'd stick to real bird watching.

Besides, after Zoë's thank you kiss, Harry decided looking at girls up close was way better.

R.J. Harlick, *an escapee from the high-tech jungle, decided that solving a murder or two was more fun than chasing the elusive computer bug. This is her second story to be published in the* Ladies' Killing Circle *anthologies. Another story, "Lady Luck", won third place in the 2002 Bony Pete Awards.*

I'm Forever Blowing Bubbles

Lou Allin

When Bill opened the grocery bags Myrna had tossed onto the kitchen table, he knew his paycheque hadn't vanished at the supermarket. A dozen boxes of Kraft Dinner, several cans of no-name peas and one head of rusty lettuce.

"Finally, the discus are getting their own display," she said, setting up the new hex tank in the only open corner of the living room. All of the chairs and the sofa had been shoved into the basement storeroom. "Their spectacular colours disappear when they're cluttered up with the rest."

Bill squinted through his bifocals at the receipt on the table. Four hundred dollars. Every set of breeders had a separate home: mollies, swords, catfish, characins and angels. The fifty-gallon tank was reserved for Bubbles, the African clown knifefish, too fond of her fellows.

Five nights later, while his wife ate her noodles directly from the pot in order to watch the fish feed, Bill decided he couldn't stomach another supper of ersatz cheese sauce and mushy vegetables. What could he make? He recalled taking Myrna to Pancho Villa's on her fiftieth birthday. "Flaunting poverty. A cuisine based on tortillas and beans!" she had snorted after the meal, forbidding him to leave a tip.

His taste buds tingling, he drove to the supermarket for

ingredients, then dared to toss together a hot chili: pintos, tomatoes, onions, jalepeños and a handful of five-alarm powder. The redolence filled the house, and he was stirring home-made cornbread for the private feast when a shriek came from the living room. "You idiot! Look what your stinky food is doing!"

He put down his Corona beer, saved from a Christmas splurge, and joined Myrna to inspect the tank. The fish, normally passive at night, were swimming up and down. "Don't think they can't smell that foul air when the pump is spewing it all over. Are you trying to poison them? Open a can of Spam and make a sandwich." And she rushed to the kitchen, grabbed the boiling pot and hustled it outside, where she dumped the contents contemptuously into the garbage can, slamming the lid like a cymbal. Then she arranged a portable fan and opened all of the doors. After anticipating the chili, Bill didn't feel like anything else, so he took another Corona and sought refuge in Bret Harte's *The Luck of Roaring Camp*. Too bad they didn't live near a major dam site, he thought. Flash floods had their good points.

Later, in a rare social gesture, Myrna subjected Bill to fish imitations. While he read, she peeked out from behind a chair and then retreated when he looked over. "Guess who?" Spot, of course, the shy catfish. Then she rubbed her knuckles over Bill's close-cropped grey head like Bubbles scratching herself on the coral. Building to a climax, she concluded with a pantomime of the meanest small fish in the tank, the bumblebee cichlid, aka the Terminator. Her breath hot with sherry, she rushed at Bill and butted him in the chest, cackling like a demented parrot.

Myrna rarely spoke to Bill except about the daily problems with the fish. "Bubbles is outgrowing her tank again. We've got to get that one-hundred-gallon job," she wailed as Bill limped in from the 37°C record Toronto heat. Buses had broken down, the fans were off at work, and his ancient Aries needed new ball joints.

"Why not give her back to the store? Maybe they'd trade for that needlefish you've been wanting," he offered, picking up the mail from its pile under the slot. It was stifling in the house, but Myrna wouldn't allow an air conditioner to alter the tropical conditions. Tonight was his washing and ironing night, he remembered with dismay as he stripped off his wet shirt.

Myrna dipped into a small holding tank for Bubbles' supper. "Are you kidding? Even if she bullies the others, she's the queen of her species." As she warbled "I'm Forever Blowing Bubbles," her ritual during feeding time, the mammoth jaw of the twenty-inch leviathan vacuumed up the feeder guppies.

The costs escalated with the new glass fortress. Along with lavender gravel, Myrna had to have the latest bionic filter system, which required constant monitoring for weeks to establish a balanced chemical cycle. Bill would come home to her stunned face peering at a murky test tube. "Not more ammonia! She's swimming in a toilet. Time for another water change." And out snaked her Python syphon hoses to drain and refill the tank. No bath for Bill until midnight. And if it wasn't ammonia, it was too much chlorine or iron. Delivery men lugged in spring water in gargantuan proportions. Subscriptions to Freshwater Aquariums and Tropical Breeders littered the coffee table. That was where she learned about the fluval, a costly refinement which sold so rarely that the pet store owner made a mark on the wall when one left the shelves. "Now I can relax at last," she said. "This baby will filter out anything!" And the new toy hummed away.

In fact, everything hummed day and night. And Bill, never

a heavy sleeper, lay tossing for hours, Peggy Lee's "Is That All There Is?" running through his mind. One night when he got up for a glass of milk in the wee hours and switched on the kitchen light, Myrna was crouched in the living room with the glow of the tanks giving a ghastly pallor to her skin. "Douse that, jerk!" she yelled. "I just got the boys and girls settled. The reflection is confusing them. Look at Bubbles, gone behind the condo, just as I dropped down her favourite tiger shrimp." A grinning plastic skull coughed up air as its teeth met and parted.

Deciding on a drink instead, Bill overturned the ice cube tray into a tumbler, added a double thumb of bourbon, then took a long swallow. Several minutes later, he was relaxing in bed with *The Outcasts of Poker Flat*. Blizzards, he thought. Convenient, quiet. Easy to run off the road in deep snow, leave Myrna, go for "help." How long would it take come January to drive up to the wilderness north of Sudbury? Six hours tops! Suddenly he gagged. "What is this?" he yelled as he pulled bits of pale ragged flesh from the glass.

Myrna appeared in the doorway, a smile flickering. "Silly Billy. Just some cod I froze for Bubbles for slow release. Won't hurt you."

A few weeks later, when Bill tried to use his VISA at the Shell station, it was rejected. Myrna, responsible for paying the accounts, blamed an oversight. But then he found the warning letter from the tax department and handed it to his wife, who was crumbling white mosquito larvae. "So sue me," she said, tapping on the glass at an inquiring discus. "Do you know how long it takes a bank to foreclose? Nearly two years. By then, your GIC comes due."

"Myrna," Bill said, a catch in his voice, "I saved that for a fly fishing trip to the Yukon."

Myrna didn't answer, admiring her new red cap oranda, its

lumpy pompon plastered on like an exterior brain. It was lurching around the tank, gobbling whatever came near. Bill blinked at his wife's henna hair, sculpted eyebrows with that perpetually surprised look, exaggerated lipstick outline. Only Lucille Ball got away with that.

Later that month, as Bill watched Myrna flipping through *Getting Started in Salt Water Aquariums* and making an ominous list, he could see his last dollar sinking faster than the loonie. And when the nursing home called to tell him they hadn't received the monthly check for his mother's care, cold sweat formed on his brow and his chest pumped like the Aries going up a hill. Not Mom's trust fund! "Did you send out the Happy Valley payment?" he asked.

Myrna clipped a romaine lettuce leaf to the tank for Annie the ancistrus and hummed a little tune. "Don't worry your pea-brain about that. Bunny Bagshaw says everyone's doing it."

"Doing what?" Bill gasped, his knees weakening.

"Liquidating, of course. That way the government picks up the tab quite nicely. The supplement for indigents kicks in. What a country."

"Indigents! You mean you told them Mom is broke? It meant everything to her to pay her own way! She trusted us!"

"Don't be a fool. She doesn't have to know, but she will have to leave her semi-private for a quad. Big deal. Give her more company anyway." She attached the Python hose and began to suck up Bubbles' tank, swirls of debris forming miniature tornados.

Bill braced himself against an onset of vertigo. As Myrna started the refill, with a strange and sudden focus, he saw the dangling electrical cord for the immersion heater. He had connected the system and knew the dangers. What would cause Myrna to be careless? The death of one of her favourites?

Bubbles? Yet Bill hated to see even a guppy suffer. He heard Myrna open the front door. "I'm going to Popeye's for some Fung-All," she called. "The barbs have been scratching." The door slammed, and the Aries groaned into action.

Bill rummaged in the basement freezer. There it was, a nice medium sized Pacific salmon languishing through the months since Myrna had stopped cooking. He gently removed the wrappings and scrutinized it from all sides. It resembled Bubbles, or would with the lights off.

Back upstairs, he removed the cover from the big tank, disconnected the electrical cord and set to work. First, he dipped down with a big net and hauled out Bubbles, placing her in a full, lukewarm bathtub. Then, with dark thread the same colour as the fish, he tied the salmon among the heavier plants under the large heater tube. He connected the thread to the tube and unscrewed the heater until it rested perilously in place. "CAUTION: Do Not Immerse Beyond This Point!" it warned. Finally, he replugged the main cable and waited, turning off all the lights in the house.

As soon as Myrna opened the door, he yelled, "Come here! The power's off, and there's something wrong with Bubbles!" Myrna rushed over, bugged out her eyes and plunged her hand into the tank, pulling the heater element with her. "Bubbles!" was her last word.

In the ten minutes before the ambulance came, Bill shut off the main breaker, chopped up and flushed the helpful salmon and thread, set up the fluval, and dabbed a bit of cayenne into the corners of his eyes. "I took the big fish out of her tank to give the walls a good cleaning. I guess Myrna didn't see her, panicked and reached in to move the plants," he told the attendants, and later the police as he blew his nose. "That fish meant the world to her."

Bill was given the week off to make arrangements for the funeral. Along with the obituary, he included a note that, in lieu of flowers, donations could be made to the African Knifefish Rescue Association.

Back from a weekend of trout fishing, he made plans to return his charges to the pet store. The tanks might make attractive terrariums for the nursing home. Then Bubbles hove into view. The large, placid fish had missed her guppies and was staring out through the glass, clown dots undulating along grey velvet folds, eight on one side and six on the other. She is a beauty, Bill thought, counting the circles as he felt his heart rate slow; the tight metal coil had disappeared from his chest. Bubbles swam so gracefully...and so sadly. With an underslung jaw and limpid gimlet eyes, the fish could have been pouting. Bill went to the fridge and returned with a Corona and shrimp bits. "Don't worry, Big Girl," he said. "Daddy's home."

Lou Allin *introduced amateur sleuth Belle Palmer in* Northern Winters Are Murder, *followed by* Blackflies Are Murder, *which was shortlisted for an Arthur Ellis Award for Best Novel, and* Bush Poodles Are Murder. *Her short stories have been published by* Storyteller, Sou'wester, *and* The Dalhousie Review, *and her poetry has appeared in over forty literary magazines. Visit her at* www.louallin.com.

Fry, Fry, Fry

He was out every night at a bar
Cheating like any rock star
And his wife Peggy Sue
Tried to think what to do
when she watched him pick up his guitar.
He had started a habit, you see,
Picked up from his hero's E.P.,
Of soaking in the tub
With his guitar unplugged
And plucking away silently.
He yelled out that with her he was bored
"I found someone else," had her floored.
It's obvious to you
What she then had to do
Yes, she plugged in the dangling cord.

Joy Hewitt Mann

Brian's Song

Linda Wiken

L ast night, I'd seen Garry Boyce for the first time in fourteen years. This morning, his body was found floating face down in the Rideau Canal. By one p.m., the Ottawa Police had tracked me down. At this point, the reality had not yet set in, but one thing I did realize—Detective Frank Czenko found the fact that I'd been the last person to see Garry alive extremely interesting. I hastened to point out that the murderer, not I, fit that category.

"So, you left him at about midnight, is that right, Ms. Landry?"

"Yes, officer, that's right. We left Darcy McGee's, where we'd met for a drink after he'd taken in a CD launch at the NAC's Fourth Stage."

"And you had one drink, a scotch, and talked…business. Right?"

That slight pause and his suggestive tone made me nervous, as did the fact that he'd been grilling me for the past hour. Okay, so maybe it wasn't quite a grilling. But try feeling calm and collected in such a situation. Not that I had anything to hide.

"You've got it. He was to have been my guest on my radio program tonight, and we were doing it live. I wanted to tape some atmosphere to blend into the studio interview, and I wanted to go over some things first. Make certain we were on the same page."

"And why wouldn't you be?"

Oh boy, if he needed a motive, I might be handing him one. But first I wanted to set the scene. "We met at that hour, at that location, at his request. He'd been totally tied up in this opera he was writing, which was to have been our topic, by the way."

"I see." He stared while I talked, then he scribbled like mad in his notebook between questions. "So, were you concerned the program wouldn't go too smoothly? Is that why you met with him beforehand?"

"Something like that. He was known to have a short fuse, and I wanted to check if any areas were off limits."

"Like what?"

"His new writing partnership with his one-time rival, for one. Our past relationship, for another. What was happening with his old partnership? Things like that."

His pen hung in mid-air. "What relationship would that be, Ms. Landry? Or do you mind if I call you Terri?"

Now I was really worried. Wasn't that a sure sign you were heading to the top of the suspect's list? Call them by a first name, be friendly. Suspect, in gratitude, blurts out a confession?

"I don't mind, Frank. It was years ago, in university. Garry and I were an item for about a year. Maybe not quite that long. Anyway, he met a friend of mine at a party, and she became the new hit."

"That can rankle. Had that happen a few times myself."

I'll just bet. He hadn't asked a question, which meant I felt no need to provide an answer. We sat looking at each other for about a minute, then he caved.

"Were you still bitter?"

"Hardly. It's been a long time, detective. I have had a few relationships since then. And I haven't seen him since then."

"So, why now?"

"I told you, I wanted to interview him for my show. I do an arts program on the CBC, and it's not every day that a country music star turns his pen to writing the lyrics and libretto for an opera. Besides, he's a home-grown star, which adds extra interest, around here anyway."

"And you left him at what time?"

"Around midnight. And I came straight home."

"Anyone verify that?"

"No. I live alone, and my landlord's out of town for the weekend."

"And where did Mr. Boyce go after that?"

"I have no idea. He didn't say. I left him at the door and walked to my car, which I'd parked on Albert."

"Any ideas as to how he ended up face down in the Rideau Canal?"

I'd been trying not to think about that. "None."

"Any ideas as to enemies or the like?"

"None. I just told you, I hadn't seen him for over a decade. I have no idea what's happening in his life, except what I read and hear."

He stood up, almost knocking my new Ikea Oland armchair over. I tensed, wondering if he'd be pulling out handcuffs. Instead he stuck his big hairy hands, complete with notebook, in his pockets and headed to the door.

"I'll be getting back to you, Ms. Landry."

*   *   *

I watched the night tick past in increments of fifteen minutes.

The overnight temperature dipped to the mid-twenties, and my air conditioner wasn't working. Of course, it had to happen when my landlord was away. I'd positioned two fans to blast away at me, not that they helped very much. But what really kept my eyelids glued open were thoughts of Garry Boyce. The not quite handsome but oh so romantic Garry in our senior year at Carleton University. The late night rides in his old MGB, top down, racing along Highway 15 with a long stopover at the Burritt Rapid Locks. A pauper's picnic on the cramped wooden balcony of the two-bedroom apartment he shared with a fellow music student. Rooting for the Carleton Ravens in the pouring rain, followed by the mad crush in the celebratory victory at Roosters.

It had been fun, but at no time had I thought it would be long-term. That's why when Garry suddenly announced he and Crystal, my roommate, were now an item, I was steamed but not totally heartbroken. Nor did I rant and tear my hair out when they were married. I also felt pleased for him when success came his way. Detective Frank Czenko had it all wrong.

Maybe it was a mugging gone wrong. Garry's short fuse had led to several fist fights during the time I was dating him. Or maybe it had something to do with his career. If so, his former partner, Harley Soames, might know something.

*　　*　　*

I didn't stop to think about the wisdom of my getting mixed up in a murder investigation. If I had, I know I would have stayed put in my toasty apartment the next morning. But I needed to know what had happened to my friend. Because when all was said and done, Garry Boyce and I had been lovers at one time.

Also, I wasn't totally convinced that my new "friend", Detective Czenko, had my best interests at heart.

I found Harley Soames at the studio he'd shared with Garry, in the Market above a trendy restaurant that opened and closed early, which went well with the music makers' penchant for starting and ending late. They'd been a writing team for close to ten years, with songs on the chart for over half of them. Although my watch said one p.m., it looked like Harley had just dragged himself out of bed. Or maybe it was a bad case of "hat hair". The remnants of what had probably started life as a black fedora lay crumpled on the desk next to the door.

He pulled a chair out from behind the electric piano and pushed it towards me while he perched on one of the stools parked between the two acoustic and one electric guitar propped up to one side of the room. He'd managed to keep a Tim Hortons cup upright throughout. He sucked back some caffeine before answering my opening shot.

"Well, we parted on friendly terms, if that's what you're getting at, Terri. Actually, we didn't really part permanently, just a short separation while he got that fucking opera out of his system." He heaved a deep sigh, took another swig, and slouched down even further.

"Why do you think that opera was so important to him?"

"I'm damned if I know. I'd have thought the award would have done it for him." He looked over at the impressive glass and nickel Juno statue on top of the mixing console, the award they'd shared for the best songwriter of the year earlier this spring. "We finally hit the big fucking award time, but that's not enough for Gar. Probably because Whiteside and him had that rivalry going on for so goddamned long. I don't know what's behind it all. 'Cause even though we've done good with country music, Garry was always moaning about being second rate, that classical was more legit or something. Probably because that's Whiteside's gig."

I almost missed his next comment. "I could've beat the crap out of him whenever he got going on that."

I hadn't realized there'd been a serious rivalry between Garry and Jordan Whiteside. I did know they'd had some history since long before I'd entered the picture. We'd even double dated a couple of times, but that hadn't been enough to get me an interview with Jordan when I'd called him last week. I hadn't seen Jordan since those days, even though he was a somewhat successful Canadian composer.

"It's odd that they'd collaborate, in that case."

"Well, Whiteside wasn't hot to trot. Garry really had to push him, but I guess he finally pressed the right button. Or maybe it was his snagging the Juno that did it. Anyway, the thing was half-finished."

"What was the plot? Garry was very vague when discussing it."

"Well, I'm not sure. I think he switched it somewhere along the line. But that's all I know. You oughta be talking to Whiteside about this."

"You're right. I have only one more thing to ask...about Garry's private life. I know he and Crystal were splitting. Do you know why?"

He shrugged. "Well, I think they just got tired of each other. It happens. That's what it sounded like, anyway."

"Did Garry have any other women in his life?"

Harley laughed. "Well, you didn't know him very well if you have to ask that. He attracted women without even trying. Something boyish about him that women like, and being in music never hurts when it comes to scoring." He smiled at his pun. I let it pass.

"But was there anyone special? Anyone recent?"

"He'd been getting some calls, which he usually cut short. Could've been a woman. If so, it wasn't someone he wanted to talk to. On the other hand, there was one he'd call every day."

"Do you know her name?"

"Well, I can guess, but I wouldn't tell you without being certain. And since I don't plan to ask the lady, you're outta luck."

"Did Crystal know about her?"

"How the hell would I know? There's not much else I can tell you. And like I said, I had no grudge against Garry, even though he ticked me off the odd time. I was using the break to stockpile some tunes, and he'd just have had to catch up with the words when he was ready to."

Harley Soames didn't strike me as a man with a motive, no matter how big a pain Garry could be. As I left his studio, I reminded myself that I'd met many accomplished liars in this business, so best to keep an open mind.

*　　*　　*

I finally got to talk to Jordan Whiteside due to sheer persistence. I literally camped in front of his house until he put in an appearance, going out the front door, Monday around noon. He recognized me, of course, and agreed to a short talk when he realized I wouldn't pull my foot out of the open front door.

"Of course, I was shocked about Garry Boyce. I feel badly because we were friends and also, I have to be candid, because our opera will never be finished."

"I thought you'd been reluctant to do the opera."

"Had been is correct, Terri. I had my own career track

planned and an opera, especially a country one, wasn't on it. But Garry convinced me it would be a good move for both of us. And as you probably remember, he could be very persuasive when he wanted something."

I tried to put thoughts of Garry and his persuasive ways, especially within the confines of the front seat of his MGB, out of my mind.

"May I ask why you wouldn't talk to me before?" Not that it had anything to do with the murder, but I wanted to know.

"I'm a busy person, Terri. I just felt an interview wasn't worth the time to me. Sorry, no offence intended."

"None taken." Like hell. "Would you tell me what it was made you decide to do this opera with Garry?"

"Sure. Money. It wouldn't have hurt my reputation either, if it became a big hit. But Garry, always the practical one, made me see there was the potential for a lot of money in this."

I looked around me. From where I sat—on a teal leather sofa in a family room that put my entire place to shame—I couldn't imagine Jordan being in need of money. But he hadn't said that. I suppose no one's immune to making money, even if you have plenty. Mind you, he could be mortgaged and line-of-credited to the hilt. And then there was the beautiful Amanda Whiteside, always the latest in glam whenever I'd seen her. It would take big bucks to keep her in the latest styles.

I was just leaving, poised to step out onto the porch, when I asked my final question. "Do you know if Garry had a girlfriend on the side?"

Jordan bristled. "How the hell would I know that?"

The interview was ended. This time I moved my entire body out of the doorway quickly.

*　　*　　*

Back in my car, I pulled out my cellphone and punched in the CBC number, asking the receptionist for the one person I knew lived and breathed opera, the local host of the Saturday afternoon opera program. She'd be the best bet to answer my question. In fact, she confirmed my suspicion that there wouldn't be a windfall of cash coming from this opera unless it took off, like the crossover rock opera *Tommy* of a few years before. And neither of us could make the stretch to a country opera with music coming from Whiteside. And, even if they could manage to produce such a piece, we both had serious doubts about how successful it would be. So, what was the real reason he'd capitulated? And did it have anything to do with the murder?

I decided to give Harley another try and hope for some additional answers this time. Unfortunately, he wasn't able to produce a copy of the script for the opera.

"The police cleared out Garry's desk," he said, "and Crystal said they'd done the same at the house. Why the fuck's it so important anyway?"

"I don't know if it is. I just thought I'd read it over and see if they sounded like million dollar lyrics."

"Well..."

"You did read them?"

"Well, no. But you know, we always make three copies of our songs. One stays here, one goes home, and the other is mailed to a post office box. In case of fire or theft. I'll just bet good ol' Garry did the same thing this time."

"Do the cops know about this?"

"They didn't ask."

I smiled. "Could we go check it out?"

He smiled. "Be my fuckin' pleasure, ma'am."

It took about three minutes to walk the two blocks to Desjardins Pharmacy, boasting one of the few postal outlets in the Market. Harley cleared the box, tossing out the usual flyers and junk mail, and was left with two envelopes; one stuffed with folded papers, the other a thin version of the first.

"That there's Garry's writing. This must be it. Not sure what this one is though, it's his writing, too." He waved the thinner one in my face

"Hmm, it's sealed, and opening it might be considered tampering with evidence, even if it proved to be nothing."

I looked at Harley. He looked at me, and a slow smile inched across both our faces.

"Well, I could say I just opened it along with the other mail, not looking to see who it was meant for."

I nodded. "Just what I was thinking. Let's head over to the Second Cup, my treat."

We each ordered a cappuccino. I paid, then searched out a table while Harley waited for our cups. The place was about half full, but I by-passed the spots with a view for the single booth with the padded bench towards the back. Harley had tucked the envelopes in his jacket pocket, so while I waited, I tried to dredge up some obscure fact that I'd buried in the back of my mind which was now teasing me to be let out.

Jordan's reaction to my final question had sparked it. Garry and his girlfriends. I knew nothing about his current love life, except that he had an active one. What I did know was his past, starting in reverse order with Crystal, then me, and who had I replaced? He'd talked about her a few times, which had steamed me, as I recalled.

Come to think of it, I'd been ticked off at him quite often, which would account for my not being too fazed when he paired off with Crystal. There was one double date with Jordan, though, which had led to a doozy of a fight on my doorstep. Mainly because Garry had gone all surly and uncooperative when Jordan turned up with his new date, Amanda Brown, who was now Amanda Whiteside…who had been Garry's squeeze before me. That was it.

Now what it meant, I had no idea, unless Garry and Amanda had taken up where they'd left off. It would have been pretty dumb of Garry to jeopardize the new partnership he'd wanted so badly. Interesting thought, though.

Harley arrived with our drinks, then ripped open the thick envelope first. He glanced through it, then passed it over to me. "Well, it's the opera, all right. Call's it *Brian's Song*. He'll have to come up with something catchier than that though. Fuck, guess he won't have to." He gave a short, embarrassed laugh.

I started reading but turned to skimming until page 5. "He's changed the font for a few pages." I thumbed through four of them until it went back to Times New Roman.

Harley took more care opening the second envelope. He pulled out a yellowed newspaper article and started reading. I went back to my task.

I'd finished one page when Harley filled me in. "It talks about a car accident back in the mid-eighties. Some music student at Carleton U drove his wheels into that cement abutment coming down Bank Street at Billings Bridge. He died on the way to the hospital. Wonder what that's all about."

I reached for the clipping. Brian Swenson had been 23 the night he died. Same age as the Brian in the story I held in my hands. Brian Swenson, as I recalled, had been Garry's roommate at the time of the accident, the year before we became an item. I went back to reading the libretto.

I needed another cappuccino to steady my trembling hands. Harley joined me in drinking, but didn't say a word as he watched me over the rim of his cup.

I took a final sip then said, "I think I know who did it."

"Well, are you gonna to tell me?"

"Not until I'm certain."

*　　*　　*

I arrived at the Whiteside residence as Amanda was leaving. Her face was a dead give-away that things were not right in her world. She pasted on a weak smile and ushered me through the door, then left. I should have suggested she don some dark glasses until the puffy eyelids and redness disappeared.

I heard movement in a room towards the far end of the dazzling foyer. I called out Jordan's name as I reached the door. Then knocked. The door swung open and Jordan glared down at me.

"*Now* what is it?" he asked. This wasn't going to be easy.

"I'm trying to get my show pieced together, and I just wanted to ask you a couple more questions. Did Garry show you what he'd written?"

"I'd seen some lyrics. I've written four numbers so far, but he'd only finished one. I think he was concentrating on the libretto."

I'll say. "And had he shown you any of that?"

"No."

"Told you what was in it?"

He moved over to the massive walnut desk that commanded the entire half wall between a fireplace and the doorway, and leaned against it. "Some. Why do you ask?"

"I was just reading over what he'd done so far, and it's a bit odd. He has two versions on the go, almost like he can't make up his mind."

Jordan picked up a pewter letter opener and started turning it over, top to tip, between his hands. "He did say something

81

about not knowing which way to take it. How much had he written?"

"Enough for me to know why you'd agreed to go in on the project."

"Is that so? Why don't you tell me all about it, Terri."

I stood up, partly to show some assertiveness but mainly to get into position to make a break for it if need be. Since he stood between the hall and me, it would have to be the patio. "It's called *Brian's Song*...did you know that?"

"No. That's just his working title. We hadn't gotten around to discussing it."

"It's a good choice, since the story seems to be about a young music student named Brian who died in a car accident. However, the interesting part is that Brian had written a composition that he was about to enter in the CBC Young Composer's Contest. And the twist is that the song was entered, but under someone else's name. And it won first prize. That person, named Jody, goes on to become a big success in the music world or at least, that's where I think Garry was taking it."

Jordan strolled towards me. "I had no idea Garry could plot intrigue. It might have been a success after all."

"Except that it's based on a true story, isn't it, Jordan? I remember Garry talking about his former roommate Brian Swenson. In fact, I've been remembering a lot from those days, like how Garry and Amanda were once an item."

He flinched but kept walking. I'd begun to inch over towards the French doors behind me. I'd spotted what looked like a heavy-duty statue of an Irish Setter on a small table along my flight path.

"I've no time for reminiscing, Terri."

"No, I guess you've got to get busy covering your tracks. It won't take the police long to reach the same conclusions once they see the libretto plus the newspaper clipping Garry had saved. What did you do, rig Brian's car to crash for good measure?"

Jordan's mouth stretched to a tight line. "Garry had it coming. He was blackmailing me to do the opera with him, and the bastard was screwing my wife on the side. And now, it's your turn…you always were too nosy, Terri."

He lunged at me with the letter opener. I grabbed the statue and knocked the knife out of his hand, then gave him a swift kick between the legs, right where it counts. He lurched forward and smashed through the glass doors just as Detective Czenko and his boys rushed into the house.

"You okay, Terri?" Czenko watched as one officer, gun in hand, checked the bloodied body of Jordan Whiteside.

"He's alive." The other officer radioed for the paramedics.

Czenko hadn't waited for my answer. He knelt next to Jordan, made sure he was coherent and then read him his rights.

I stood there and thought about Garry and Jordan, Garry and Amanda, Garry and me while I tried unhooking the wire the police technician had taped under my sweater.

Linda Wiken *is owner of Prime Crime Mystery Books in Ottawa. Her short stories have appeared in the four previous Ladies' Killing Circle anthologies (she was co-editor of* Cottage Country Killers) *as well as other mysterious publications. She has not aspired to singing opera, although she is a member of the Ottawa Police Chorus.*

Summertime

Audrey Jessup

It rained solidly the first three days of our holiday at the cottage on the Rideau Lakes. After doing all the chores to get the place shipshape, we had to try to entertain ourselves. We never had a TV at the cottage. Mom figured it did us all good to live without it for the summer. So she worked on her quilting, Dad and Donny played chess, and I built a model generator. Donny was always real smart at theory and brain games. I was better at practical hands-on stuff. Mom says even at the age of four, I had figured out I had to look after my brother, although he was three years older. I was the one who knew where the cereal was kept. Donny was the one who could figure out the guidelines for assembling the prizes that came in the cereal boxes. Now, at thirteen, I was okay at following written instructions, but Donny was going to be one of the people who write the instructions in the first place.

Being holed up in a cottage in the rain is not great for family togetherness, but before we got real snarky with each other, the weather cleared. On the fourth day we woke up to sunshine, and we all went for a swim. Afterwards, Donny and I took the canoe out to see what was new on the lake since last year. As we tied up the canoe at the dock and climbed the slope to the cottage, we could hear them arguing. Mom, her hair covered with that dye stuff you could smell a mile off, was leaning over the porch, holding a cocoa tin. She was shouting at Dad, who was hunkered down on an old plastic sheet with bits of machinery scattered all around him.

"It's only down to the village and back, for Christ's sake," he said. "He'll be back in five minutes."

"But you know he's not supposed to drive without a licensed driver with him. What if he's stopped for some reason? We'll all be in trouble."

"Well, I can't go. I've just got the lawnmower apart, and if I leave it, I'll never remember where anything went. Besides, I'm up to my elbows in grease. You'll have to go."

"How can I go with all this black goop on my hair? I don't imagine you want it all over the car."

"Then it'll just have to wait until the goop's finished, won't it?"

"I can't wait that long. I've already started the recipe. I have to have the cocoa now. I've got all the other ingredients mixed and ready. I promised Grampa I'd make him his favourite cake for his party."

Dad just shrugged. "There's always ice cream."

"I am not going to celebrate my father's birthday with a dish of ice cream." A little pulse throbbed in Mom's neck, and her face was beginning to go pink.

"Well, then, you'll have to let Donny go. Just give him the money and tell him what you want. Tim can go with him to keep an eye on things. Right, sport?" He winked at me. "Whistle for the dog and take him, too. He always likes a car ride." He tossed the car keys to Donny. "Drive carefully, now. No racing up and down, revving the engine."

Mom fussed a bit more before she finally caved in. "You will be careful, won't you? The roads may still be slippery after all that rain."

"Sure, Mom." Donny turned away, giving me a high five. "Let's go. Get Alfalfa."

I didn't have to "get" Alfalfa. As soon as that old dog heard the clink of car keys, he was in the back seat before anyone else had a chance.

"You'd better sit in the back with him," Donny said. "I don't want him poking his head over my shoulder and distracting me while I'm driving."

He made it sound very important.

I sat in the back with my hand through Alfalfa's collar. He wanted to put his head out of the window behind the driver's seat, but I wouldn't let him. I pushed him over so he'd stick his head out the other side.

The lane from the cottage to the highway was all blotchy with sunlight coming through the leaves.

"Gee, it must be harder to drive when you can't see the bumps and things," I said.

"Naw," said Donny. "You get a feel for these things."

Yeah, right. Ten driving lessons and a few hours behind the wheel, and you get a feel for these things. Mom had let him drive part of the way to the cottage and he'd done okay, even with Mom sitting stiff as a board beside him. She'd done okay, too, only told him to be careful once because the old gateposts at the end of our road made the turn very sharp.

It was only five kilometres to the village. We went to Murphy's General Store, and while Donny bought Mom's stuff, I got three ice cream cones, chocolate with chocolate chips. The third one was for Alfalfa. Otherwise I'd never be able to eat mine in peace. Even at that I had to be fast.

Donny still had most of his ice cream when we'd finished ours. He was driving home along the main street, taking a lick at his cone now and again, driving with one hand. We were almost out of the village when two ladies with three little girls stepped onto the road ahead, and he slowed right down to let them cross over. Suddenly, Alfalfa lunged for Donny's ice cream, knocking the cone into his lap. I made a grab for Alfalfa's collar. The car leaped forward, and there was a thump. A Raggedy Ann doll hit the window on the passenger side, the red hair all spread out like a halo.

Donny's foot must have jammed on the gas pedal, because suddenly we were racing through town. I looked out the rear window and saw people bending over something in the road.

"Donny," I said.

"Shut up." The cords on the back of his neck were rigid.

"But..."

"Just shut up."

We drove back to the cottage in silence. Even Alfalfa knew better than to move. But my mind wouldn't stop. I kept seeing the people bending over something in the road. Surely it was just the doll. It must have got broken. Yeah, that was probably it. I should never have let go of Alfalfa's collar.

Donny parked beside Mom's car. As soon as I opened the door, Alfalfa took off as if he knew he was guilty, too. But we couldn't both crawl under the porch and hide.

"Take the bag for Mom," Donny said.

I took a look at the front of the car as I went by. The right headlight was broken, and there were a few scratches. There was no blood. So maybe it was okay.

"Everything all right?" Dad asked me as I went by.

"Sure," I said. "Except Donny spilt his ice cream down the front of his pants."

Dad grinned. "That'd be a bit of a shocker." He called over to Donny. "If I'd known driving solo was going to make you dirty your pants, I'd have gone myself." He laughed. "Tim, do you want to give me a hand afterwards? This lawn mower is turning out to be more complicated than I thought."

"Do you have the book? Donny could work it out from that."

Dad didn't have the lawn mower book. I don't know whether Donny could have concentrated on it, anyway. I helped Dad with the machine, and I had a hard time keeping my mind on the job. Donny took Alfalfa and went out in the canoe.

By lunch time, we had the mower fixed, Mom's hair was its usual brown, and Grampa's favourite chocolate cake was cooling on the counter.

Mom frowned at Donny pushing his sandwich around on the plate. "Are you feeling okay?" she asked. "You look a bit pale."

I jumped in. "Too much sun," I said. "Swimming this morning and the canoe ride after. It was hot out there. And we did have the ice cream."

"Well, ice cream doesn't seem to have spoilt your appetite, young man," Mom said as I finished my sandwich.

"Oh, damn," Dad said. "I wanted to check if it had marked the upholstery. I'd better take a look. It's easier to get out before it sets."

Donny got up and went into the bathroom.

I kept my head down, but I heard the screen door bang behind Dad. When he came back in, his tread was heavy.

"How did the headlight get broken, Tim?"

I swallowed. "We...we hit the gatepost as we came in." I said it fast, as if that would make it more true.

"I knew something was upsetting him," Mom said. "He was so quiet, even for Donny." She looked at my father. "He was probably afraid to tell you he'd damaged the car. Poor kid must have been going through agonies." She got up and went to the bathroom door. "Donny," she called. "It's okay. Tim told us how you broke the light. It could happen to anyone. Come out, and I'll give you something to settle your stomach."

His voice was muffled. "I'll be out in a minute." We heard the water running in the basin.

"Why didn't you tell us you'd hit the gatepost?" Mom said as soon as he opened the door.

Donny looked at me.

"Dad asked me how the headlight got broken," I said quickly, before he could say anything. "So I told him how we took the turn a bit too wide."

"We really should take down those posts, Jack. I've always found the turn difficult myself." Mom put her arm round Donny's shoulder. "You should have told us. It's not the end of the world, you know." She looked at my father. He didn't say anything. "Will the insurance cover it?" she asked.

Dad shook his head. "We can't use the insurance. We could lose all our coverage if they find out we let him drive on his own."

"Well, we don't have to tell them that. I could say I was with him when it happened."

"It would still send the rate for him sky high, and it's costing enough already." Dad frowned. "It will be better if I say I did it. I guess it's really my fault, anyway. I should have just left the damned lawnmower." His chair scraped on the floor as he pushed it back. "I'll go and have a look at the post so I can get my story straight." Donny and I looked at one another. He was as pale as his white T-shirt.

"Come on, Donny," Mom said. "I want you to go lie down for a while. You look dreadful. Clear the table, Tim, will you."

As I stacked the dishes, I could hear Mom making him take a couple of aspirins. Dad seemed to be gone a long time.

When he came back in, he walked slowly over to the table and sat down. "Where's Donny?" he said.

"Mom made him go to bed. She's giving him some aspirins. She thinks maybe he caught cold swimming."

"I checked both posts." His voice was flat. "There are no..." He stopped talking abruptly when my mother came back into the room.

"He looks really ill," she said, frowning. "I hope he hasn't caught something." She turned to me and put her hand on my forehead. "You seem okay. Do you think you could sweep the porch and straighten things up before Grampa arrives?"

"Sure," I said. I was glad to go.

When I was finished, Mom told me to change my T-shirt, and in the bedroom I told Donny about Dad going down to look at the gatepost. "He started to tell me there were no marks, but then Mom came in and he clammed up. Do you think I should sneak down when it's dark and hack at it a bit with the axe?"

"Naw, it wouldn't be any good. He'd be able to tell. It wouldn't be the same kind of marks."

I was glad Grampa was coming that afternoon. I thought it might help lighten things up a bit. He was always so cheerful. "What's the use of complaining?" he would say. "If you can fix a problem, fix it. If you can't, get over it and get on with other things." Could we fix this problem?

He arrived about four o'clock, carrying a bunch of pink flowers for Mom and a bottle of wine for Dad. He was all excited.

"I could hardly get through the village for cops," he said. "They were all over the place, and stopping every car. Apparently there was a hit-and-run accident this morning, a little girl. They've taken her to the Children's Hospital. Sounded serious. I stopped to get you guys some ice cream. Chocolate with chocolate chip, right?"

I saw Donny tense. "Great, Grampa," I said. "I'll put it in the freezer for later."

"Yes, fellow in the store told me about the accident. The worst kind, hit-and-run. I hope they get the bastard. But it seems the police have found something that will help."

"What kind of something?" Dad asked in a tight kind of voice.

Grampa shrugged. "He wasn't sure. Glass, maybe, tiny piece of the car, perhaps. They could probably get paint chips from the little girl's clothes, too. They can tell a lot from those, you know."

"Do you want to go for a canoe ride, Grampa?" I said. "There's a new cottage down at the end of the lake. They have a sailboat. Real nice. We saw it yesterday."

Grampa smiled at me. "Maybe later, Tim. What else have you boys done since you got here? C'mon, tell me what you've been up to, Donny."

"Donny's not feeling too well, Poppa," Mom said quickly. "In fact, I'm going to take him in and give him another aspirin. I think he should lie down before dinner."

In the end, Dad and I took Grampa for the canoe ride.

Altogether, I guess it wasn't the best party Grampa ever had. Mom and I tried to keep things going, but Dad seemed to have trouble concentrating and would have to jerk himself back into the conversation. Donny stayed in bed and just came out to say goodbye.

The next morning, we both stayed in bed until Mom banged on the door. We didn't feel like an early morning swim that day.

As we sat down at the breakfast table, Dad looked at

Donny. "How are you feeling this morning?"

"Fine. I'm fine."

"Fine enough for pancakes and bacon?" Mom asked.

"Oh, boy," I said. "Sounds good. Is that what you're making, Mom?"

"Coming right up." She smiled at me.

While she was serving breakfast, Mom suggested we might all go to the July First celebrations in the village later. They always had a little fair and fireworks at night.

We were finishing our milk when Dad switched on the radio for the local news. There was something about a strike, then the July First celebrations, then: *Four-year-old Tammy O'Neill, who was involved in a hit-and-run accident yesterday, is still in a coma at the Children's Hospital. Police are looking for a light-coloured sedan which was travelling west along the main street of Ostanga, a village north of Kingston, yesterday morning. If you have any information, please contact the Ontario Provincial Police.*

"Oh, those poor parents," Mom said. "Imagine what they must be going through."

Donny slumped in his chair with his eyes closed.

Mom jumped up to go round the table to him, but Dad waved her back. "Leave him."

"But he's sick."

"Leave him." Dad's voice was harsh. "He's going to tell us how the headlight got broken."

"For heaven's sake." Mom was getting annoyed. "He told you he hit the post. What more do you want?"

Dad looked at her and shook his head. "There are no marks on either of the gateposts, and there's no broken glass."

They stared at each other for what seemed a very long time. Then Mom looked at Donny, still crumpled in his chair, and

I could feel her looking at me, too. I kept my head down. Very slowly, she sat down.

"Surely you don't think..."

"Tell us what happened, son." My father's voice was gentle now. I saw Donny swallow, trying to speak.

"We stopped to let these people cross the road," I said. "Donny had his ice cream cone in his hand, and suddenly Alfalfa jumped forward to snatch it, and the ice cream fell off into his lap, and I guess it startled him so much his foot jerked on the gas, and then suddenly there was this bang on the side of the car."

"Why didn't you stop? Donny, why didn't you stop?"

He raised his head. "I wasn't supposed to be driving on my own, and I didn't really know what happened. The people had already crossed the road. I knew it would be big trouble for you and Mom if anyone asked for my licence and they found out I only had a beginner's permit. I thought everything would be all right. It was only when Grampa told us..." He started to cry.

Mom got up and wrapped her arms around him, cradling his head against her stomach. She looked over at my father. "What are we going to do? We'll have to call the police."

Dad ran his hands through his hair. "If we call the police, he'll probably be arrested. Hit-and-run is a very serious offence." Mom's grip on Donny tightened. "We could be sued, too, you know, by the girl's family. I don't think the insurance would cover it."

"But surely, when we explain he didn't stop because he was trying to protect us..."

Dad just shook his head.

My voice came out all squeaky. "It was really my fault, because I was supposed to be holding Alfalfa in the back."

"And I should have left the goddamned lawn mower," Dad said.

There was a long silence. Nobody looked at anyone else.

Suddenly Donny pulled his head away from Mom's arms. "I'm sorry, Dad," he said. "I've really screwed things up, haven't I?"

"We all have, Donny," Dad said. He got up from the table. "Why don't you boys go outside and get things tidied up. I'll help your mother in here." As Donny went by, Dad put his hand on his shoulder and squeezed it.

As we swept the porch and wiped the dew off the chairs, we could hear the murmur of their voices. Suddenly Dad burst out loudly, "Don't you realize, if we say we allowed him to go, it will probably mean the end of my job? What company wants to hire a financial advisor who admits encouraging his own son to break the law?"

We heard Mom saying "Shush. He'll hear."

"What do you think you should do, Donny?" I said.

He shook his head. "I don't know. It's not just me. What would we do if Dad lost his job?" He looked at me. "And you'd always be the brother of that kid who ran over a little girl and ran away. How do you think you'd like that?"

I'd always figured I was the one who had to think about looking out for Donny. And now it was Donny the Dreamer trying to look out for all of us.

After that we just sat, staring at the lake. It looked so calm and peaceful.

The cottage door banged, and Dad came out, got in the car and drove away. A minute later we heard a crash and then the car came back. The right front fender was all crumpled.

"I guess Dad decided that was the best thing to do," I said. "He won't lose his job. Everything will be all right."

Donny just looked at me.

We could tell almost right away everything wasn't all right. When we went in for lunch, Mom's face was set, and her mouth was a thin straight line. I figured Dad hadn't told her he was going to smash the car into the gatepost. Dad was on the phone.

"Okay if we take our sandwiches down to the dock?" I asked. She just nodded.

As we walked away, we heard Dad say, "Yes, Charlie, the day after we arrived. It was raining so hard you could hardly see. If you'll put in the claim, I'll bring the car in when I come back to town in a couple of weeks."

Charlie was our insurance man.

We sat on the dock, and I ate my sandwich. Donny threw his in the lake.

We didn't go into the village for the celebrations. Dad said he had a headache, but I think we all knew he didn't want to have the car stopped with its crushed right fender.

Mom stretched out in a deck chair with a book, but she didn't seem to be turning the pages very fast. I tried to get Donny to help me with a ship's model I was building, but he really wasn't interested. We could hear the fireworks over in Ostanga around ten p.m., and after that we all packed it in for the day.

When I went in to go to bed, Donny was lying facing the wall. I didn't think he was asleep, but he didn't answer when I said his name, so I got undressed as quietly as I could.

Around midnight, something jerked me out of a deep sleep. It was Mom and Dad arguing. I guess they thought we would be too fast asleep to hear. Mom was mad at Dad for smashing the car on the gatepost and telling the insurance man he'd done it the day after we arrived.

"Don't you realize you've taken away any chance now for him to go to the police?"

"But I thought you didn't want him to confess and go into juvenile detention," Dad said. "You sure as hell hung onto him when I said that might happen."

"But we never really discussed it," Mom said. "You just went off and did it. We should have phoned someone to find out if he really would be put in jail."

"Like who?"

"Well, a lawyer, I suppose." Mom sounded as if she was getting really mad. "Don't you have lawyers on staff?"

Dad sighed. "Yeah, sure. I'm going to phone someone in the company and let him know the mess I'm in."

"The mess you're in! It's Donny who matters."

Dad's voice had that tone he used with us when he caught us doing something stupid. "Are you telling me it won't matter if I lose my job? Would that help him?" He banged a drawer shut. "How do you think I feel? I was the one who said we should let him go."

There was a long pause, and then I heard Mom crying. "Oh, God," she said, "I don't know what we should do. I only know now we have two criminals in the family."

I looked over at Donny's bed. He was sitting up with his head in his hands.

Things really fell apart after that. Everybody was edgy, and Mom and Dad snapped at one another for no reason. Donny looked like a ghost with big dark circles under his eyes. And it started to rain again, not even a good pelting rain, just a slow miserable drizzle that would stop for a while then start again just as you thought it was all over. After two days of it, I got Donny to come out in the canoe with me, even if we did get wet.

"It's kinda nice to get away from the cottage for a while,

isn't it?" I said.

"Yeah. And it gives Mom and Dad a break from having to look at me."

Every day, the radio carried a bit about the police still exploring leads to find the hit-and-run driver. Mom and Dad tried at first to listen to the news when we weren't there, but Donny had a little radio of his own, and he'd go off alone for a walk in the woods with it under his yellow slicker, so they gave up. He'd take Alfalfa with him, but he didn't want me along, and I didn't know what to do to help him. I tried to keep busy giving Mom a hand to reorganize the kitchen shelves or restacking the wood for the fireplace, but that didn't take long, and catching frogs or netting sunfish isn't much fun on your own, especially in the rain, so it was pretty boring.

Then the report came that Tammy O'Neill had died and that the police had been able to identify the make of car from paint samples taken from the victim's clothing. We were sitting around after breakfast, and when Donny heard that, he just got straight up from the table, grabbed his yellow slicker, and walked out the door. I got up to follow him, but we heard him tell Alfalfa to stay. I hesitated for a while, but I figured if he didn't even want Alfalfa along, he wouldn't want me, either, so I sat down again.

He still wasn't back at lunch time.

"Don't worry about it," Dad told Mom, frowning. "He probably doesn't realize what time it is."

"He forgot his watch this morning," I said. "It's still on the dresser."

"There, you see. Tim and I'll go and look for him. Right, sport?" We got up from the table to put on our raincoats. "And then this afternoon we'll go fishing. They say some fish bite better when it's raining. They probably figure humans are too smart to be sitting there in the rain." He was talking to keep Mom from worrying.

"Yeah, great," I said.

But as we walked down towards the dock, we saw the canoe bobbing offshore. There was no painter trailing from the bow. My heart started to hammer in my chest. I should have followed him. I was supposed to look out for my brother.

"Alfalfa," I shouted. "Find Donny."

He found him in the woods hanging from a tall maple with the painter round his neck and rain streaming down his yellow slicker.

Audrey Jessup *was a founding member of The Ladies' Killing Circle and co-edited two of their five anthologies. Her work also appeared in* Storyteller *magazine and the anthology,* Life Music. *Audrey died in January, 2003.*

Rock-A-Bye Baby

Susan C. Gates

Janet was expecting. Joy coursed through her swollen belly and thick ankles—which were currently propped up on the arm of her sofa. Soon, she'd be holding her new baby. She couldn't remember ever being this happy.

In truth, she'd been expecting all her life. Her earliest memories were of playing mommy to a gaggle of dolls and stuffed animals. Her mother claimed she never showed an interest in blocks or cars and became hysterical if any of her babies went astray. At the age of three, she had peppered her mother with detailed questions about her aunt's pregnancy. Later, Janet had crouched low on her heels, as only a toddler can, grunting at periodic intervals. When her mother had asked what was wrong, she'd said she was delivering a baby. That incident gained an honoured and amusing spot in the Anderson family lore, trotted out for clan celebrations or on those rare occasions when Janet brought a boy to the house more than twice.

She'd loved being the shepherd to her flock of younger cousins. She watched out for them, kept them occupied and in line while their beleaguered parents enjoyed a few moments of solitude or adult company. Babysitter, au pair, aunt, volunteer—all that experience felt irrelevant next to Janet's fervent belief that every cell of her being was programmed for motherhood.

Janet set the open book of baby names on top of her rounded belly and stretched sideways to pick up a coiled notepad from the coffee table. A folded page of computer paper fluttered to the floor. Groaning with the effort, Janet rolled onto her hip to retrieve the list she'd assembled of pediatricians in their new neighbourhood. Not for the first time, Janet marvelled at the power of the internet and slipped the sheet back into her notebook.

The front of this book was reserved for girls' names, the back for boys'. She had meticulously recorded her favourites, along with their meanings and ethnic origins. Today, she was narrowing down the choices. They'd been given such plain-jane names in her family, she was determined to find something original, but dignified. Research and contemplation were ingrained in her nature, but Janet believed that, in the end, the baby's name would only be revealed once it was in her arms, gazing up into her face.

Looking back, Janet was glad that she had waited to start her family. She had worked hard at her accounting career and was now more than ready to make the sacrifices necessary for this child. The baby would be the centre of her world—not an afterthought, or an obligation, or yet another checkmark on her life's To-Do list. Always wise with money, Janet had scrimped and saved, investing shrewdly. She would be a stay-at-home mom.

The phone rang. After some frenzied groping under the sofa cushions, Janet came up with the cordless. "Hello?" she gasped.

"Hey, Jan, just checking in on you." It was her sister-in-law. "How's it going?"

It seemed to Janet that Marie had assumed the role of unpaid, and unsolicited, mid-wife. Marie acted like there was some sort of karmic connection between them ever since Janet had been present for the birth of her third baby, and Marie had continued to draw Janet into the minutiae of child development and infant achievements.

"About the same. How are the kids?" Janet could make out the sound of *Sesame Street*, drumming and the wails of at least one toddler.

"About the same!" Marie laughed. "How'd it go with old Doc Weatherly today? I still can't believe that you go to him after he made that crack last year about your eggs getting old. 'Use 'em or lose 'em!'—he should talk. Wasn't he in training pants when Queen Victoria was crowned?"

"My appointment's not till after lunch," Janet said. "You should relax, Marie."

"Me? Relax?"

Janet had to hold the phone away from her ear to protect it from the familiar shriek.

Without taking a breath, Marie continued. "I'm not the one having a baby out of wedlock at the grand age of forty-one, missy. I still don't understand why you didn't consider adoption."

"I considered it, but I'd be waiting in line behind all the married couples. Talk about having Methuselah for a mother."

"Not adopting, you ninny, giving it up for adoption."

Tears stung Janet's eyes. Marie mistook her silence as a licence to continue.

"It's not like you couldn't have married, if you'd set your mind to it. You had some boyfriends. You just scared them all off with your overwhelming desire to have kids. John says guys can smell that desperation vibe a mile away."

"Just which one would you have suggested I marry, Marie?" Janet struggled to steady her voice, glacial ice infusing each successive word. "The one who finally confessed, after six months of dating, that he was already married? Or perhaps Tom, who was blatantly and continuously unfaithful? Probably Larry, right? You both liked him, didn't believe me when I told you he favoured ending our arguments with his raised fist."

"Jeesh, Jan, I didn't mean to upset you. It's just that raising kids is so damn hard, and I have John to help me. I can't imagine doing it alone. It'd be simply impossible."

"You think I haven't heard that argument before? Every goddamned, well-meaning parent from here to Kalamazoo has told me that! You know what my answer is to you and the rest of them? You already have your kids! How impossible would your life be without them? Imagine that!" Janet hung up the phone.

Launching herself off the sofa, she padded into the kitchen in search of a nice, soothing cup of herbal tea. The phone rang again, but seeing her sister-in-law's number on the display panel, Janet refused to answer it. She didn't want to explain herself to Marie, or anyone else, any more. Sure, she could have married, Marie was right. But a stable, calm environment was important for children. How many of her mother's friends had languished in acrimonious matrimony? And look how many of her own friends' marriages had expired before the warranties on their wedding gifts. Janet sighed. More steam was now shooting from the kettle's spout than from her ears.

She'd really packed on the pounds. A few months ago, her morning snack would have been ice cream and a hand-full of cookies or a box of snack crackers. With the help of a registered dietician and strict adherence to her prescribed food plan, the cravings had subsided. On top of that, Janet's rising excitement had all but banished thoughts of eating.

Eyeing a frosty carton of Sara Lee cherry cheesecake, Janet was tempted right now. Instead, she firmly closed the refrigerator door with her spreading hips, stopping to admire the ultrasound photo stuck to its front panel. The baby's position during the procedure had prevented a determination of its sex. She'd always wanted a girl—but at this stage either would be welcome. She traced the shape of the baby's head from the forehead to the base of the skull and then gently tapped the location of the heart. "See you soon," she whispered.

Janet took her cup of lightly steeped Lemon Zinger tea into the guest room. This was where she had stored things for the baby. There were neat piles of soft, thin face cloths and receiving blankets. "You can never have enough of these spit-up blankies," her cousin Diane had advised. She fingered the fuzzy warmth of sleepers in shades of mint and yellow and peach, burying her nose in the scent of the Ivory-laundered fabric. She recounted the number of tiny, white diaper shirts, hoping a dozen would be sufficient. Janet wanted to have the basics on hand, because you never knew about the timing of a baby's delivery. "Be Prepared" was still a good motto for her life, Janet thought.

A musical mobile of woolly, pastel lambs hung from a ceiling hook above the window where a spider plant had swung in the breeze. Janet twisted the mobile's mechanism to start the hushed strains of "Rock-a-bye Baby" and angled her grandmother's rocking chair at the window so she could see the school playground across the street.

Her little house had been a steal ten years ago—not many people, it seemed, enjoyed the squeals of happy children at play the way Janet did. She'd recently sold it, contents and all, at a handsome profit to an engineer arriving from Pakistan. Her baby would be starting out life with all new things, in a brand-new home. So they wouldn't have to move until after the baby arrived, Janet had negotiated a rent-back agreement with the new owner, who was amenable since he was still waiting for his immigration papers.

Janet propped her feet on the corner of the spare bed, sipped her tea and watched the shenanigans of the afternoon recess crowd. She knew she should rest. All her friends had warned her.

"You think you're tired now? Ha! Wait till that baby comes."

"Sleep through the night? We're still waiting! Start praying for that miracle now, Janet!"

Like the fasting monk petitioning God for the gift of His grace, she knew what the real miracle was. At night, when she was able to quell her elation and anticipation, dropping off into a fitful sleep, Janet saw it in her dreams. She was working diligently and reverently on the day-to-day care of her infant, she smelled its newborn warmth, caressed its downy cap of hair, heard it suckle.

The soft notes of the lullaby and the cooing of the mourning doves on the hydro lines soothed Janet's busy mind. She had waited so long, had thought perhaps her dream of a child would never materialize. But her delivery day was near.

Shrill ringing jarred Janet from her thoughts. She snatched up the portable phone. It was Michelle, the director of the neighbourhood Youth Centre where she was a volunteer.

"Just wanted to make sure you hadn't gone off to the hospital yet. I know you've started your Mat Leave. How are you feeling?"

"No baby yet, but I'm ready for it to happen," Janet said. She heard the rolling wheels of a desk chair and the hum of a printer.

"You'll be in later then? Remember, today's the day Crystal's bringing in her special guest."

Janet flashed on an image of Crystal, a pretty child with mocha-coloured skin, solemn brown eyes and a mane of corkscrewed curls. A Grade Four student, she showed initiative and leadership potential during the Centre's programs—this undoubtedly because she was the eldest of five. It saddened Janet to see a child whose spirit was so flat and leaden. She appeared to carry the weight of the world on her slight shoulders.

The only time Janet recalled seeing Crystal smile was several months ago. On that day, she had brought in a picture of the new baby in her mommy's tummy. She had been animated and enthused, hopeful—yet resigned to the heavier responsibilities.

When Janet asked her if she was going to have a baby brother or a baby sister, Crystal had whispered, "We don't know for sure. But Travis says it better be a boy, he don't father no bit...well, um—girls."

"I've got a few things to do early this afternoon, but I'll be there in time to set the food out before the kids arrive," Janet said to Michelle.

Janet's official role in the After School Program was to feed the kids a snack and help them with their homework. Her greatest contribution, she felt, was as a sounding board, listening to them tell of their day's accomplishments and troubles—the idealized fifties-style mom waiting with chocolate-chip cookies and milk, a smile and a hug.

"Is there any chance that you could come in a bit early? We have a little something for you," Michelle said.

Janet smiled. "A little something" she now realized was code for "we want to give you a baby gift."

"Sure, see you between three and three fifteen?"

It was quiet across the street. Recess was over. Janet struggled out of the low-slung, armless rocker. *What to Expect*

When You're Expecting and all the other baby bibles urged pregnant women to have their bags packed well in advance of their due dates. Janet checked her list of basic necessities, placed the last few items into the suitcase and zipped it shut. Bumping it down the stairs, Janet wheeled the case into the front hall and parked it beside her black brief case and the brand-new diaper bag.

She pulled on the navy-blue wool coat that barely covered her new girth. Yes, Janet thought as she squeezed behind the steering wheel of her silver Camry, the decision to volunteer at the youth centre had been a fortuitous one. Life was pretty good—when you stopped thinking and hoping and stewing— and set some goals for yourself. Things were working out, with only a few alterations to her long-held plans. Janet's only regret was that her parents wouldn't be around to watch this grandchild grow up.

*   *   *

The wait at the doctor's office wasn't any longer than usual for an old-style family physician who still insisted on delivering his own patients' babies. Florence, Weatherly's nurse and wife, directed Janet into the examination room with a kindly pat on the arm after their obligatory trip to the scales and after the "filling of the cup", as Florence so delicately put it.

"How are you today, dear?" Weatherly shuffled through lab results and pages in her file, not meeting Janet's eyes. "Any complaints?"

"I've been tired and achy. My ankles swell, and the back pain has returned."

"Well, that's to be expected. You can try lying on the hard floor, rather than the chesterfield. You still going to those

Aquafit classes?" he peered over the top of his half-moon glasses long enough to see Janet shake her head.

"They ended two weeks ago."

"Keep up the walking then." Weatherly plopped onto a stainless steel stool and gave Janet his full attention. "Good news, bad news, my dear. Your weight seems to have topped out. That's a good sign. Did you follow through with the referral to the dietician?"

Janet nodded assent.

"Very good. Important to take control of your carbohydrate and sugar intake at this stage. The bad news is your blood pressure is still slightly elevated, which concerns me. I'd like to see you again in two weeks. I know you're against the use of drugs, but we may need the meds to get things moving in the right direction. At this juncture, it's best that you're off work. See Flo on your way out, she's got the letter you requested."

With that, Janet was dismissed, and Weatherly was out the door to his next patient.

*   *   *

She found the Youth Centre's director sorting craft supplies in the storage cupboard.

"Janet!" Michelle wiped her dusty palms across the seat of her jeans. "We need to talk. Feel like a cup of herbal tea? A cold drink, maybe?"

Uh-oh. Am I in trouble here? Janet scrambled to recall all of her recent contacts with the kids, searching for any incidents that may have given cause for concern. Hand pressed to the small of her back, Janet struggled to keep up with Michelle as she hurried down a short hall to the kitchen. It wasn't like Michelle to take time out for chats, she was far too busy trying to hold the Centre together on meagre funds and waning volunteer interest. What was going on?

"I'm sorry, I should have made time for your annual review earlier, but...you know how it is around here." Michelle shrugged and smiled, setting out mismatched mugs for tea and plugging in the electric kettle. "Can you tell me how this experience has been for you?"

God, I hate these open-ended questions, she thought. What did Michelle want her to say?

"It's been great, very rewarding." Janet ran her index finger, back and forth, in a semicircle along the base of the mug facing her.

"Well, that's good. I have to admit I have been concerned," Michelle said.

Janet's eyes shot up to meet Michelle's warm hazel ones. "What about?"

"During your application interview, you mentioned how upset you were over the end of your match as a Big Sister, how you wanted this volunteer position to be a less intimate one, more of an arm's length relationship."

Janet nodded. She had been matched with a seven-year-old girl, Ashley, and it had been a heart-wrenching experience. The Little Sister had told Janet that people were hurting her. A child welfare investigation uncovered both sexual abuse by an uncle and physical abuse by her mother's live-in boyfriend. Taken into protective custody, Ashley had eventually been adopted by her foster parents, a couple in their late forties.

"Are you still in touch with your Little Sister?" Michelle's voice softened, and she reached across the table, covering Janet's hand in hers.

"No," Janet slipped her hand away from Michelle's. Using

both damp palms, she batted back the hair that had fallen in her face. The hair was easier to wrangle than the waves of depression that had enveloped her when Ashley had been excised from her life. "The adoption official claimed that she needed a fresh start."

"That must have been very difficult for you, after all you did to help that child." Michelle's tone implied that this was a question, not a statement.

"Well," Janet forced a short laugh, "that's when I decided that I could probably do better than a lot of the single mothers out there—like Ashley's mother, for example." If she told the truth, Janet would have to admit that she had made the decision to abandon her ideal of a two-parent family in a period of anger and frustration.

"I've noticed that you give Crystal a lot of special attention. I'm worried that perhaps you're being drawn into her family's difficulties." Michelle's steady gaze appraised her.

"She is a great kid, but what more can we do? We've sent over food baskets, made sure all the kids have visited the ClothesLine, alerted Children's Aid." Janet paused. "I can tell you one thing—it makes me count my blessings, knowing that I'll be able to provide a better life for my baby."

Michelle's face broke into a warm smile. "I think that's a very healthy attitude, a good sign that you're moving ahead with your own life. If we're lucky enough to have you return as a volunteer after your baby's born, you need to remember that our focus here is on group programs. We all have our favourites, of course, but we need to treat all the children equally. So no more little gifts for Crystal, okay? Besides, it's against Centre policy."

"Of course, sorry if I caused a problem. That wasn't my intention." Janet wiped a trickle of sweat from her temple.

"And I honestly can't make any promises about returning."

Michelle stood and went to the cupboard to the right of the sink. "Everyone at the Centre wishes you the very best, Janet, and though it's not much, we'd like you to have this." She set a brightly wrapped parcel in front of Janet. Michelle checked the time on her watch, "Well, the kids'll be arriving soon, guess we'd better get back out there. I'm really grateful for your contribution here, Janet. Thanks again." Michelle swept out of the kitchen, stopping to confer with another volunteer.

Relieved to have the interview concluded, Janet opened an upper cabinet and started to count out the correct number of plastic juice glasses, setting them in neat rows on a scratched brown tray. That went well, she thought. The baby monitor was an interesting choice for a gift.

Shortly after four o'clock, Crystal lugged her baby sister into the building. The kids clustered around as she set the car seat on one of the plywood tables. Without letting her friends crowd the baby or maul her with their germy fingers, Crystal supervised the infant's unveiling. She unzipped the worn, soiled bunting bag and slipped off the greyed-white knit cap so the others could admire the baby's full head of frothy blonde hair.

Crystal's mother had entered the Centre with them but hung back at the double doors to the gym. She was a fair-haired, child-sized woman, probably younger than Janet, but she looked ancient, malnourished, defeated. A fresh bruise was forming along her left jaw-line. A mottled yellow-green semicircle decorated her lower right eyelid. A black cloud hung over the woman as staunchly as the bouquet of cigarettes, stale laundry and beer that enveloped her. Michelle approached Crystal's mother, inviting her to join them in the kitchen for a coffee or a juice. Declining, the woman mumbled, "I'll be outside havin' a smoke," and bolted for the front door. The director and Janet exchanged looks. Michelle sighed and returned to her tiny cell of an office. Janet cleared tables of the muffin, milk and banana remnants from the afternoon's snack, wiping them down in readiness for the crafts volunteer.

The blast of a whistle diverted the group's attention from the baby. The kids were ready to blow off some steam and clamoured around as Henry, a student from the university, set up the basketball drills. Crystal whispered a reassuring phrase to her dozing sister, popped in the soother and ran to join the game.

Looking around carefully, Janet ensured that all was in order. Her duties were complete, and it was time to head out. With a last look at the happy faces of her flock, she slipped unseen out the back door into the afternoon's cold, early dusk.

*   *   *

Once the "Fasten Seat Belts" sign had been extinguished, Janet picked the baby up and cradled her in her arms, rocking back and forth.

Their Air Canada tickets were open-ended, so Janet was amazed that the last-minute seat assignments had found them alone in the forward row. Doc Weatherly's letter confirming her obesity had entitled Janet to a second seat free-of-charge. The infant's car seat was belted into the third. Most of her anxiety had evaporated once the plane was airborne. Everything would be perfect if only the briefcase containing the bearer bonds, cash and their new identity papers were closer at hand. A helpful flight attendant had stowed it in the overhead compartment during pre-boarding.

Slightly more than an hour ago, Janet had been tossing trash. It had taken no time at all to drive home, change her daughter into her homecoming outfit with the sparkling new snowsuit, and summon a taxi. On impulse, Janet had raced back upstairs, grabbed the mobile from the guest-room window and stuffed it into the outside pocket of the waiting suitcase. She'd left the keys to the house and the Camry on the kitchen counter for the new owner.

Now they were en route to Vancouver, where she had a car waiting to take them over the border into the American Northwest. This was a region with a hundred small, isolated towns accustomed to a steady influx of new residents running from some previous life, starting fresh, vague about their origins.

The baby's blue-black eyes held her gaze. Janet experienced a jolt of recognition—this same quizzical look had passed between her sister-in-law and nephew in the delivery room. She stroked and snuggled. She pressed her lips against her daughter's forehead and cheeks. Janet used the pad of her thumb to track a path from the bridge of the infant's nose up through the tangle of golden silk over the soft tissue of the fontanelle to the nape of the baby's neck. She manipulated her index finger so the child would clasp it tightly in its tiny fist. Tears leaked out the corners of Janet's eyes, flowing over fine lines—the foremothers of crows' feet.

"Faith," Janet murmured, "Faith will be a fine name, my girl."

Susan C. Gates *is a recovering public servant, a reformed banker and a volunteer with two organizations serving children. She shares her Ottawa home and varied music collection with two discerning Shih Tzus, Molly and Murphy. An earlier version of this story received an Honourable Mention in the 2001 Capital Crime Writers Contest.*

Jagger He Ain't:
The Saga of a Rock Wannabe

He purchased a car like his hero's
But he never would let me get in:
"You are much too old for this beauty."
Ooo, the chill in my haemoglobin.

His black leather pants almost killed him
As he sucked in his low hanging gut,
He told his young pals "That's my mother,"
And made fun of my widening butt.

He was always away on a club date
Getting "Satisfaction" in some sleazy bar,
And refused to discuss his big problem
This dream that he'd be a big star.

When I was finally able to tell him
How his delusion affected my life,
How he was only heading for heartbreak
His dismissing words cut like a knife.

Now the look in his eyes was pure madness
As he told me to pull in the claws.
"Your job is to look after my needs
And not constantly whine about yours!"

The next morning he jumped in his sports car,
Taking off in a great whirl of dust,
To chase his past youth like a demon,
To be like Mick Jagger or bust.

Making light of my worries was wrong, Hal,
So I've set up a big concert for you,
You'll be rocking with the devils in Hell, Hal,
'Cause the brakes on your car are cut through!

Joy Hewitt Mann

Let Me Drive

Violette Malan

You want me to steal a car?" I placed my cup and its bone china saucer on the desk that separated me from the Boss. All without my hands actually shaking.

"Ms. Caine, please." The Boss spread his hands. "Not just any car. A collector's item, a cultural icon about to be shabbily used."

"I don't want to argue with you, but I'm a grifter, not a car thief."

"My people are otherwise occupied, and in any case, I prefer to use someone who owes me a favour."

"Tommy didn't actually kill anyone," I pointed out.

"If he had, I would simply have collected my percentage and...persuaded him to return to his own lucrative line of business. But your brother only pretended to be a killer, and took money to perform that service, money that should legitimately have come to my people—you can see how I can't allow that."

Sure I could. Anybody could. Except Tommy.

"Do you know where your brother is?"

"For all I know, he's sitting in his apartment watching *Voyager* reruns," I said.

The Boss narrowed his eyes, his cup of coffee held halfway to his mouth.

Here it comes, I thought. In real life, no bad guy can take

your word for it that you don't know anything, they always have to torture you to be sure.

Not that I'm calling anybody in the Firm a bad guy, you understand.

Still, I wasn't as frightened as you might think. Usually, in this kind of situation, women have more to worry about than being tortured and killed. They have to worry about being raped, tortured and killed. But the Boss had three daughters, and it was well known that he disapproved, some said violently, of any kind of molestation of women. So rape wasn't on the cards. The Boss was a gentleman, he'd just kill me.

Maybe I could come back and haunt Tommy.

Finally, the Boss nodded. "Since your brother is unavailable, you will have to obtain this automobile for me."

I tried my best to agree without looking like I was thanking him. The Boss didn't need to spell out that the killing option was still on the table. Like he didn't need to spell out that he'd let my family operate in his territory for years without even asking for a percentage. The Boss was what social historians call a benign despot. He had all the power, but he was usually fair and equitable about how he used it. In the past, people had made the mistake of thinking that fair and equitable were synonyms for soft and easy. No one made that mistake any more.

Two men in spiffy suits dropped me off at my place. My answering machine was blinking, but at the moment what I needed to do was stand in my living room and call Tommy every name I could think of while kicking the sofa. I repeated a couple of the names for good measure.

Who would have thought that not being a hitman could get a person into so much trouble? Certainly not my brother. No, as Tommy Caine would put it, "it seemed like a good idea at the time."

That's what Tommy usually says. And, as usual, he was getting away with murder, metaphorically speaking, while big sister Lillian was called on the carpet. Story of my life.

Don't get me wrong about Tommy. His heart's in the right place, and he's honest-to-god not as thick as he seems. After all, on the surface, pretending that you're a hitman specializing in the removal of awkward spouses is a pretty good grift. And, again on the surface, foolproof. Even if the mark realizes she's been taken (it's more likely to be a woman, men usually manage to kill their spouses themselves), what are they going to do, go to the cops?

Still, I was well aware that I had no time to waste being annoyed with Tommy. The Boss had given me a week to work in, but what I'd told him was true; I'm a con artist, not a car thief. I stuck on my latest blues CD, hoping the music would relax me enough to come up with a plan. By the third song, I found myself smiling. Ah, for the days when my biggest problem was a cheating boyfriend! I almost laughed when I found myself singing along with the chorus of the seventh cut, "Move over honey, let me drive".

That's what I needed, some way to get the owner to give me his car and let me drive. Some way to persuade a shrewd operator—strictly in the business sense—to give me his vintage Aston Martin. And not just any Aston Martin, but the car actually driven in *Goldfinger* by James Bond himself, Mr. Sean Connery. Hmmmm.

I stopped singing and picked up my pen.

The next afternoon found me on a job site. A vintage loft building on Church Street was being turned into a restaurant. I had on a nice suit, the skirt just short enough to distract without being so short that people would wonder how I thought it possible to walk around a construction site. A couple of phone calls had told me who was insuring the place, and a walk through their office let me pick up the right letterhead. It's amazing what people will let you do when they think you're there to service the photocopiers.

Now, with my clipboard, my little skirt and my bouncy blonde curls, I was ready to take a walk through for the insurance company.

The guys were only too happy to down tools, lecture me about site safety (which of course was the reason I hadn't worn hard hat or safety shoes), and tell me all about how well they'd followed the building, plumbing and fire-and-safety codes. They were also happy to tell me when the car was due to be installed, who was building the installation, and when the security would be in place.

I knew that skirt would do the trick.

The very next day I was sitting across a very impressive glass desk from Guy Travelle, the owner of both the car and the theme restaurant in which it was to be installed as an attraction.

This was the desecration from which the Boss wanted me to save the car. Go figure.

I'd had some cards printed, and my cousins Nicola and Sarita were lined up to look after the telephones. Travelle wasn't the kind of guy who'd check these things, but he was the kind of guy who would have an assistant who'd check these things.

At this stage of the game, play could have gone a couple of ways. Ideally, I would have conned the guy into giving me the car—you know, letting me take it somewhere, and by the time I didn't bring it back, it would be too late for him to do anything about it except confess to the cops how stupid he'd been. A surprising number of people don't want to do that, especially men, and especially businessmen with a reputation for being hard-nosed.

It took me about thirty seconds to figure out that I would have to go with Plan B.

"As I told your assistant," I said, crossing my legs, "CatsEye Productions is doing a documentary on the Aston Martin, to air over the next month on *Car Week*. We've pretty well completed filming, but it's come to our attention that you have a famous example of the car yourself, and we'd like very much to include it in our documentary." This is called "make the mark think he's doing you a favour". For some strange reason, people are more suspicious of you when you try to give them something, less suspicious when you're asking them for something.

"Including your car would really underline the importance of the Aston Martin as a cultural icon," I said, wishing the Boss could hear me. "We'll want to film outside and inside the restaurant, will that be a problem?" Notice how I took it for granted that he'd agree? That's a trick marketing people use, and it hardly ever fails. On marketing people, that is.

"Hey, happy to help." I could see the dollar signs flashing in Travelle's eyes.

"We'd like to film on Wednesday the ninth, that way we can guarantee to get your segment in." He had no way of knowing that I already knew the car, and its fancy security system, was due to be installed on the Thursday.

"No way you can film on the tenth?" he said, brow furrowed as he saw his free publicity going up in smoke.

Frown prettily, tap lower lip with Montclair pen. "If it was just me, no problem, but I have to get the film and sound crew. We'd like to interview you on the spot, much more effective, and the ninth is the only day they'll give me."

I watched him add it up. The security system couldn't be installed earlier, as I'd found out from a call I'd made that very morning. Just how risky was it, Travelle was thinking, weighed against all that free publicity?

Just how greedy was this guy, I was thinking.

"Of course, filming on the ninth would mean that the segment would air on that Saturday's show," I said, giving him the clincher I hoped would seal the deal. The restaurant was scheduled to be opened on the Friday. This kind of coverage the very next day was as good as money in the bank.

I saw all of that pass through Travelle's mind.

"Let me make a call," he said. "Jason! Get Barb on the phone...Barbie? Guy Travelle. Can I get delivery on the ninth? I can? Great." He turned back to me. "It's a go."

"Perfect. Let me call my people." I got out my cell phone, called the number on the business cards and almost smiled when Nicola answered, right on cue, "CatsEye Productions."

"Call up the crew," I told her. "We're a go for the ninth."

The next phase was in place when I ran into a snag in the form of the Boss's son-in-law sitting in my kitchen, drinking my imported beer.

"Have any trouble breaking in?"

"I'd watch my tone if I were you, Lillian. I'm not my father-in-law."

He was the eldest daughter's husband, and at the moment the only son-in-law. He wasn't exactly next in line for the throne—I think the Boss was hoping the other daughters might do better—but you might call him the heir apparent. Most people were hoping the other girls married soon.

"About the car," he said. "What's been done?"

I debated saying that I wasn't about to report to him, and then decided not to push it. He'd already as good as told me I couldn't rely on his having any of the Boss's gentlemanly instincts.

I got myself a beer and sat down across from him. No point

in making it obvious that I was scared.

I filled him in on everything I'd done so far.

"I didn't see a way to get the guy to give me the car," I concluded. "I don't have time for that long a set up. The way I've worked it, he'll put the car in place a day before the security system is ready. So I'll just get it the old fashioned way. I'll steal it."

"You'll go in overnight?" He nodded, chewing on his upper lip. "I like it. Maybe you shouldn't go to any trouble, though. I'll get my people to take the car."

I got a real cold feeling in the pit of my stomach.

"You think that's a good idea?" I asked. "The Boss asked me to do this."

"I think it's a good idea you do what I tell you," he said. "I think it's a good idea if someone does something for the old man, it should be me."

I wanted to argue some more, but something about the way he picked up his empty beer bottle by the neck told me that wouldn't be such a great idea.

I waited until he was gone, and I had the door locked and bolted and the alarm on before letting myself think about what had just happened. I was so scared I didn't bother to call him names and kick the sofa. I leaned against the locked door and hugged myself. Talk about a rock and a hard place. This was going to be a lot more complicated than I thought.

The sun wasn't up on the morning of the ninth when there was a pounding on my door. I thought it would be the son-in-law, and I was wondering if pretending I wasn't home would work, but when I checked the peephole, it wasn't the son-in-law I saw.

It was Tommy.

The good news was, the minute he'd heard I'd been

summoned by the Boss, he'd headed back. The bad news was, I wasn't off the hook.

"I haven't got the money," Tommy said, helping himself to the last of the coffee. "I didn't even make the pick-up on the last mark, she's the one who blew me to the Boss."

I shook my head. "I don't think it would make any difference. We'd still have to run the game. We're paying off our fine for encroaching on the Firm's territory."

"Paying off my fine, you mean." Tommy rubbed his face with his hands.

I opened my mouth to tell him to hit the road, get in the wind, his being here couldn't help me and might hurt me, if not himself. But then another song lyric sang its way through my head, "You've got to share the driving if you want to make good time".

I looked Tommy over carefully. Good haircut, recent shave. A real grifter, my brother, ready for anything. "Can you get your hands on a good suit?" I asked him.

To meet Guy Travelle at the restaurant, I dressed in typical film crew gear—in other words, like a goth commando. To say Travelle looked alarmed is an understatement.

"Not to worry," I said. "I'll be filming my questions at the studio. This," I swept my hand over my clothes, "is just to show solidarity with the crew." I indicated the people hauling cameras and microphones out of a van. All three looked as if they'd borrowed their clothes from someone much bigger and then slept in them for a week. As of course they had. "Union," I mouthed at Travelle.

Travelle nodded like what I'd said made sense. People will accept the most ludicrous explanations if they involve political correctness. This whole PC thing is a godsend to the con game.

The real point, of course, was that I didn't look anything

like the cute blonde the construction guys had seen before. Today, they never gave me a second glance.

Still, I didn't really feel at ease until the flatbed arrived with the car. For a moment, I could almost understand what the Boss was on about. As a piece of machinery it was beautiful, but it was more than that. It wasn't just a car from a movie, it was a car from a better world.

Then I snapped out of it. This was a car that was going to get me killed, if I wasn't very lucky indeed.

The delivery guys drove the car off the truck and positioned it right in front of the restaurant's glass doors, where we could get a good shot of both the car and the big sign. Just as Travelle was getting his businessman's smile ready for the camera, a tall, thin blonde man in a very good suit marched up and cleared his throat. He had the thinnest lips I'd ever seen on a human being, and he looked like trouble.

"Mr. Travelle?" Without waiting for an answer, Thin Lips handed Travelle a business card. I caught a glimpse of a familiar-looking letterhead.

"I'm from Shipstone Mutual. We received word that you were taking delivery of the Aston Martin insured under policy number CD45597 today instead of tomorrow."

"Hey, I called you people yesterday. Talked to the man, I'm covered." I lifted my eyebrows, but the Thin Lips took it in his stride.

"That's as may be, Mr. Travelle. I have a disclaimer and supernumerary rider here which needs your signature before you can proceed." Thin Lips waved some documents under Travelle's nose. "We'd also like you to explain what additional security arrangements you've made, since we understand the alarm system doesn't go in until tomorrow."

This was just what I needed.

"Hey, no problem, I got the firm that covers my offices to give me a guy for overnight with the car."

Oh my god, I thought.

"I suppose that will do, Mr. Travelle, if you'll just initial this note to that effect, thank you very much."

"Hey." We all turned to look at the cameraman. "Can we get the car moved forward ten feet? Yeah, and can we get it turned around? Like, facing the other way? Look more British, like, you know?"

"I'll move 'er." One of construction guys stepped forward. He looked a little familiar to me, and I didn't think it was from seeing him on the job a few days before. He looked an awful lot like someone who'd been playing cards in the room outside the Boss's office. Or maybe driving the son-in-law's car.

I couldn't take any chances. "Oooh," I said, "let me drive it. I'd love to."

Smiling, Travelle was opening the door for me, when Thin Lips butted in.

"This is most irregular. Nothing was said in our policy about the car being driven. I'm afraid I can't allow it."

"I was driving it until this winter," Travelle argued. "That policy's still in effect until July." Thin Lips continued to look sceptical. "Look, if it's theft that's worrying you, why not drive it yourself," Travelle said, smiling, "Then you can be sure it's safe."

My crew came out of their huddle. "Hey, like can you drive it through the parking lot and then circle around? We want like a shot of it pulling up, you know, like James Bond is coming in for lunch."

We could all see how well Travelle liked that suggestion. In minutes, Thin Lips, the insurance man, was behind the wheel, doing his best 007 impersonation as he pulled into the parking lot and exited onto the side street, squealing the tires.

"He's going a little fast," Travelle said, stepping off the curb to signal to the car.

"Hey, even the insurance guy's got a little soul when it comes to a car like this."

Travelle turned to smile at me, so he didn't see the car speeding up still faster as it came around the corner and headed right for us. I didn't believe it myself, and I was looking right at it. In the very last minute I pulled Travelle out of the way of the speeding car and skinned both my elbows as we landed heavily on the sidewalk.

We lay there and watched the Aston Martin disappear up the road.

*   *   *

Several hours later, I pulled into the underground parking of the big Delta Chelsea Hotel downtown. I knew better than to go home right at the moment. No way to know who might be sitting in my kitchen.

I'd left Travelle full of assurances and numbers where he could reach me. He was getting on the phone with his insurance people when I left. I wondered what they'd say. The police had given me no trouble. I had ID up to the eyebrows, my phone numbers were all legit, and I'd even obtained a permit to allow us to film on a public thoroughfare. By the time they figured out only the permit was real, my little documentary director would be long gone.

I pulled into a parking space next to a vintage Aston Martin.

Tommy was keeping the space empty for me, looking like a mechanic in his dirty coveralls. His insurance clothes were in a suit bag, ready to sling into my car.

He had the biggest grin I'd seen in days, and somehow his lips didn't look thin at all.

"This is a great car," he said, giving me a hug. "You sure we can't keep it? Nobody's expecting us."

"Are you insane?"

"Hey, even the cops think somebody stole it. How's the Boss going to know any different? Worse comes to worst, we blame the son-in-law."

Like I said, Tommy gets good ideas, but he never seems to see what the worst might come to. I'd figured out that the Boss could protect me if I pissed off the son-in-law, but who was going to protect me if I pissed off the Boss? I plucked the keys out of Tommy's hand.

"Move over honey," I said. "Let me drive."

Violette Malan's *published fiction includes mystery, romance, fantasy and erotica. Violette won the inaugural short story contest at the 1999 Bloody Words Crime Writer's Conference. Her mystery fiction is included in the noir anthology* Crime Spree, *the Ladies' Killing Circle's* Fit to Die, *and the all-Canadian issue of* Over My Dead Body.

Them There Eyes

Coleen Steele

You always notice the pretty ones.

It was at Rye's Pavilion in Peterborough, during our Glenn Miller medley, that I first spotted her. A gorgeous little number, with long, wavy, chestnut hair, glossy red lips and smouldering eyes. The Ava Gardner type, dark and sultry. And she had a body to match—all dangerous curves.

But she was young. Very young.

Playing the same songs night after night, you don't need to watch the music every minute. You have plenty of time to check out the dancers. Actually, that's probably why it took me as long as it did to notice her—she wasn't dancing. Just standing by herself, watching the band all evening.

I saw her again a week later, at the dance hall in Dunsfield this time. Again alone, not dancing. During a rest in "I'll Get By", I let my eyes wander. When my gaze swung her way, we made contact. It was like a shock to the system—those big dark eyes staring at me unwaveringly. Though disconcerted, I managed a smile. It wasn't returned.

A kick from Bill Dinsmore beside me made me jump. I had missed my cue. Leaping in, I blew a clinker, earning a glare from Sammy, our bandleader. Those big eyes had done more than make me forget my place, they had made me forget to breathe. With a bit of concentration, and no further glances in her direction, I played through the rest of the piece without any mistakes. But it was a struggle—I could feel her staring at me, studying me.

Then suddenly she was out on the floor. Some lucky guy had coaxed her to dance. I watched, mesmerized, as she surrendered herself to the music, skirt fanning out, revealing long shapely dancer's legs even Betty Grable would have envied. Her lithe body swayed and twirled like nothing I'd ever seen. She had to be a professional, but what was she doing here, I wondered? I also wondered what it took to get more than a dance from her.

That was the only time I ever saw her dance. After that display, the guys lined up to ask her, but she shot them all down. And for the rest of the set, whenever I glanced her way, I found her eyes upon me.

I made up my mind to approach her at the break. I didn't dwell too long on the question of why I'd caught her eye when she could have any guy in the place at her feet. I didn't want to think about it. Not then. I ignored the fact that being in this business for over twenty years had taken its toll, and I didn't have much to attract a dish like that. I put it down to luck and convinced myself that some girls just had a thing for seasoned trumpet players.

When the set finished, and I bent to put my horn on its stand, Bill nudged me. "Who's the doll with the big eyes? I wish she'd give me the once over like that."

I grinned. "Don't know, but I'm gonna find out."

Pushing past, I stepped down from the stage, only to find she wasn't where my appreciative gaze had left her. I scanned that room from top to bottom, but she wasn't anywhere to be seen. Disappointed, I shrugged and turned back, following the last of the boys out through a side door for a breath of fresh air and a smoke. She'd probably gone to the ladies room to freshen up. Provided one of the young guys that buzzed around her didn't get too lucky, there'd be time later to catch up with her.

But not that night. I watched until it was time to pack my horn away; she never returned. By the time our last set ended, I was disappointed and feeling deflated. Girls like that didn't come around often. When Bill asked if I wanted to join some of the boys for a drink and suggested we might get some female company, I hesitated at first.

"All right. Sure. Why not?"

I packed up and threw my jacket over my shoulder, but didn't escape quick enough.

"Pretty sloppy tonight, Finley."

"Sorry, Sammy, I had something on my mind."

"Well, you'd better get it off your mind quick. We're playing Dunn's in three days, and I don't want any screw ups."

"Sure, Sammy."

*   *   *

The next day five of us, our instruments and our luggage piled into Bill's old '43 DeSoto and headed west to Bala. The tiny resort town, a jewel set in the Muskoka Lakes, where every summer the rich came to play, boasted Dunn's Pavilion, one of the swankiest dance halls in the province. Playing Dunn's was always a highlight of the summer tour. When I stepped through those doors, my mind couldn't help but conjure up all the greats that had played there over the years—the Dorsey Brothers, Les Brown, Glenn Miller, Guy Lombardo, Count Basie.

Dunn's had a house band, of course—this summer it was Ozzie Williams' Band—but almost every week a big headliner would play a night or two. This week it was us. We weren't the Dorseys, but we could assure just a big enough draw to get the booking.

One of the reasons I had hooked up with Sammy's band was because of the touring we did every summer. We were always on the move, sometimes playing two or three halls in a week. Some of the fellas preferred getting a steady booking at a resort like Bala for the whole summer. They'd bring their wives and families north and rent a cottage, spending their days fishing or lazing in the sun. Me, I needed to move around. I tried settling down, even marriage once, but I wasn't good at it. I got itchy.

When we took to the Dunn's stage, I couldn't help but scan the crowd, searching for those red lips and luminous eyes. She wasn't there, of course. Bala was a long way from Dunsfield. I ignored the little pang of disappointment and breathed a sigh of relief that I could concentrate on my playing. It was all smooth sailing, and I really hit a groove. Until the final set.

I was blowing my way through "Swinging on a Star" when I got a funny feeling I was being watched. Now, of course, being on stage, someone was always watching me, but this was different. It sent a chill down my spine. I scanned the dancers crowding the floor and then the onlookers beyond. There she was, standing just inside one of the doorways leading to the wrap-around veranda, with those beautiful eyes fastened on me. I shot Sammy a glance to see if he had noticed the little squeak my trumpet made at the sight of her. When I looked back, she was gone. I spent the rest of the evening searching for her. A couple of times I thought I caught glimpses, but it was so crowded, I couldn't be sure.

*   *   *

After a couple of days' rest, the tour moved on again. The Dardanella in Wasaga Beach was next on our list. It didn't have the same stature as Dunn's, but it was always fun. Surrounded by an amusement park and the longest freshwater beach in the world, it couldn't help but have a carnival atmosphere. This year, when I took my trumpet out of its case, I didn't feel quite so festive. You see, I was beginning to feel spooked.

Most guys would have thought me damn lucky to have a doll like that showing such interest. Part of me was, I guess; you know, flattered and wondering if I was going to get a chance with her. But the other part was spooked. It was disconcerting to see that girl popping up in dance halls across the province. Don't get me wrong, we have fans that will catch our show a couple of times during the summer at different halls, but this girl was trailing us. Or, I should say, me. I do play a pretty mean trumpet, but nothing that should persuade a dish like that to traipse around after me just to see me blow. And if she was interested in more than just the way I handled a horn, why the disappearing acts?

I waited all evening in Wasaga, never easing up enough to get into the swing of things. She never showed.

We played a few smaller beach towns along Lake Huron, but I didn't see her. By the time we reached Grand Bend, I had begun to relax and believe maybe it had all been in my imagination. I allowed myself the pleasure again of letting my eyes wander over the dancers in search of pretty girls and shapely legs, without fear of seeing those eyes upon me.

"Don't look now, lover boy, but your mystery girl's back."

That feeling of unease returned as I followed Bill's gaze. There she was. As gorgeous as ever. She strolled in, turning heads, and once she found a spot for herself, swung her attention immediately to the band. Her eyes sought me out, and when she saw me watching her, one brow arched gracefully, as if she were amused she had caught my attention. It was the first time I'd received any acknowledgement. It should have pleased me, but instead it made the hairs on the back of my neck quiver.

"Boy, she must have it bad for you. When you gonna land her?"

The look I gave Bill shut him up quickly, and he left me alone for the rest of the night. I finished out the set, of course, but my heart wasn't in it. All the fun had gone out of playing.

The last note had barely finished when I jumped off the stage, horn in hand, and struck out for her table. She started to get to her feet to make her escape. I was determined to catch her this time. I would have made it too if some guy hadn't stepped in my way.

"Hey, I saw you play with Trump Davidson and Bobby Gimby too, didn't I?"

"Yeah, I've been around." I tried to brush past him, but he called in the recruits, and I was suddenly swarmed by his pals. Past them, I could see my quarry heading for the door.

"See, I told you I knew him." He smiled broadly at his friends. "These are my friends, Mike and Al and Tony."

"Nice to meet you guys, but I'm kinda in a hurry."

"Sure, sure. By the way, what's your name?"

"Harry Finley. Look, I've really got to go."

They finally released me, their enthusiasm cooled by my chilly manner. I knew I'd put them off, and Sammy wouldn't be pleased if he found I'd been less than friendly to some fans, but I didn't care. I needed to catch that girl.

I couldn't see her, but I ran as best I could through the

crowd and out into the night. She had vanished. I hunted amongst the cars that were beginning to pull away and peered down the lane at couples strolling back to their cottages and motels, but without success.

"Lookin' for something?" came a husky, feminine voice behind me.

I swung about frantically.

The girl sauntered into the light cast by the parking lamp. She was long-legged, curvaceous and inviting; the type any sane man would be grateful to find.

But she was blonde.

The girl took a drag on her cigarette and tried too hard to look sophisticated, coolly looking me up and down. A couple of girlfriends giggled behind her. My frustration and disappointment must have showed, because her composure started to crumble, and she took a step back.

"Sorry, doll-face. Not tonight," I said. "Any other night, but not tonight."

When I returned to the stage to collect my case, Sammy was waiting.

"Finley, you better get your act together. You want to chase girls, fine, but you do it on your own time."

Considering what I had just turned down in the parking lot, I thought that funny. Chasing girls had been the last thing on my mind lately. I just wanted this one to stop chasing me.

In London and Port Stanley, she didn't put in an appearance, but still I didn't relax. I knew I'd see her again. My music was suffering. I couldn't concentrate, wondering each time I played if she'd be there watching me. The summer season was almost over, and for the first time in years I was glad to see it end. I wanted to get back to Toronto. I don't know why, but I felt that once I got there, this would all be over. She wouldn't follow me there. I could concentrate on my music again. Well, we just had two dates to go—Crystal Beach and Port Dalhousie. I bet she'd wait until the last night, in Port Dalhousie to make one last show. I was wrong.

The Crystal Ballroom was one of my favourites, and like Dunn's, it attracted the biggest names. But it wasn't just that; the crowd was always fun. Could be because it shared the beach with an amusement park, or it could be because of all those Americans who ferried across the lake to dance and have a good time. They came from Rochester and Buffalo and little towns in upstate New York, and something about being in a foreign country seemed to really make them want to cut loose.

The ballroom itself was huge—1,500 couples could dance at one time—and crowded to capacity that evening. But I spotted her. Perched in one of the balconies like some divining angel, she stared down at me all through the Glenn Miller number and the Hoagy Carmichael song that followed. I had my eyes fastened on her and didn't let go, but when we slipped into "You'll Never Know," she slipped back into the crowd and was lost to me. Twice, later in the evening, I glimpsed her on the main floor, but she didn't dance.

Tonight was the night. I knew it in my heart. My stomach knew it too—it fluttered and jerked through the second set and clenched tightly through the third. My nerves were shot, and it showed in my performance. Several bad notes and a butchering of "Stormy Weather" earned me glares not only from Sammy, but the rest of the band. Even our singer, mild-mannered Cliff, shot me a look of reproach between numbers. I didn't care. I just wanted it all to be over.

With the last note still hanging in the air, I chucked my horn into its case and jumped to my feet. She was still there, near the refreshment counter. Tonight I'd catch her.

"Can I have a word with you, Finley?"

It was Sammy blocking my path. "Can it wait?"

He shook his head, and my heart sank. Not at what I knew was coming, but because she was getting away.

Sammy pulled me towards the rear of the stage, where we wouldn't be overheard.

"I wanted to wait until the end of the season, but tonight's the last straw. When I took you on, I thought you were a pro, but you've been off most of the summer. It's not fair to the rest of the guys. I'm letting you go now."

"But Sammy, I've just had a problem I've been working through."

He eyed me with contempt. "That girl you've been dragging around? Do her parents know what you're doing?"

"It's not like that. I don't even know who she is—"

"Look, I've had enough. Come by in the morning, and I'll pay you off."

There was no choice but for me to take my horn and go. I glanced at Bill, who was still packing up, but he wouldn't meet my eye. Great, not only was I out of a job, I was out of a ride back to Toronto. Actually, I was more worried about a ride than a job. A trumpet player with my experience shouldn't have any trouble picking up work. Maybe I'd try Bert Niosi at the Palais Royale. I'd heard one of his trumpet players, Ross Archer, was talking of retiring, heading back to Winnipeg.

I didn't spend too much time troubling about it. Not then. It could all wait, but my chance with that girl was fast disappearing. She'd probably be long gone by now, and if she planned on following me to Port Dalhousie, she'd be disappointed.

Wading through the diminishing crowds, I stumbled out into the parking lot, where many were trying to find their cars.

Gales of laughter reached me from the docked ferry as it loaded up to deliver exhilarated partygoers across the lake. Even without the music to accompany them, many were continuing their dancing onboard. At least they were having a good time.

I hunted through the rows of cars. And I found her.

She was sitting in the passenger seat of a shiny new Pontiac with the door open. Poised sideways, she had one high-heeled pump resting on the ground, her stockinged legs crossed and tempting.

"Would you like to drive me home?"

I almost didn't hear her. Her voice was low and sultry, like a summer breeze, and it was almost swallowed up by the firing of the engine in the old Packard beside me. But the keys she dangled from her fingers told me that I'd heard right.

I hesitated only a moment. Taking the keys, I watched appreciatively as she swung those luscious dancer's legs into the car. Closing the door, I walked around to the driver's side and climbed in. She didn't say anything, just looked at me with those smouldering eyes, the way she had been doing for the past two months. I could have got out then. Maybe I should have. I turned the key.

The engine purred to life. "Yours?"

"A friend's."

Hmmm. Some friend. I put it in gear and eased it into the line exiting the lot.

"My motel's down this way," she said. But I'm not in any hurry. We can go for a drive if you'd like. If you want to try out the car."

The car was nice, but it wasn't really what was on my mind. We drove about for a while with the windows down, feeling the night air cool against our skin after the heat of the dance hall. We didn't speak much—she didn't appear to want to. It was late when we pulled into her motel parking lot. She invited me in.

I trailed close behind her, opening the door to room eight when she handed me the key. She slipped past, and I followed her in. The uneasy feeling I always got whenever she was near flared worse than ever. Glancing around, I suddenly wondered if she shared that room with anyone, maybe her "friend". I wasn't in the mood to fend off a jealous husband or boyfriend.

"You got the room to yourself, honey?"

"Sure," she said, casually flinging her purse on the floor by the room's one dresser. Taking a seat on the bed, she crossed her legs and leaned back invitingly.

Seeing no obvious signs of male occupancy, I put my horn down by the door, and took up the offer, sliding in close beside her. But when I attempted to put my arm around her, she wiggled away.

"Not yet."

"All right. You tell me when. In the meantime, why don't you tell me what this is all about."

"Come now. I'm sure you've been in girls' motel rooms before?"

"Sure. Lots of times. But not with someone like you. Not with someone who's been following me. What gives?"

She appeared put out by my bluntness, those luscious lips that I had not yet tasted, pursing together. "I like music. I like to dance. Your band's good."

"That doesn't cut it. We're not that good. And I know you can dance; I saw you once. But you don't dance; you watch. You watch me. Why?"

She stood up abruptly. "Would you like a drink?"

I sighed. "Sure, honey. Whatever you've got."

Two glasses and a bottle of Canadian Club sat waiting on the nearby dresser, almost as if she'd been expecting company. Of course, for all I knew, she always brought someone home with her. With a face like that, there wouldn't need to be much arm twisting.

"Someone once told me about you," she said, her back to me as she poured the drinks, "and I was curious." I thought I heard her voice quiver a bit. But that wouldn't be so strange. She was just a kid.

"You could have got to know me a lot faster if you hadn't been so quick to leave each night."

"I wasn't ready." She turned to me, a drink in each hand.

She didn't strike me as the shy type, but I didn't comment. "And now you are?"

"It's time."

"So what's this all about? Who told you about me and got you so interested?"

An answer didn't come right away. She made me wait before throwing me the first piece of the puzzle.

"It was a woman who used to sing in one of your bands."

"Sammy's?"

"No. Another one you were in years ago."

"What was her name?" I asked, but she sidestepped.

"She collected pictures of you." The girl put her drink down on the nightstand beside the bed and picked up an envelope. "I have them here, if you'd like to see."

I seized the envelope from her outstretched hand and dumped the contents on the bed beside me. There were about half a dozen newspaper clippings, most pretty faded and worn. I picked up the first one and sure enough, there I was with a few other members of a band I'd played in years before. I glanced through them all and noted that except for a couple of more recent ones, they dated back more than fifteen years. Taking a closer look at the older ones, I saw they were all of the same band. I identified some of my cronies from that period— Ferde Scott, Arnie Wilts, Bill Harrington, Bob Mowry. It was funny seeing them there. Most I hadn't seen or thought of in years. Ferde Scott was the only one still in the business.

I looked at the girl for some kind of explanation. She handed me my drink.

"It was Irene Driscoll that collected those pictures. The earlier ones at least."

Her expression was almost triumphant; as if she had just made some great revelation that explained everything. I nodded slowly, remembering. "Pretty blonde with a big voice?"

"She was."

Irene had been more than pretty. She'd been a real knock-out, and she'd had talent to go with the looks. The female singer with one of the first bands I'd played in, I'd known Irene for a couple of years before she quit and dropped out of music. I couldn't remember why. Some sort of accident or something, I thought.

"Something happened to her, in the late thirties, early forties?"

"She got cut up. Someone took a knife to her face."

"Oh." I glanced down at my drink, holding it with both hands. "Too bad."

"But you knew her when she was beautiful, didn't you?"

"Sure. She was gorgeous. A real looker. All the guys in the band were crazy about her."

The girl raised her glass to her lips and nodded meaningfully at mine. She sipped the pale amber liquid and then said softly, "But you were lucky enough to date her."

"Me? I wish. She barely noticed me."

"But it was you that she went with. You that she loved."

"Are you kidding? She only had eyes for Arnie."

Her hand shot out and clutched my arm. I had just been about to deliver my own drink to my mouth. Instead, rye splashed all over my hand and onto my jacket sleeve. "Are you crazy? What'd you do that for?" I was on my feet, trying to dry myself with my handkerchief.

"Who's Arnie?"

"Arnie Wilts." I disentangled myself from her hold. "They went steady for a year or two. Arnie played trumpet as well."

Her face had gone pale. I thought she might be ill.

"Look." I pulled a photo from the pile and pointed him out. "He's here in these photos too."

She stared blankly at the clipping a moment, then frantically started scrambling through the pile. When she found the one she was looking for, she thrust it in my face.

"This is you, right? The guy circled?"

"Nah, that's Arnie. I'm the guy next to him."

"But it says it's you."

I looked at the names listed below the photo. "Someone got it wrong. Story of my life."

A look of panic and disbelief marred her face. She looked wildly around the room then made a dash for the purse she'd thrown on the floor. Rifling through it, she pulled out her chequebook. From inside it she took another photo. This one wasn't a clipping, but a glossy photo from someone's Brownie. There was Arnie's handsome face, mugging for the camera.

"Arnie again."

She stared at the photo. "Oh, God," I heard her say softly. She stood there immobile, lost in another world.

I put my wet handkerchief aside and raised my glass to my lips.

She screamed and struck me. The glass was smashed from my hand, its contents showering the floor.

"What the hell's going on?" I touched my fingers to my bruised lip, half-expecting to find blood.

Her eyes were big and round, terrified.

I raised my wet hand to my nose. It smelled strange. It smelled like rye, sure, but there was something else. "What was in that drink?"

"I thought you were him. I thought that was you in those pictures."

She looked ready to tune out again. I grabbed her wrist. "So? What difference does it make? Who are you?"

She sank down on the bed. "Norma. Irene's daughter."

I tried to put the pieces together as I watched her begin to sob. Irene's daughter. It took me a minute, but I got there.

"You're Arnie's girl, aren't you?"

"He left her once he found out about me," she choked out. "He just left us to manage on our own. After I was born, she couldn't handle it. She had no money. And she was so ashamed. When another guy came along and was willing to marry her, she jumped at it. She'd never have looked at him twice otherwise."

"The guy was no good?"

She shook her head vehemently.

Things were starting to fall into place, for me anyway. "Is he the one that cut her?"

"Yes. She got another job singing. He didn't like the way men looked at her when she was on stage. He was afraid she'd find someone else. So he cut her face up so she couldn't work. He cut it up so men wouldn't look at her any more."

She quieted for a moment and I waited, sensing there was more she'd tell me when she was ready.

"A few months after that, she killed herself."

"What happened to him?"

"I didn't find out until later, but he died a couple of years after her in a car accident."

"So you wanted revenge on the man that started it all. But you got the wrong guy." I put my hand to my nose again. "What did you put in that drink?"

"Rat poison."

"Christ!" I jumped to my feet and raced into the bathroom. I scrubbed my hands until they were raw, and the new bar of soap was merely a sliver. Just in case a drop had actually touched my lips, I bathed them and rinsed my mouth for good measure. When I was finished, I leaned on the sink, staring in the mirror, wondering what to do next. She had tried to kill me.

When I returned, the girl was lying on the bed, still crying. I stood there, not knowing what to do. She looked so young. If she was Arnie's girl, she could only be about seventeen or eighteen. I suddenly wondered about the beautiful dress she had on and the others I'd seen her in, and thought about the new car sitting outside, but I tried not to think too hard about how a girl like her would get those things.

I walked to the door and opened it. Picking up my horn, I glanced at her once more. I threw her a bone. "Arnie's dead, by the way. He died just last year, knifed by a jealous husband."

Outside, the air felt cool and clean. Rubbing at the hand that had been splashed, I set off across the parking lot, the gravel squelching noisily in the quiet of the night.

Irene's girl. Irene's gorgeous blue eyes swam up in front of my face as I recalled how beautiful she'd been when I'd known her. Irene. I hadn't thought of her in years. I'd been half in love with her. I remembered that now. But I never stood a chance.

I remembered that summer we'd toured together; it must have been about 1935. She'd been crazy about Arnie; she'd barely noticed me.

My steps faltered.

Arnie had missed part of that tour. About two weeks, because of pneumonia.

I stopped.

The Brant Inn. We'd played a week there. She'd been lonely, and angry with him over something—probably another girl. I had thought I was the luckiest guy in the world.

I hesitated.

Norma. Irene's daughter.

Those eyes.

I tugged up my jacket collar and walked on.

Yes, I'd go see Bert Niosi about a job next week.

Coleen Steele *writes crime and mystery fiction from her home in Bowmanville, Ontario. Two of her stories were awarded Honourable Mention in the Writer's Digest 2001 Writing Competition and she has been published in* Storyteller *magazine. Coleen's fascination with film noir and old radio shows often creeps into her writing.*

Who's Sorry Now?

Her pretty backup singer, Lee,
She killed at twenty-two.
At thirty-one, the deed was done,
She killed Lee's partner, Lou.
When she was barely thirty-four
She slew the third one, Tim,
And shortly after forty-one
The last singer followed him.
She did it all so carefully
And covered every clue
She'd get away with murder
And she would get what's due
She'd get all the glory—
As last one left alive—
Until Lee's cousin, the cop, showed up
And her career took a dive.
Now she's got a hundred partners
And the spotlight's on each night
But there's no one she can sing to
And not one fan in sight.
And so the moral of this story
If you care to lend an ear—
When no one's left to back you up
You land hard on your rear.

Joy Hewitt Mann

Two Little Girls in Blue

Sue Pike

Y ou awake, Stu?"

Stu lurched upright in his chair, rubbing his hand across his face and finding to his horror he'd been dribbling down his chin. Worse still, there were tears on his cheeks. Damn. He must have been dreaming about Belle. Or Joanie, maybe.

"Guess I dozed off."

"You remember you called me?" Franklin helped him to his feet and steadied him a minute until the blood made its way to his legs. "Something about the stove not working?"

"What? Oh, right." Stu leaned on Franklin's arm and pushed toward the kitchen. "The elements have been overheating something fierce. Last week after Joanie left, I nearly burned the place down just trying to heat some canned stew." He grimaced. "Damned if it wasn't one of her pots I ruined."

"I guess we've all done that at one time or another. How is Joanie, anyway?"

If Stu closed his eyes, he could still picture Franklin and Joanie all those summers ago, Joanie in her blue cotton bathing suit, her blonde pigtails streaming out behind as she ran down the hill to the dock with Franklin close behind. He could hear their shouts again, part fear, part triumph as they swung out over the lake, clinging to the ropes he'd tied to a couple of big oak limbs overhanging the water. Out they'd fly, while he and Belle held their breaths, afraid the kids would hang on just a second too long and tumble onto the rocks.

"She's okay, I guess." Stu let go of the other man's arm and leaned against the kitchen counter. "You mind having a look at those elements?"

"Already tested them while you were getting your beauty sleep." Franklin grinned. "There isn't a thing wrong with them. They seem to be working just fine."

"Yeah, well. I guess I probably knew that. I just kind of hoped I could tell Joanie something else had caused that little meltdown." He turned and looked out the window over the sink. He counted two pine grosbeaks on one feeder and half a dozen goldfinches nibbling safflower seeds on the other. There were shadows gathering down at the dock and thunder clouds building up over the far shore of the lake. It was the best time of day to catch a bass. He'd try that new lure Joanie gave him for his birthday.

He turned back from the window. "Thanks for coming, anyway. I appreciate it. How much do I owe you?"

"Forget it." Franklin frowned. "I don't like to see you so worried, though. What's got you all riled up, anyway?"

"Aw, it's just Joanie. She and that—that fellow she lives with." Stu sank into a chair in the breakfast nook and began shuffling the salt and pepper around. "You've met her new guy, haven't you?"

Franklin chuckled. "Sure. I was at their wedding. Must've been ten years ago now. Remember?"

"Oh, right. Well, he's some kind of geriatric psychologist, whatever in God's name that means." He shrugged. "Anyway, Joanie listens to every goddamned word comes out of his mouth, especially when it's about me. Made me take some kind of memory test, and I guess I didn't exactly come off with flying colours. Anyway, now they think I'd be better off in a seniors' home with folks my own age." He snorted. "Makes me sound like a little kid."

"I sure don't want to take sides here, Stu, but they might have a point. It's maybe not such a good idea you being out here all by yourself."

"I'm only here for the summer, and besides, there's people in the other cottages."

"A lot of these places have changed hands recently. They're mostly weekend cottagers, and I'll bet you haven't met many of them yet. Knowing you, I'm not so sure you'd call on them for help, even if you did run into trouble."

"There's nothing wrong with me, and if something does happen, you're welcome to carry me out in a box." Stu didn't want to talk about it any more. He got up and took Franklin by the arm and pushed him toward the screen door. "You've got better things to do than stand around chewing the fat with an old fellow like me. And besides, I've got some fish to catch."

Stu saw the younger man off then gathered his rod and tackle from the shed and made his way down the long flight of stone steps to the water. He was loading everything into the old aluminum rowboat when the Pilon kids from next door sidled onto the dock. They were dressed in identical blue bathing suits. The older one asked what he was doing.

"Well now, I'm getting set to go fishing. There's a big old bass out there just waiting to be caught."

"Can we come?" She'd told him her name a couple of times, but he couldn't think of it now. She sure did make him think of Joanie when she was a kid. "We've never been fishing."

"Aw, you're better off staying here with your mom."

"She's gone shopping." The smaller one spoke up. She was

about five, Stu guessed. "Sarah's the boss of me until she gets back."

Stu wasn't really listening. He'd forgotten to bring the net down. He'd never be able to land a bass without it, but it was going to mean struggling up that hill again.

"Say, you wouldn't do a favour for an old man, would you? I left my fish net in the shed."

"Well..." Sarah scrunched her face up and stared up the hill.

Oh, boy, he could see it coming. The kid couldn't be more than ten or eleven, but she was a born negotiator. Stu knew that from previous encounters. Just the other day he'd had a run-in with her about riding her bike through his tomato plants. He'd asked her to stop, and she'd given him a big song and dance about him not being the boss of her.

She had her hands on her hips right now. "We might get it. But only if you take us fishing with you."

"We're bored," chimed in the little one. "We got nothing to do."

He weighed the pros and cons of having to put up with two kids in a boat against the prospect of climbing that hill.

"Okay. But you better run over and tell your mother."

"Don't you listen to anything?" Sarah rolled her eyes and gave an exaggerated sigh. "We told you, Mom's gone to the village. I'm in charge, and I say it's fine."

The two girls ran for the stone steps, their bare legs flashing in the pre-storm light.

Once he got them settled in the boat, Stu fired up the old Evinrude outboard motor and crossed to the other side of the lake. He tried casting, but the girls kept shifting in their seats, throwing off his aim. He had to shush them, explaining that bass have good hearing and would be scared away by their high-pitched squabbling.

"I'm bored," the little one complained.

"Well, boring's what fishing's all about. You shouldn't have come if you didn't want to sit still."

Her bottom lip quivered, and Stu relented. "Tell you what, there's a place I haven't been to for a coon's age. It's kind of hidden away. But I'm pretty sure I could find it again." Stu smiled at the memory of long-ago trips to Mosquito Creek with Joanie and Franklin. They used to love scrambling down the water-washed boulders where the upper lake spilled into the creek.

"Take us there. Please!" Both girls began to chant, "Please, please, please."

Stu looked over at the clouds mounting above the northern shore. The leaves were turning in the quickening breeze. "It's going to rain for sure."

But the girls only increased the volume. "Please, please, please."

Stu turned away to start the motor, but the chanting was getting on his nerves. He gave it too much gas and flooded it. "Joanie! Stop that this instant," he shouted.

Sarah looked at him through narrowed eyes. "Who's Joanie?"

He was startled and a little frightened. What in the world had made him say that? "She's my daughter. I just got mixed up for a minute." He pulled the rope, and the motor caught. "Hold on. We'll be there soon."

The outlet from Mosquito Creek was concealed by acres of reeds. You had to know the route through the five-foot high vegetation to find it at all. Stu turned off the motor, lifted the prop out of the water and let the boat drift until he found a small gap. It had filled in considerably since he'd last been here, but he managed to pull the boat through with his hands. Once past the shallow mouth of the creek, he fitted both oars in the locks and rowed past floating clumps of lily pads. He asked Sarah to lean over the bow and yell if she saw any stumps or deadheads in their path. When they got to the waterlily meadow, he cast his line, and almost immediately a bass hit the lure. The girls screeched with excitement as Stu struggled to get the net under the flailing fish and haul it in. He grabbed it under the gills, yanked the hook out of its mouth with pliers and dropped it onto the floor where it thrashed, flapping against the seats and sides of the boat. Laughter turned to screams as the girls cringed together in the bow. "Get it out of here," one of them demanded. He'd forgotten which was which. "Throw it back in the water."

"I'm not throwing it back. I promised Belle I'd bring a big one back for supper." Stu looked up and realized the younger one was now crying in earnest. "Tell you what. I'll kill him, and then he won't bother you." He stood up and pounded the butt end of an oar onto the bass's head. It twitched a couple of times and then lay still.

"Gross! I'm going to throw up." The older one started making retching noises.

Stu was seriously rattled. "Here's what we'll do. I'll let you kids off at the waterfall. You always have fun there, don't you, Joanie?"

He started the motor again, driving the boat into the tall grasses at the base of the rushing water and helping the girls to step out onto land. Fat raindrops began splashing off their bare arms and dark blue circles appeared on their bathing suits. "All right, you and Franklin play here for a while, and I'll see if I can catch another fish before the rain starts in earnest. I'll be back before you know it."

The girls looked at him with wide, frightened eyes, but said nothing.

"You awake, Stu?"

Stu lurched upright in the armchair, his heart pounding. "Good God. You trying to frighten an old man to death?"

"Sorry to wake you, but Joanie's been trying to phone, and you didn't answer." Franklin unzipped his yellow slicker and hung it over the back of the rocking chair. "She's been listening to the news broadcasts and wanted me to make sure you were okay."

Stu snorted. "I must've unplugged the phone. It's the only way I can get any rest around here."

"You've missed everything then." Franklin ran a hand over his wet hair. "It's the damnedest thing. Some kids have gone missing."

"Kids?" Stu felt his stomach contract. "Not Joanie. You did say she's okay, didn't you?"

"She's fine. Been trying to call you from the city." Franklin bent over and peered into his eyes. "Are you all right, Stu?"

"Who's missing then? You said someone's missing."

"It's the Pilon kids from next door. Their mother left them on their own while she went shopping in the village. When she got back, there was no sign of them." He went to stand by the front window. Stu struggled out of his chair to join him. It was pitch black out there. Through the rain beating against the glass, he could just make out a string of lights bobbing far out on the lake.

Franklin sighed. "Everybody with a boat's out there. The rest of us are searching the woods behind the cottages." He picked up his coat. "We're worried about some of those old feldspar pits. The area's riddled with them. And there's been a few bear sightings near here this summer."

"Wait a minute. I..."

"What is it?"

"I don't know." He turned away from the window. "There's something...uh, you sure Joanie's okay?"

"I told you. She's fine."

Suddenly, it felt like a skid of bricks was pressing down on Stu's chest. He'd never experienced such pain. His knees began to buckle, and he could feel the room tipping, feel Franklin's hand under his elbow. He mustn't lose consciousness, though. There was something important he wanted to say. Something about blue bathing suits.

Sue Pike *wrote her first crime story, "Murder Isn't Right", at the age of seven. After a long sabbatical, she began writing again, and her more recent stories have appeared in* Ellery Queen Mystery Magazine, Storyteller, Cold Blood *and all five Ladies' Killing Circle anthologies. "Widow's Weeds" from* Cottage Country Killers *won the Arthur Ellis Award for Best Short Story of 1997.*

When Laura Smiles

Liz Palmer

Oh, God. Here comes Carol, our activities director. She needn't think she can wheedle me into playing bingo.

"Hi there, Ruth. I've got something interesting for you today." She radiates energy and efficiency.

I force a smile. She has a tough job trying to keep us busy. Most of us in the nursing home want to be left alone, to remember…or forget.

She lays the *Winnipeg Free Press* in my lap.

"Isn't that the same house as the one in the photo on your dresser?"

Even without my glasses I recognize Grove House.

"It's my grandparents' home. Every July they waited there for me." I point at the step. "With Great Aunt Muriel tatting lace in the rocker. As I ran towards them, Pop would turn to Nana and say, 'I guess it must be the first day of summer, because our ray of sunshine has arrived.'" Carol is smiling patiently, and I see I have told her this story before.

"Well," her eyes sparkle, "a skeleton's been found there, hidden in a secret tunnel. Let me read you the article." She is about to pick up the paper when one of the fellows across the room starts yelling. She scoots over to sort out the problem. I have no need to read the story. I close my eyes and remember the first time Nana and Pop were not waiting for me on the steps. I was ten.

*   *   *

Sitting on the bench, feet swinging to and fro, I watched the second hand tick round the face of the station clock. In seven minutes, I'd be getting on the train and travelling to Merton all by myself.

"Sit still, Ruth, I've something to tell you." I stopped counting the ticks and waited, expecting yet more of Mother's instructions on how to behave. Instead, she said "You will not be the only child at Grove House this summer."

"What do you mean?" Summer had always been me with Daddy's parents, and Great Aunt Muriel.

Mother's lips compressed the way they did when she was cross. "Your cousin, Laura, will be there."

"You never told me I had a cousin called Laura."

"Because I was unaware of her existence until I received a letter this morning. Eleven years old, and she's only just turned up." Mother obviously disapproved of such unorthodox conduct. "Aunt Muriel writes that Laura's had a very difficult life, and Nana and Pop want you to be especially nice to her."

"Where has she been? And why has her life been difficult?"

"Her mother died last year."

"Oh." I edged closer to my mother. "Does she live with her father?"

Mother shook her head. Her fingers tapped against the stiff brown leather of her handbag. "She hasn't got a father either."

"She's an orphan!" I couldn't imagine having no parents. "Does she live in an orphanage?"

"No, with a foster family. Now that times are hard, they

can't afford to keep her, so she's going to live with Nana and Pop." Mother stood up as the train came into the station, hissed out its steam and came to a shuddering stop. She helped me put my bags into the carriage. "I'll see you in a month." We hugged. "Be a good girl and be kind to Laura."

I waved until she became a dot in the distance, then sat in the corner and watched the fields go by. A cousin might be fun. She'd be able to do things Nana and Pop couldn't, like climb trees. I'd share my toys with her, and she'd be grateful. I wasn't sure I liked the idea of her living with my Nana and my Pop.

The train slowed as it approached Merton, and I dragged my luggage to the door. Through the glass I could see Old Joe, Pop's general handyman, waiting with the buggy and the brown mare. It didn't take long to load up, and soon we were trotting down the dirt road towards Grove House. Joe steered the buggy through the wooden gates. The horse broke into a canter, and Joe shouted "Whoa" at her and hauled on the reins. We'd arrived.

I swivelled round to wave at Nana and Pop. They weren't there. Great Aunt Muriel sat alone on the verandah, a long ribbon of lace falling over the arm of the rocker. She smiled and nodded at me.

A small lump of fear formed in my stomach. I climbed slowly down from the buggy, very slowly in case they hadn't heard us coming.

Joe hitched the horse to the railing and lifted my bags out. Finally, the screen door opened and Pop appeared, leading a girl by the hand. Nana held the girl's other hand. They came and stood in a row at the top of the steps, Nana and Pop beaming proudly at my new cousin.

"Hey, Ruth, come and meet our little ray of sunshine."

Laura smiled at Pop when he said this, and the lump in my stomach hardened. She kept hold of Nana's and Pop's hands, and I hesitated at the bottom of the steps. How could they hug me, if she didn't let go? Then Laura looked down at me. She had dimples and big blue eyes colder than the wind in our Winnipeg winters.

"She doesn't like me." Her voice trembled, and she buried her face in Nana's flowered shirt. Nana's arms went round her.

"Of course she does, darling. You do, don't you, Ruth?" Nana and Pop both glared at me as though I'd done something bad.

"Yes." I mumbled, staring at my sandals, knowing I hated her just as she hated me. Knowing my summers at Grove House had changed forever.

Within the hour, the pattern had been set. Laura led the way to my room. Tucked under the eaves near the top of the stairs, it had sloping walls and a wide window seat. Years ago, Pop had painted my name on the door. My books were on the shelves, and my toys were in the closet. Except they weren't. And the eiderdown with the yellow roses wasn't on my bed either.

"Where are my things?" I pointed at the empty shelves.

"Laura borrowed them. We knew you wouldn't mind."

I did mind. I minded not being asked.

"I'm very sorry." Laura hung her head. "Please forgive me."

"Well said," Nana smiled and patted Laura's head. "And you with nothing to apologize for. Ruth, I'm sure you're going to be generous and share with your cousin. I'll get the juice and cookies ready for when you're finished unpacking." The door closed behind her.

Laura glanced from me to the mirror. "No one would think we were cousins," she said. She sounded pleased, and I didn't blame her. I was skinny, with crooked teeth and straight brown hair. Laura had white skin with rosy cheeks and long golden curls like my best china doll. Nana and Pop couldn't help but love her the most.

"I'll fetch the books and the puzzles. The rest of the toys stay in my room."

"No," I said. "You bring everything here to share out."

"Suit yourself." She shrugged and left the room. I took the dresses Mother had placed in the top of the case, shook them, and hung them in the closet, wishing all the while that Laura had never been found.

The door crashed open. "Ruth," Nana snapped, "did you tell Laura to bring your things back?"

"Yes, but…"

"To think you could be so selfish, Ruth Cummings. When I found Laura crying outside the kitchen, I told her she must have made a mistake. However, I see it's Pop and I who have made the mistake. You, young lady, have been spoiled."

Tears filled my eyes. I tried to explain, but Nana wouldn't listen. During the next few days, this happened time and again. Laura would twist my words and turn me into a monster while I, I could only stutter my protests.

Night after night I cried myself to sleep. Laura had cast a spell on Nana and Pop. Like the Ice Queen, she'd planted a sliver of ice in their hearts, and they'd forgotten how happy we'd been before. I longed for a good fairy to arrive to melt the ice. Gradually, I withdrew into myself.

Sometimes the sounds of Pop and Laura singing the songs he used to sing with me drifted through my bedroom window. He and Nana knew lots of songs and dances from their time on the stage. That's how Pop met Nana. She'd starred in a travelling show that played in Winnipeg when Pop was very young. He fell in love with her and ran away to join the troupe.

I didn't have anywhere to run to. Mother spent every July

in Regina caring for her father while her sister had a holiday. Daddy never stayed in Winnipeg in the summer. He took his students to the far north to study rock formations. I prayed Grandpa would die so Mother could come home, then cried with shame for my awful thoughts.

The third week of that dreadful month arrived. I'd taken to spending the days reading in the old maple behind the stables. On the Wednesday morning I'd finished making a sandwich to take with me and gone into the pantry for an apple when Pop and Nana came into the kitchen.

"When Laura smiles at me, I'd do anything for her," Pop said.

"I know what you mean. She just melts your heart." Nana sighed. "I wish Ruth hadn't grown into such a sullen, unattractive girl. It would be lovely for Laura to have a friend."

"Ruth isn't happy unless she's the centre of attention." Pop's voice faded as they went out to the garden. Tears streamed down my face. The sandwich fell to the floor as I sobbed into my hands.

The pantry door opened, and soft arms held me close. "There now." Aunt Muriel patted my back. "Don't cry so. Come along with me."

"Why, Aunt Muriel?" I cried. "Why don't they love me any more? Is it because I'm not pretty?"

Aunt Muriel wiped my eyes with her lavender scented handkerchief. "No, my dear. Sometimes grown-ups make mistakes. Nana and Pop made one a long time ago, and Laura suffered. Now they are trying to make amends, and unfortunately, you are caught in the middle."

Aunt Muriel had her rooms in the round stone tower on the south side of the house, and for the rest of the holiday they became my refuge.

It rained every day the last week of that July. Laura played spillikins with Pop and skipped rope on the verandah, with my rope. In the stone tower, Aunt Muriel took a black-bound ledger out of her bookcase. "I've a puzzle for you." She put it down on the gate-legged table by the window. "First you must promise to keep what you learn a secret." She sounded very serious.

I stared at the ledger. "Cross my heart and hope to die," I said.

She nodded. "I believe I can trust you. When my great-uncle first came here, he lived in a small hut. He planted the trees to remind him of England, and he dreamed of a strong stone house."

I wriggled to the edge of the chair, wishing she'd hurry.

"Life was precarious in pioneer days, and when Uncle James drew the plans for this tower, he incorporated an escape route in case he should ever be trapped."

My toes curled with excitement. "A secret tunnel?"

Aunt Muriel nodded and passed me the ledger. "See if you can find where he hid it."

The wet week went in a flash. I measured walls, tapped stones, consulted the plans and lay sleepless in bed working on the problem. I didn't find it that year, or the next.

*   *   *

I found it in 1934, my twelfth year.

We, at Grove House, had settled into two camps. Laura ignored me, providing I didn't interfere with her domination of Nana and Pop. She allowed me Aunt Muriel. After that first devastating summer, I found I preferred being with Aunt Muriel. She encouraged me in my efforts to write poetry and, to hone my mind, she taught me the intricacies of bridge. I learned to tat and proudly presented my mother with a lace doily for her birthday. The evenings I devoted to deciphering the cryptic references in the plans.

July 8th I walked over to the fireplace and pushed the stone beneath the mantle. The one closest to the chimney breast.

A small section of wall swung open with a screech. I held my breath and waited for the household to come running. Aunt Muriel said the walls were too thick for the noise to penetrate.

Stomach churning, I peered inside. I could see a couple of steps leading into a dank smelling blackness. "Where does it go?"

"To the stables. Tomorrow we'll oil the mechanism, and I'll give you the keys to the doors. There are two. One at the foot of the stairs and one at the far end. You mustn't go down there without my knowledge. If you were to have an accident, I'd never forgive myself."

While the novelty lasted, I went to and from the house via the tunnel, thus avoiding Laura. The secret gave my sagging self-confidence an enormous boost.

*   *   *

September, 1936. Because Merton had no senior high school, Laura came to live with us during the school term.

She fascinated the other students, especially the boys. She had inherited Nana's musical voice and captivating laugh, and at fifteen she'd learned how to use her beauty to her advantage. Few people realized her lovely exterior concealed a self-centred manipulator. On the rare occasion when a boy became interested in me, she switched her charm full on. It never took long for him to defect.

Until Richard.

We met in November, 1942. Mother and I had moved to Regina to be with her sister while Daddy did something for the war effort, in Ottawa. In the three years away from Laura, I'd crept cautiously out from my shell and made a few friends.

Dragged by a girlfriend to a musical evening for lonely British airmen, I was half-heartedly doing the actions to a raucous rendition of "Knees up Mother Brown" when someone spoke from behind.

"Is this your kind of music?"

I turned and looked up into warm brown eyes set in a thin, tanned face.

"Not really." I hoped it wasn't his favourite.

"So let's go somewhere else."

We talked and talked. Richard missed his home and family in England. He had been in Regina for over a year training pilots for the Royal Air Force. We discovered a shared love of poetry, history and Bach. The best, most magical winter of my life flew by with every spare moment spent with Richard.

At Cambridge University, he'd belonged to a quartet specializing in Elizabethan madrigals. One late spring evening he brought a guitar over and sang to me while I sat dreamily working on a lace collar.

"When I see you tatting, I feel I'm in another era." He lifted my chin and kissed me. The world stopped for a moment, and when it started again, we were engaged.

Until then I'd managed to keep him out of Laura's way. I hadn't been to Grove House in two years, not since Aunt Muriel had died. Now Daddy insisted I take Richard to meet Nana and Pop.

"This," I told Richard on the train, "will be a very short engagement. Once you've seen my cousin, that will be that." And I told him all about Laura.

"Have some faith, my love." He grinned. "I can't wait to meet this siren."

Laura made a play for Richard as soon as they'd been introduced. Head on one side, eyes wide and innocent, she lured him away from me with apparent ease. I crawled straight back into my old shell.

Immediately after supper finished, I slipped away, unnoticed. The tower rooms had been kept for my use. Aunt Muriel had insisted and, to give them credit, Nana and Pop had agreed despite Laura wanting to use them herself. The lawyer for her estate had given me the only key and now, desolate and bitter, I shut myself in.

Hardly a minute had passed before someone hammered on the door. "Help. Open up."

I plodded over and unlocked it. Richard rushed through and closed it quickly behind him.

"Whew." He leaned against the heavy wood. "Why did you ditch me?" He studied my face. "Ruth, love, you didn't think I'd fallen for her, did you?" He pulled me to him. "Silly sausage. I love you." He kissed me. "You. Got it?"

Life bubbled up again. He'd met Laura and still loved me. How could this be? Apart from Aunt Muriel and my parents, this hadn't happened before.

"Laura's gone to help your grandmother wash the dishes. Seeing the surprise on Nana's face, I suspect it's not normal. Let's sneak out for a walk while she's showing what a good little granddaughter she is." He grabbed my hand, and giggling like children, we crept out.

In the fading summer light we strolled in the woods behind the stables. I showed him my childhood hiding places, but I kept my promise to Aunt Muriel. The tunnel remained a secret.

After the weekend, letters from Laura arrived daily at the base.

"What am I going to do?" Richard showed me half-a-dozen

fat pink envelopes. They smelled of roses.

"You could write and ask her to stop." I itched to know what she'd written. When I asked, Richard ran a hand through his hair and reddened.

"Stuff about being in love. Nonsense really." He didn't pass me the letters to read.

"If you returned them unopened she'd get the message." I couldn't tell how he really felt. Flattered, perhaps. Whatever it was, I sensed danger.

"Good idea." He looked relieved, and I relaxed a little. Loving him wasn't enough, I had to have faith in his love for me.

July and August were busy for both of us. Richard had a new batch of conscripts to deal with, and in the Red Cross, where I volunteered, many of the workers had come down with a summer flu. He never mentioned Laura's letters during our fleeting moments together and I, content to be with him, never thought to ask.

Her arrival in Regina came as a shock.

"Didn't Richard tell you?" She sat on the chesterfield in our parlour. Her blue suit intensified the colour of her eyes. "I'm going to be staying in a hostel and working on the entertainment side."

"Entertainment side?" My mind had gone numb. Richard hadn't said anything. What else was going on?

"Yes. Entertaining the airmen. You know," she gave a husky laugh, "singing, kicking my legs, taking their minds off the war."

As soon as she'd gone, I phoned Richard at the base.

"Sorry, Miss. I'll get him to call when he comes in."

I paced round the kitchen, trying not to panic. Why hadn't he told me? I couldn't bear to lose him to anyone, let alone Laura. She'd crunch him up and spit him out later. I'd seen it so often in the past. Desperate men pleading with her to tell them what they'd done wrong. I wouldn't let it happen to Richard.

The phone rang, and I snatched it up.

"Ruth? What's the matter?" Richard sounded out of breath. I rarely called him during the day.

"Why didn't you tell me Laura was coming?" My voice cracked.

"Your cousin? How would I know?"

"She sounded surprised you hadn't told me." I swallowed a sob.

"Put the kettle on, I'll be there shortly." The line went dead.

Before the tea had time to steep, the roar of his motorbike reverberated down the road.

He erupted into the kitchen and uptilted a bag on the table. Pink envelopes, still sealed, tumbled out.

"I never got around to returning them. I meant to write and ask her to stop." He spread his hands. "I suppose she thinks I've read them."

"I thought…"

"I know what you thought, and it hurts me. Particularly since you've had so much experience with Laura's little games."

We comforted each other, and I promised him I'd always check before accepting anything Laura said.

By Christmas, she had become the sweetheart of the entire airbase. Laura, however, was obsessed with Richard. She would wait for him outside the hangar, shivering in the wind. Badger him into going to her concerts, where she would sing love songs to him. Richard, my chivalrous love, couldn't bring himself to be unkind.

When Laura promised him a real prairie Christmas with Nana and Pop in Merton, he reminded her of our engagement. She went alone but cut her visit short, and on her return she started to dog Richard again.

I'd had enough and confronted her. "Why do you always try to take people away from me?"

"You don't understand anything, Ruth. You've been wrapped in a cocoon all your life. I love Richard, and I'm going to fight you for him."

Over the months, as Richard continued to rebuff her, she lost weight and I began to believe she truly cared for him.

February, 1944. Nana and Pop were killed in a road accident. Richard, preparing to return to England, made time to come to the funeral with us. He was very gentle with Laura.

"I wish she'd meet someone else, Ruth. This is going to be tough for her. She didn't have a real family until she came to Grove House. She never had a father, and she was put in a foster home while her mother struggled to support them by acting and dancing. Her mother died, and the money stopped coming. Then the depression set in, and the foster family couldn't keep her. Not much of a childhood."

I wondered why her rotten childhood had given her the right to ruin mine and, more to the point, when she'd confided this mournful history to soft-hearted Richard. I didn't say it aloud. "She'll have some security now with the house and the money from Nana and Pop."

"Yes. That will help keep her mind off me leaving." Richard was due to go in three days. We'd discussed our wedding. I wanted it now, but he thought we should wait. Although he never said so, I suspected it was in case he didn't survive the war.

I will never forget the reading of the will.

Our great-grandfather, the lawyer explained, had decided Pop was irresponsible and had left everything to his daughter. Aunt Muriel had given Nana and Pop the rights to use the house and the interest of the fortune while they lived. I was her sole beneficiary.

Laura fled from the house. I sat, stunned. I'd won it all. The house, the money and Richard.

"I'd better follow her." Richard headed for the door. "She may do herself a mischief, the state she's in."

"Tell her I'll make provision for her," I called after him. I got tied up with the lawyer, and it was late when we finished. Richard still hadn't returned, and I thought he must have gone straight to his hotel room in Merton.

In the morning, I wandered round the house waiting for him and worrying about Laura. She had stayed away all night.

She walked into the tower room just before lunch, a pale waif in a crumpled black dress. I rushed to speak, to reassure her.

"I'll arrange for you to have the house, Laura, and half the money. I won't need it in England."

Laura lowered her eyes. Her hands stroked the wrinkles in her dress. "I stayed with him last night, Ruth. He has to marry me now. He's coming to tell you soon." She yawned. "I came by to get some clothes."

Richard had finally succumbed to Laura's smile.

The deep anger which had smouldered inside me for years, ignited. She wouldn't win this time...

*   *   *

"Ruth, Ruth, are you okay?" I hear a voice calling. "Take a breath, dear."

I open my eyes. Carol is patting my hand, a frown creasing her forehead.

"I'm fine." I whisper. I feel on my lap. "The paper. Where is it?"

"Here it is." She bends down and picks it off the floor. "Would you like me to read it now?"

I shake my head. "Read it to her." I point across the room. My cousin, Laura, sits in the chair beside the window. The best chair in the room. She's been here since the death of her third husband. Two old men are dallying close by.

She pats her yellow curls and smiles as Carol goes towards her, but her eyes are on mine. I'm glad she will finally know what happened. We hold each other's gaze while Carol reads the story.

Then Laura gets up. Leaning on her cane, she shuffles over to me.

"When you told the military police you'd sent him away, I believed you," she says. "Didn't you ask him what happened?"

"Ask him?" My hands start to shake. I am gulping for air. A vice is squeezing my lungs.

She stares at me. "You didn't." She laughs, "Oh, Ruth, I never slept with him. We spent the night drinking stewed tea in the mess. I said I was going to tell you we'd spent the night together, and you know what he told me?"

I cannot breathe. I clutch at the pain in my chest. My heart is breaking.

"He said, 'Ruth won't believe anything you say without checking with me'. He was wrong, wasn't he?"

Liz Palmer *writes from her home in the Gatineau Hills. She has had stories in three of the previous Ladies' Killing Circle anthologies. She won the Capital Crime Writers short mystery contest in 2001 and placed 2nd in 2002. She loves to kayak on still mornings.*

Sing a Song of Sixpence

Sing a song of sixpence
A socket full of die
Mabel fixed the outlet
To make her husband fry.
When the plug was shoved in
Brad began to roast
Oh, wasn't it a dainty dish
To make her husband toast?

Joy Hewitt Mann

Three Coins in the Fountain

Pat Wilson and Kris Wood

The cramped vestry was airless and hot. Under my heavy robe, I could feel a trickle of sweat running down my back. Trust the Koff-Carstairs wedding to be on the steamiest day of the year. I wondered how Father Donald was going to stand the heat once he put on his vestments. And where was Father Donald? The wedding was due to start in less than ten minutes.

The door crashed open, hitting my elbow and knocking Sunday's bulletins off the table. "Oh, shoot! Did I hit you with the door? Dear Charles, my faithful lay reader, you're always here first." Father Donald lumbered in like a huge over-inflated beach ball, the illusion heightened by the striking orange and yellow striped shorts and pistachio green T-shirt he was wearing. His flip-flops squeaked in protest at every step.

"Dottie's idea," he beamed, holding out the hems of his shorts and looking down at himself proudly. I doubted his sister Dorothy had ever suggested such an ensemble. "Well, not really her idea, but she encouraged me to dress coolly, that is, as coolly as you can dress on a day like this, although I'm not sure she really meant shorts, but then who will see them, except you, although on the other hand, I suppose if something untoward were to happen, and I had to remove my vestments, although, knowing what I'm wearing…"

I threw the alb over his head, mercifully muffling whatever he was saying. I confess that I pulled the cincture rather tighter than necessary around his middle, effectively cutting off his breath, his words and his train of thought, if he ever had one.

"Ooof! Easy there. I'm not a sack of potatoes, you know, although I might look like one, or perhaps a sack of flour, what with the alb being white and all, and…"

The door banged open again, this time, striking Father Donald rather smartly on his ample rear.

"Oh, sorry, Rev'rint Peasgood. I didn't see you there." I wondered at the blindness of anyone who could miss the mountain of white in the middle of the vestry.

It was William ("Call me Billy…") Koff, father of the bride, resplendent and sweating heavily in his white rental tux garnished with a deep purple cummerbund. "The Missus just reminded me that I had to give you a little somethin' for your services today." His eyes slid over to me, and I felt the dealer's appraisal of his glance. "You and your sidekick here." I winced. I'd been called a lot of things since I started serving with Father Donald in St. Grimbald's, but never a "sidekick". He handed me a large white envelope. "Money's tight right now, what with the wedding and all, and little Krystal and the Missus wanting nothing but the best…" The seams on the jacket strained as he searched fruitlessly for a handkerchief and finally pulled out the purple fan of silk in his breast pocket to wipe his crimson face. "…and sales is down everywhere," he continued, stuffing the now damp piece of silk back into the pocket, "and the business is no exception, so when I noticed that you hadn't bought tickets to the reception, why, me 'n the Missus thought you'd just as soon come and join in the festivities, as our guests, so to speak."

I opened the envelope with a sinking feeling. When two

garish gold and purple pieces of card fell into my hands, I kissed my new LaFlamme omelet pan goodbye.

"Oh, how thoughtful!" Father Donald grabbed one of the tickets. "A buffet! My favourite!" There go the profits, I thought. The latest trend in weddings seems to be to sell tickets to the reception, the takings of same either offsetting the wedding costs or going to the bridal couple. "Dottie's off to the A.C.W. meeting tonight, so I was going to have to fend for myself, although she always makes up a salad plate, but I think that a person needs something more substantial after a long day, not that a wedding is such a long day, although, on the other hand, it probably is for you…"

I threw the heavy white and gold chasuble over his head, once again cutting off the flow. The sounds of taped synthesizer "Pachelbel's Canon" floated in from the church.

"Uh-oh, that's my cue," Billy smirked. "Sounds pretty good, eh? Cheaper than an organist, that's for sure."

And so the wedding began, in all its inexorable awfulness. From the canned music to the purple and gold, gum-chewing bridesmaids, to the soloist wearing skin-tight black Capri pants and crooning to a karaoke version of "Wind Beneath My Wings", and the ever-so-tasteful unicorn tattoo clearly visible on the bride's ample bosom, the wedding was all one might expect from the union of the only daughter of the proprietor of Billy's Bargain and Auction Barn ("Bid High, Bid Low, It's All Got to Go"), to Trevor Carstairs, owner of Carstairs Fine Antiques and Collectibles ("Rare coins our specialty"), and only son of retired shipping magnate, Richard Carstairs.

Nowhere was this more apparent than in the two front pews. On the bride's side, Billy sat with a selection of female relatives, each sporting a large, purple silk orchid corsage. On the groom's side, Elaine and Richard Carstairs sat alone.

Elaine, grim-faced, wore a cream Chanel suit without the requisite orchid. Richard was in a wheelchair and looked pale, but then I'd heard his recent heart surgery hadn't been all that successful. They neither spoke to, nor looked at, any of the Koffs. Come to that, they didn't speak to each other, either. I'd heard rumours of trouble between them, partly due to Richard's iron control over the purse strings and partly to Elaine's obsessive devotion to Trevor. In fact, at one of our Wine Club meetings, Edith Bricks had confided to me that Richard said he would cut his son off without a penny if Trevor married Krystal Koff. I wondered how Elaine would handle this blow to her precious boy's future.

Krystal and Trevor's affair had been the talk of the village for months, particularly Trevor's inexplicable infatuation with Krystal Koff, a miniature (if one can use that word to describe a 180 pound young woman) of her mother, Rita. For a man who'd inherited his father's love of fine things, Krystal seemed an unlikely acquisition for Trevor. The affair, much encouraged by the Koffs, culminated in an announcement of impending parenthood and today's gala event. The rumours of Trevor's disinheritance had obviously not reached the Koffs, and who was Krystal to flout the convention of shot-gun weddings in our parish? Trevor seemed too besotted to care about either.

In just under thirty minutes, Father Donald, despite several enormous gaffes and slip-ups, had delivered enough of the marriage ceremony to make the union legal. The wedding party headed off for a quick spin around town, horns blaring, sans Carstairs, then to the Lions Club Centennial Park and Playground for photographs, with the Carstairs. Father Donald and I made a quick stop at the Rectory so he could slip into something more appropriate for a wedding reception at the Lodge.

Only the fact that the reception was at the Lodge impelled me to accept the ticket for the wedding dinner. I was neither a member, nor had I ever been invited to this secretive old building on the edge of town. This was a golden opportunity to inspect a small piece of local history. Last I'd heard, Billy was the current Grand Poo-Bah or whatever the head honcho is called, and so, no doubt, got the Lodge cheap for the reception.

By the time I'd got Father Donald decently attired and to the Lodge, everyone else was more or less assembled. I was horrified to be greeted by Billy, bow tie hanging, cummerbund undone, not in a receiving line as one might expect, but seated at a card table, where he was enthusiastically selling tickets for the drinks. Another money-maker.

Next to the table was a large bird cage on a stand, lavishly decorated with purple doves and orchids.

"Oh," said Father Donald, "what an interesting gift for the happy couple. I'm giving them a set of church mugs, well, not me, but Dottie and me, well, actually just Dottie. She does all that sort of thing, gifts and such, although I often suggest ideas to her, not that she listens to them, well, she listens, but doesn't usually take up my ideas, although I thought the one about giving a lifetime subscription to *St. Grimbald's Gleanings* was pretty good, that is if you like to read, or read things like *The Gleanings*, and I must say, Dottie is an amazing writer…"

"It's a money cage," Billy interrupted.

"A what?" Father Donald gaped at the cage.

"A money cage. You put in a twenty and I write your name on one of these slips of paper, and at the end of the evening, we have a little draw, and you could be the lucky winner of a new toaster oven." He winked at me. "Got two of them as wedding presents, they did, so I says to myself, let's just do a deal here."

Sure enough, the bottom of the cage was covered with twenties. I figured there was nearly a thousand dollars in there already. I briefly toyed with the idea for St. Grimbald's organ fund.

"Oh, I'd love to. I know Dottie could use a new toaster oven. Oh, shoot! The Bishop. Doesn't like raffles. Not that I'd tell him, but if he were to find out from someone here perhaps, although I doubt anyone here talks to the Bishop much, not that they aren't the Bishop's kind of people, or that the Bishop wouldn't talk to them…"

"That's all right, Rev'rint. It's just my way of getting a little extra folding green for the happy couple. Now, what's your poison?" Billy brandished the roll of drink tickets.

In a moment of rashness, I asked for a glass of white wine, not expecting French, mind you, but willing to settle for California.

"White wine? Sorry, pal. We're offering beer, made it myself, or Swish and mix. Three bucks a ticket or four for ten dollars."

I purchased tickets for ginger ale. At a dollar a can, it looked like glasses were extra. I noticed the Carstairs had done the same, although Elaine had somehow managed to acquire a straw.

Father Donald bounced off to inspect the buffet, and I wandered around the large barn-like room, decorated in an eclectic mix of moose antlers, lodge banners, and purple and gold rosettes, bells and streamers. I was drawn to a strange glow from the west wall.

It turned out to be the wedding cake, illuminated by a number of small plastic spotlights clipped to a gilded trellis. The cake was huge, made up of many layers, not only on top of each other, but also scattered around the table and joined by golden ladders. The symbolism of the ladders escaped me. The largest cake tier perched over a fountain spewing forth pale mauve liquid. I wondered if the ladders were for rescue attempts should the plastic bride and groom on top fall in. On impulse, I pulled a coin from my pocket and threw it into the fountain. I smiled. Billy had missed this money maker. It would be interesting to see how many others followed suit.

Throughout the dinner, I kept an eye on the fountain, and sure enough, nearly everyone who inspected the cake threw in a coin or two. Even Father Donald lifted his face from his plate long enough to borrow a loonie from me. I noticed the Carstairs ate sparingly. Perhaps the smoke-laden atmosphere had spoiled their appetites, or perhaps they didn't care for the cabbage rolls, macaroni salad and meatloaf entrees.

In the lull between the speeches and the beginning of the dance, I decided to wander around and take a look at the rest of the Lodge. I left Father Donald enthusiastically helping the DJ set up his equipment.

I opened one door and found myself in a huge kitchen full of secondary female Koffs, scraping plates and making up "doggy bags" of leftovers to take home. I edged around them and saw Elaine Carstairs heading out what looked like a back door. No doubt, like me, she was hoping to get a breath of smoke-free air. I waited a moment to give her privacy, then followed.

I pushed the door ajar and found myself in the utility room. I stepped back abruptly when I heard voices from the shadows behind the furnace. Far be it for me to interrupt some amorous couple, although I personally would have chosen an atmosphere more conducive to romance.

"No, no. It's the big one on the left! Look, I'll tie a bow on it." It was Billy Koff's voice. Not wanting to know or hear any more of Billy's amorous advances, I closed the door quietly, and wondered if the woman with Billy could possibly be the fair Elaine.

Later, back in the hall, the festivities continued in their time-honoured rituals. Bride danced with Groom. Bride danced with Father. Groom danced with Mother. Bride's father and groom's mother danced. This one was worth watching. I noticed Elaine was having trouble keeping Billy at arm's length. Plainly, his little episode in the utility room hadn't depleted his energies.

It was well after nine-thirty when I began to look for Father Donald. With any luck, no one had told him about the eleven o'clock buffet. I found him at the Cake/Fountain, looking hopeful. I was pleased to note that the fountain bottom was covered in coins.

"It's not real cake," I told him. "It's all made of styrofoam. They scrape off the icing and use it again."

"Not real..." His face fell. "Oh, shoot! I was just thinking that it must be time to cut the cake. I always like a piece of wedding cake, and Dottie will be so disappointed if I don't take her a piece home to put under her pillow..." I found it hard to imagine Dorothy Peasgood dreaming of an unknown lover. "...not that she wants to get married, although I suppose if the right one were to come along, on the other hand, you'd think he would have come along by now, if he was going to, I mean..."

"Perhaps we can stop at the Donut Shop on the way home," I told him. "They close at ten, so we should leave right away." Secretly, I congratulated myself on my cleverness. I'd have him out of here in no time. As we walked away, the Carstairs took our place at the fountain, Elaine wheeling Richard's chair. She checked her watch against the large clock on the wall, and I thought she must be as anxious as I was to make an escape.

"I'm sure I saw a 1908 gold sovereign in there, Richard," I heard her say, as he angled his head for a good look into the bowl.

It hadn't occurred to me that someone might toss a rare coin into this particular fountain, that a Koff of any ilk would have such a thing, but then, they probably thought it useless junk and cheaper than the real thing. I hung back a moment, thinking of a pleasant chat with the Carstairs, but then decided it was more urgent to get Father Donald away.

"Let's make our farewells and be on our way," I said to Father Donald. I looked around for Mrs. Koff, whose large purple presence had been all too obvious throughout the evening, but she wasn't in the room. It would have to be a Billy adieu.

Ticket sales were still brisk, and I noticed that the Money Cage was nearly half full of twenties. Obviously the fundraiser/wedding was a great success.

Father Donald was just in the middle of thanking Billy profusely for the delicious buffet when the lights went out. Several people shouted rude comments, better not remembered. There was a lot of raucous laughter and a few girlish shrieks. Obviously, this was someone's idea of a party game. It occurred to me that the party was moving into a new phase, and Father Donald and I were leaving just in time.

The card table went over, hitting Father Donald, who cannoned backwards, knocking me to the floor. In a moment, we were joined by a third body with an unidentifiable metal object that smacked me sharply in the ribs.

"Oh, my soul! Oh, my stars! Oh, shoot!" Father Donald flailed helplessly.

"Get off me!" I shouted.

A stream of blue language erupted from the third party with us. I recognized Billy's fruity tones.

Thankfully, the lights went back on, and there we were, Father Donald, me, the fallen card table, and Billy, clutching the Money Cage to his chest. It took us a moment to reorient ourselves, and as we started to disentangle, Rita Koff loomed over us, a purple mound of righteous indignation.

"Billy Koff, what are you still doing here? Rolling around on the floor with the preacher? Are you drunk? And you say I'm the dumb one," she started.

"Now, Ruby, dear…"

"Don't you 'Ruby dear' me. All that planning and treating me like a fool, putting ribbons on the switches, and when it comes right down to it, you can't even make it out the door." At this point, she realized that Father Donald and I were listening with open-mouthed attention. Her bosom heaved with anger, and she declared imperiously. "Well, what are you two gaping at? Billy, clear up this mess. This is supposed to be a wedding, not a free-for-all." She grabbed the Money Cage and put it back on its stand. "So much for your bright ideas," she snorted and walked away.

Chagrined, Billy smiled weakly. "I was only trying to protect the money," he said. "Can't trust anyone these days…"

"Oh, shoot! You don't have to tell us. You read about it in the papers all the time, well not all the time, but nearly every day, although there have times when there's been good news in the paper, not many, of course, but on the other hand…er, could you give me hand, Charles?" Father Donald was rolling helplessly from side to side.

I gave up trying to brush the dust off my good Brooks Brothers suit and heaved Father Donald to his feet.

"I'm sure you were just protecting your daughter's investment," I said icily to Billy Koff. It was obvious to me that the plot had been to steal the Money Cage. I realized that it had been Rita with Billy in the utility room, no doubt getting last minute instructions on how and when to pull the main switch. Considering that Andy Bickerton, the local RCMP officer, was the best man at the wedding, the whole scheme was pretty nervy of Billy.

Father Donald leaned towards me conspiratorially and whispered loudly. "Don't be too judgmental, Charles. Billy's a lapsed Catholic, you know, although I'm not sure how Catholic, or lapsed, come to that, but they do this sort of thing all the time."

Father Donald had lost me. What had Billy's Catholicism to do with larceny? Father Donald was usually quite open-minded about the other denominations.

"Poor old Father Clement used to do it all the time," Father Donald continued. "At the bingo, which is probably why we don't have them in our parish, bingo that is, not Catholics, although I know some parishes do, although not overtly, of course, not like the Catholics…"

I began to wonder if Father Donald had received a blow to the head in the lights-out scuffle. "What are you talking about?" I said rather sharply.

"Well, when Father Clement was priest at Our Lady of Perpetual Sorrows, if a non-Catholic was about to win the jackpot, Father would simply throw the main switch. When the lights went back on, the numbers had changed on the board. Not that I condone such a thing, but I certainly understand his wanting to keep the money in the family, so to speak, and Billy was only doing the same thing, well, not exactly the same thing, it not being a bingo but a wedding, but the principle's the same thing, although principle might be an unfortunate word under the circumstances…"

I realized there was nothing more wrong than usual with Father Donald's mental processes. And in a strange way, it did make sense.

I looked over to see how the Carstairs had survived the blackout. They were still by the Cake/Fountain, Elaine staring blankly across the hall, and Richard behind her, slumped in his wheelchair.

"Good news, Charles!" Father Donald was at my elbow. "Billy tells me that there's another buffet at eleven o'clock—sandwiches and squares. I always enjoy a little something before bed, although it's not supposed to be good for me, at least that's what Dottie tells me, what with her watching my weight and all, but on the other hand, if I bring her a little something, and maybe something for me, too…" Father Donald smiled in happy anticipation, and my heart sank. We were stuck here for at least another hour.

I decided to join the Carstairs and enjoy some intelligent conversation until the buffet was served. Father Donald, chatting about the possibility of Nanaimo bars at the buffet, trailed along behind me.

"Did you find that coin you were talking about?" I asked Mrs. Carstairs.

Elaine looked startled. "Coin? What coin?"

I felt myself redden. I'd been guilty of eavesdropping and given myself away. "Do forgive me. I overheard your telling Mr. Carstairs about a rare coin in the fountain. But perhaps I was mistaken."

"Actually, I thought I saw a 1908 Canadian gold sovereign, but we never had a chance to look for it because the lights went out." Elaine Carstairs smiled thinly at me.

Father Donald beamed. "Oh, rare coins. Shoot! You'd never believe what we find in the collection plates at St. Grimbald's. American money, always good, although it's a bother to take to the bank, and it changes so often, well, not the money, it doesn't change, unless of course, you take it to the bank. Canadian Tire money, too. Not that it's not useful, in fact, Dottie bought a new electric knife for the church kitchen, although I'm not sure it was meant for that, being in the collection and all, but on the other hand, once it's on the plate, then it's up to us to use it, and you can't bank Canadian Tire money, at least I don't think you can."

Mrs. Carstairs looked dazed. She'd obviously had few conversations with Father Donald.

Father Donald peered around her to Richard Carstairs. "I understand from Trevor that you're somewhat of a coin guru, Mr. Carstairs. We've got this funny little coin came in several Sundays ago, got a hole in the middle, not damaged, but a real hole. Covered in funny writing. Even Dottie can't figure out where it's from. I wish I had it to show you, but perhaps if I describe it fully, although I'm a little fuzzy on the actual words on it, but on the other hand, the shape should give something away, and if it were worth something, well, St. Grimbald's is always on the lookout for some extra cash, well, not cash, offerings, er…donations."

He wound down when Mr. Carstairs didn't respond. He bent down over the wheelchair and raised his voice a notch. Speaking directly into Richard's ear, he began again. "A coin!" he shouted. "With a hole. And funny writing."

He turned to Elaine and me. "Shoot! I think he's asleep." He shoved Richard's shoulder delicately. Richard fell forward out of the wheel chair and onto the floor.

"Oh, my stars! Oh, my soul! I think he's dead!" Father

Donald crossed himself rapidly several times.

"Dead!" Elaine Carstairs threw herself down beside Richard. "He can't be. He's just fainted! The shock of the blackout! Someone call 911. Get some water!" She rolled him over and began to slap his cheeks gently. "Richard! Richard, dear. Wake up."

I knelt down beside her and lifted Richard's limp hand. It was wet, and as I pushed up the French cuff of his shirt to take his pulse, I noticed it was wet also. He must have been fishing in the fountain for the coin despite Elaine's disclaimer. No doubt she was too embarrassed to admit it.

I felt no pulse and knew that he was dead.

"Water!" cried Father Donald, latching onto something concrete he could do. He looked around wildly, and his eyes landed on the fountain. "Here! I'll get some." He whipped out his handkerchief, dropped it into the bowl and swished it around energetically. Scooping up the soaking cloth, he turned, knelt down, draped it across Richard's face and began to pat the sodden mass.

"Ow!" Father Donald cried suddenly, waving his thumb vigorously. "Something cut me!"

Sure enough, great gobs of blood were now dripping onto the starched white shirtfront of the dead man.

"Step back. Step back. Let me in." It was Andy Bickerton, slipping into his official role. Obediently, people moved back, and Andy joined us on the floor next to Richard. "Dead, is he?"

"Yes," I said. "Did you call 911?"

"They're on the way, although I guess it's too late. What happened?"

"Looks like a heart attack," I said.

"I knew we should never have come to this dreadful affair."

Elaine's voice rose hysterically. "It's been wrong from the beginning. I begged Trevor, but he wouldn't listen, and Richard was so angry. And now see what's happened."

"Heart attack?" Andy frowned. "Then what's all this blood?"

"Oh, shoot! That's me!" exclaimed Father Donald, waving his thumb now wrapped in the sodden handkerchief, which was rapidly turning red. "The fountain water is full of glass. I must have scooped some up with my handkerchief. Nasty sharp little bits, too. There should be a sign, well, maybe not a sign, but some kind of warning, although on the other hand, maybe it's there to stop people stealing the money, although it's a little extreme, if you ask me, not that I'm any sort of crime expert, but…"

"Glass?" Andy interrupted. He had dealt with Father Donald before and knew how to cut to the chase.

"Yes, glass. Look!" Father Donald held out a sharp shard. "It was stuck right in my thumb. Oh dear, and I've got blood on my best jacket. Dottie will be so upset with me."

I stood up, and Andy and I peered into the bowl. Sure enough, I could see several pieces of frosted glass on top of the coins. They hadn't been there when Father Donald and I had inspected the fountain just before we made our way to say goodbye to Billy.

I reached up to adjust the nearest spotlight so I could see more clearly into the bowl.

"Careful!" Andy said sharply and grabbed my arm. "Look. The light bulb is broken. I think that's the glass in the bowl."

"This is no time to worry about a two dollar spotlight. My husband is dead! What kind of idiot would think it funny to turn all the lights out." Elaine broke into hysterical sobs. "Someone is going to pay for this!"

"Someone? What do you mean, someone?" The words

were out before I could stop them. Elaine was deliberately lying. "Mrs. Carstains, you know who turned the lights out. I saw you go ahead of me into the utility room. You would have heard Rita and Billy plotting to throw the main switch and steal the Money Cage."

"Whoa!" Andy held up his hand. "What's this about stealing?"

"When Rita Koff turned off the lights, Billy was going to make a run with the Money Cage, and no doubt, blame it on someone at the reception." A gasp went up from the circle surrounding us. "The plan failed. Case closed." I saw the bridal couple's faces, Krystal's red with anger, and Trevor's white with shock. Krystal clutched Trevor's arm and burst into loud sobs.

Trevor pushed off Krystal's hand and turned to help Elaine to her feet. Hugging her close, he said, "It's all right, Mama. Your boy is here."

"Oh, Trevor, darling. It's so terrible, but I can take comfort in knowing that you will never want for anything." I saw a glint in her eyes, not of tears, but of elation.

In a flash, I knew what had happened. Elaine had overheard not just that the lights were going out, but when the lights were going out. All she had to do was position Richard with his hand in the fountain, drop in one of the baby spots just before the appointed time, and let Nature do the rest. The hot spot would break in the cool water, sending enough of a current through the fountain to finish off Richard's frail heart.

By the time the lights were back on, she'd returned the spotlight to the trellis. If it hadn't been for Father Donald's zealous attempts to revive Richard, no one would have ever noticed one broken light or connected it with Richard's death. I was sure Andy would find her fingerprints on the spotlight clip.

I took Andy aside and whispered, "You'd better hold off the paramedics. I think this is a crime scene."

"Oh shoot! Does this mean they won't be serving the sandwiches and squares?"

Pat Wilson *and* **Kris Wood** *have been friends for over thirty years, although they've seldom lived near each other. Instead, they've run businesses, written stories and collaborated on a multitude of projects all through mail, email, fax, telephone and the occasional brief visit.*

Pat is an international speaker. Kris is a certified gerontologist. Both are published authors.

They now live next door to each other on Sober Island, Nova Scotia.

The Night Chicago Died

Bev Panasky

I t was the summer I just couldn't catch a break.

Day after day the sun beat down on the city, pushing temperatures into the high thirties and shoving tempers up with it. Cases were hard to come by—clients and criminals, everyone was staying home in air-conditioned comfort.

I stood at the window pondering the dire state of the world in general and my life in particular when a sharp knock startled me.

The office door swung open, and a woman in a crimson dress and heels stepped into the room. "I'm looking for Ronnie Wagner."

"That's me." I walked toward her, my hand stuck out. Shaking her hand was like holding a dead jellyfish.

She glanced around the office with an expression of slight disgust, as though the carpet fuzzies might come to life and attack her. "I expected a man."

I'd heard that before. "Well, you've got me. Maybe I can help."

She surveyed the diplomas on the wall before perching on the chair opposite mine. "My name is Dawn Rapture, I'm in trouble and I need to hire a private investigator."

I did a mental eye-roll; a stripper name if I'd ever heard

one. I took out a pad of paper. "What kind of trouble are you in?"

She fixed her baby blues on me. "The police think that I killed Gary Chicago."

*　　*　　*

Gary Chicago was one of the slickest, slimiest creatures ever to call Ottawa home. He liked to sell himself as the "accountant to the stars". There was no trick, no loophole he hadn't found. He could take drug or blood money, run it through the system and it would pop out as crisp as a nun's underpants. All the players respected his talents, but I'd heard it said that maybe he knew a little too much about everyone's finances for comfort.

"Why would they suspect you?" I asked.

She looked away. "Gary and I were very close."

I could just picture it—the dream of all working girls, find a prince and live happily ever after. Except that all you'd get from kissing that toad was warty lips. "Did you have a reason to kill him?"

Laughing, she pulled out a slim cigarette case. "Honey, everyone had a reason to kill him."

She ticked them off on her fingers: "Abe Ivanov was his business partner, he's the one all the clients are flocking to now. There's Salvatore Bolino—I don't have to tell you about him."

Indeed she didn't, he was just the biggest racketeer in this part of the province. He would have been a bit player in Toronto or Montreal, but around here, he was a big fish in a small pond. A very big fish with very big teeth.

Another finger flicked up. "Of course there's his wife, Nicole, and his Amazon daughter."

She crushed out her cigarette and stared off into space. "You know, he always wanted to play a certain song whenever we were together. That Barry Manilow one, you know the one, about giving and never taking." She laughed, coming back to the present. "What did I care? He did the giving."

My dad always said that you don't have to like someone to take their money. "I charge $300 a day plus expenses." I wondered how many hours of swinging the pole it'd take for her to make that kind of money.

She looked around. "A bit steep, isn't it?"

"Take it or leave it, you won't find anyone cheaper."

She pulled out a wad of cash. "When can you start?"

*   *   *

Abe Ivanov's office was on the fringe of the Byward Market in a nondescript three-storey walk-up. At the top of the stairs, I stood in front of a glass door that said "Abraham Ivanov, Chartered Accountant". Traces showed where Chicago's name had been scratched off.

The receptionist pointed me toward an ivory leather couch, where I found a copy of Car and Driver and flicked through the pages. After about twenty minutes, the door to the inner office flew open and out stalked Salvatore Bolino, two goons hot on his heels.

"Miss Wagner?" Ivanov looked tired. "Would you care to come in?"

He led me into a large office with a huge mahogany desk and hundreds of plants. I settled into a striped wing chair and set my tape recorder and business card on his desk. "Thank you for meeting with me," I said.

Ivanov shuffled over to the adjoining bathroom and came

out with a watering can. "You're looking into Gary's death?" He didn't wait for me to answer. "Some things are best left to the police, don't you think?"

"I've been hired privately to look into this matter." I hit the RECORD button.

"Ah yes, the little tramp hired you. Did she tell you that she was the one with the motive?"

"What motive is that?" I asked.

"He was going to leave her. A woman like that gets used to a certain lifestyle, and she isn't too happy about losing it." He turned toward me, a slight smirk playing at the corners of his mouth. "I'm sure you can sympathize, being a woman and all."

I wasn't thrilled with the comparison. "How is that a motive? How would she be any better off with him dead?"

He smiled. "I'll tell you what happened. They planned a little rendezvous, and afterwards, when Gary told her it was over, she shot him."

"There's one problem with your theory," I said. "Ms. Rapture was working during the night in question. I'd be interested to know where you were."

He lifted an orchid, filled its tray and replaced it. "Do you call what that woman does working? Did she tell you if she had a few hours off between performances?"

I shifted in the chair. "Mr. Ivanov, you're avoiding my question. What were you doing on the night of July 13?"

He turned to look at me, dark circled eyes staring out of a gray face, "Why should I tell you anything? Who do you think you are?" He slammed the watering can onto his desk. "I believe this interview is over."

I turned off the tape recorder, gathered the rest of my belongings and headed for the door.

"Miss Wagner," Ivanov called after me. "Stay out of this.

There are some powerful people who won't be too happy about you poking around in their business."

I stomped out of his office and down the stairs.

That had gone badly. If everyone else was as forthcoming, I figured I could skip the investigation and buy Ms. Rapture a going-up-the-river present instead. I was fuming. Opening my purse, I dropped in the tape recorder and steno pad.

"Don't make a sound, *ma belle,*" a voice said in my ear as a hand clamped my upper arm like a vise. Before I could react, I was thrown sideways into the back seat of a large dark car, where I practically landed on one of Bolino's goons.

The man shoved me into the centre seat, leaned across and pulled the seat belt over my lap. He wrapped the loose end around his massive hand.

The car door slammed, and we pulled away from the curb. "Hey!" I said, twisting to look out the rear window, "That's my purse back there!"

A big hand grabbed the top of my head and turned me forward. I clasped my trembling hands together and surveyed the interior of the car.

We travelled three or four blocks before the driver's eyes shifted to the rear-view mirror. "What you doing with Ivanov, *ma belle?*" he asked.

"Nothing," I said, "I'm not doing anything."

Frenchie smiled. "Don't be lying to me, or I will have to let Aldo get some answers from you. You don't want that."

My companion jerked the seat belt, digging it into my stomach. "Okay," I grunted. "I wanted to ask Ivanov some questions about Gary Chicago's death, but he didn't tell me anything." I licked my lips. "I don't know anything about anything. Honest."

"How do I know you are not lying?"

"Have you ever talked to that guy? He asks more questions than he answers. I need a Tylenol after ten minutes with him."

Frenchie threw back his head and laughed. "It is true. It is true. That man should learn to just say it. Like the commercial, huh, Aldo? Just say it."

He pulled to the curb. Aldo let go of the belt and shoved me out onto the sidewalk.

The front passenger window rolled down. "You stay out of this, *ma belle*. It is done. If you go looking for answers, you will only find trouble."

They pulled into traffic. Just another shiny blue Lincoln with a muddy license plate.

* * *

I found my purse lying half on the sidewalk, half on the road. I gathered the contents that had spewed out. Everything was accounted for except my cell phone. I looked around. Something that looked suspiciously like a phone antenna stuck out from under the back wheel of a red Toyota.

As I walked back to my car, I started to shake. Inside, I clutched my arms across my chest and rocked until the trembling stopped.

No case was worth that, I concluded. Then I thought about the rent and the fact that I'd only been on the job for a couple of hours. I might have earned enough for a Big Mac, but that was about it.

I decided to put in a few more hours, earn the three hundred I'd been paid, and call it a day.

* * *

I swung into the Bank Street Dairy Queen. Once I'd stopped shaking, the heat had seeped back in, leaving me rubbery-limbed and parched.

A Peanut Buster Parfait hit the spot. I sat in the almost empty parking lot and leaned back against the headrest. My neurons, no longer overheated, started firing a bit faster, and I realized there was an avenue of information that I hadn't yet tapped. Tossing the empty container in the garbage, I trotted across the parking lot to a pay phone and dialled Sophie Burch's number.

"Good afternoon, Crown Attorney Thaddeus Skipp's office."

"Hi, Sophie."

"Ronnie, what a surprise! To what do I owe this pleasure?"

Sophie was the mother of an old boyfriend. Though the romance had soured, she and I had remained friends. "Actually, I'm hoping you can tell me a few things. About Gary Chicago's death."

There was a long pause, "You know I'm not supposed to talk about anything I hear around here. I could get fired. Or even charged. It's a really big deal. Anyway, I don't know anything."

"Come on, Soph, don't give me that. You screen everything that goes into or out of Skipp's office. Don't tell me you don't know anything."

I could hear her breathing on the line.

"You owe me, and you know it," I said.

"That's not fair! I'm going to pay you back!"

"I've heard that before."

Sophie's voice shook, "I haven't been to the casino in six months. I swear to God that part of my life is over."

"Look, I just had a run-in with some of Bolino's friends, and it's left me more than a little cranky."

There was silence on the line.

"I gave you every cent I had to keep people like those from rearranging your body parts."

"I know, Ronnie!"

"The least you could do is help me out."

"I can't."

"Damn it! I cashed in my RRSPs for you!"

"All right! All right! Just a minute." I heard her door click shut.

"What is it you want?"

"Why don't we just start with some yes/no questions?"

Sophie sighed.

"I take it Ms. Rapture is the main suspect," I said.

"Yes."

"Are they pursuing other avenues?"

"No."

"Do they have decent evidence against her?"

"Yes."

"What kind of evidence?"

"These are supposed to be yes/no questions," she whispered.

"Come on, Soph, I need a hint."

She sighed. "Not here. Not now."

I smiled. We made a dinner date, and I headed for home. Time to clean up. I was having company, after all.

*   *   *

My apartment was one of many identical shoeboxes in a shabby high rise in the west end of Ottawa. Apartment 904, home sweet home. The Tweetster greeted me as I stepped through the door. Tossing seeds was his way of saying hello.

I took a quick, cool shower and slicked back my hair. It wasn't blow-drying weather. Anyway, my hairspray had already given up its last squirt, and digging the mini-bottle out of my purse just wasn't worth the effort.

* * *

Sophie arrived, a cold bottle of Chardonnay in hand. She was a cheap date; a couple of glasses and she was ready to talk.

"So you want to know what they've got on that Rapture woman, huh?" she asked around a mouthful of pizza.

"It would help me know what I'm up against." I reached for another gooey slice.

"Well, everything seems to point to her."

"Everything would be what exactly?"

"They found him in the bathroom of the hotel room. He was fully dressed except that…well…let's just say he was exposed."

"Umm…" I said.

"Apparently he looked perfectly normal except for the big hole in his chest. And the blood, of course. Whoever shot him nailed him right in the heart."

"None of that necessarily implicates my client."

"No," Sophie said, "but they found cigarettes in the ashtray with lipstick stains on them. A colour called Rubicund Red— apparently a favourite of Ms. Rapture's."

They couldn't possibly be harassing my client with only that scanty bit of evidence.

"As I understand it," Sophie continued, "they found traces of lipstick on certain other things as well." She gave me a look.

"Ah."

"Our investigator says word on the street is that Chicago

was going to drop her. He was eyeing up someone else."

I contemplated another slice of pizza but had begun to feel queasy.

"There's more." Sophie patted her throat and the back of her neck with a tissue. "They found your client's fingerprints on the doorknob and the phone. When the DNA comes back, they'll be picking her up." She raised her glass in a mock salute. "It looks like you played the wrong hand this time, Ronnie."

*   *   *

I lay awake half the night wondering why a murderer would hire someone to find out who killed the victim. Did she think I was so stupid that I'd just meddle around causing problems?

In the morning I called Ms. Rapture and didn't waste any time on preliminaries. "They found your fingerprints in the hotel room," I paused. "What have you got to say about that?"

Just as I began to wonder if she planned to reply at all, her shaky voice came over the line. "Gary left me a message to meet him at the hotel at nine. When I walked in, he was already dead."

I rubbed my temple, "You didn't think I needed to know about that?"

"Oh, God! It was so horrible!" Her voice caught in her throat. "I loved him."

"Why didn't you call 911?"

"I was going to. I picked up the phone to call," she said, "but I realized it might look bad for me. So I left him there. God forgive me, I just left him there!"

She cried while I sifted through the new information. "Why should I believe you?" I asked.

"You have to! Someone is setting me up. You're my only chance."

I sighed. "All right," I said. "I'll see if I can get the family to talk to me. But don't get your hopes up."

* * *

I called ahead, and Mrs. Chicago reluctantly agreed to meet me. She opened the door of her million-dollar-tons-of-curb-appeal home and fixed me with a stare that would have made a lesser mortal cringe. I handed her my card and held my ground. "Mrs. Chicago, thanks for meeting with me. I know this must be difficult for you."

She ignored my out-thrust hand but took the card and stepped back, waving me in. Amber liquid sloshed from her glass onto the marble floor. "I don't know why you're here," she said as I pushed the RECORD button on the tape recorder and followed her into the depths of the house.

In the kitchen, she picked up a knife and began slicing a lemon. She finished her drink in one quick toss-back.

"I've been hired to look into your husband's death," I said.

She glared at me as she dropped a handful of ice into her glass, poured three fingers of Scotch and added a slice of lemon on top. "I'd offer you a drink," she said, "but I don't like you."

"That's okay, ma'am."

"So, that woman hired you." Mrs. Chicago looked me over. "She must be desperate."

I forced a smile. "Can I ask you about your husband's activities on the day of his death?" The alcohol vapours coming off her were making me dizzy.

"He got up in the morning like usual and went to work."

"Did he seem different in any way? Was he nervous? Anxious?"

She swirled the liquor in the glass, the only sound was the tinkle of ice cubes glancing off crystal. Finally she looked at me, her face lined with sorrow. "I don't know. I was still in bed."

"What's going on here?" I whirled around at the sound of a voice directly behind me.

"Oh, Amanda, I'm glad you're here." Mrs. Chicago pointed a finger at me. "She's here about your father's murder. She's a private eye. A private dick." She uttered a short, harsh laugh and stumbled out of the room.

The woman standing behind me had to be six feet tall and built like a linebacker. I glanced down. I could see the can of pepper spray, nestled against my wallet, waiting for its chance to shine. I shifted the tape recorder to my left hand.

Dark, glittering eyes fixed me to the spot. "What are you doing here? Why are you bothering my mother? Who hired you?" The questions came short and fast.

"My client's name is irrelevant," I said.

She laughed. "Let me guess. That stripper he was running with, right?"

I didn't respond.

She tossed her briefcase on a chair. "What a joke."

"So you know about your father's girlfriend. Did your mother? Before this, I mean."

"Of course, we knew." She gathered the lemon slices and dropped them into the garbage. "She wasn't the first."

"How many were there?"

She turned toward me and shrugged. "Who knows. He did manage to survive the other relationships, though."

"There must be other suspects," I said.

"Like who?"

"Your father had some very shady clients. Do you think any of them would want him dead?"

Amanda Chicago leaned back against the counter and crossed her arms. "Why would they want him dead? He performed a service for them. You don't kill off your service workers."

"Maybe he knew too much." I looked around the huge, gleaming kitchen. "Maybe he was shuffling a few cards from the bottom of the deck."

She shook her finger at me. "No! My father had some less than respectable clients, but everything he did was strictly above board! He was well compensated for his knowledge, that's all. Everything he had, he earned."

"Okay!" I held up my hands in surrender. "It was just a thought."

"You're wasting your time. She did it. It's obvious."

Amanda herded me toward the door. "I'm sorry my mother and I couldn't help." She paused. "Actually, I'm not sorry. She did it. I just wish we still had the death penalty in this country."

I stopped half in and half out of the door. "It's all circumstantial. They won't convict her on a little bit of lipstick that can be bought from any drugstore in the country."

Amanda smiled. "I'm told that it can take months for the police to put together a critical mass of evidence. Eventually, it all stacks up. The fingerprints, the cigarette butts, the note—they all come together in time. My mother and I are patient people. We can wait."

*   *   *

I swung onto the Queensway and headed for home. All that remained of the sunset was a ribbon the colour of tomato soup in my rear-view mirror. Deep in thought, I crested Kanata Hill, barely noticing the lights of the city spread out below.

Everyone wanted to point the finger at my client. Abe Ivanov couldn't wait to see her charged. But, in reality, he had inherited a lot of big-money clients.

The family. They had plenty of motive, but could they actually do the dirty deed? Not mama. Amanda? She could have, but why? She seemed fond of her father, and apparently this wasn't his first affair.

Then there was Bolino. Had Chicago known too much? Was he stealing?

I sighed. Amanda Chicago had been right about one thing—all available evidence pointed to Dawn Rapture.

I pulled into the parking lot behind my apartment building. My brain itched with the knowledge that I was missing something. I ran through Ms. Rapture's version again: arrival, body, phone, leave. Closing my eyes, I chanted it like a mantra—arrival, body, phone, leave.

I rewound the tape of my interview with the Chicagos and hit the PLAY button.

I never did make it to my apartment. Instead, I headed downtown to have a little chat with Dawn Rapture.

*   *   *

"You ever been here before?" Dawn asked.

"No, can't say I have."

"Women come to the show sometimes. Usually with their husbands. I guess they figure it's better to be embarrassed than bored."

I shuddered. Even backstage, you could feel the thick aroma of loneliness and desperation pressing in from the other side of the curtain.

"I wanted to ask you about the message Gary left for you to meet him at the hotel."

"Okay."

"Do you still have it?"

"No."

I stood back as Dawn caked her head in hairspray. "You erased it off your answering machine?" I asked.

"It wasn't a phone message," she said. "It was a note. He must have dropped it off when I wasn't home. He'd been writing me little love notes for a few months."

My mouth went dry. I fumbled through the contents of my purse before remembering that my phone had been turned into Toyota toe-jam.

"I'm up next." Dawn headed for the door.

I snagged the cellphone that was sticking out of her purse. "Can I borrow this?"

"Knock yourself out," she said.

It was impossible to get reception inside, so I weaved my way through the bar and out onto the street.

I dialled Sophie's home number. As I waited for her to answer, I paced back and forth between the club and the neighbouring deli.

"Hi, Soph," I said when she answered.

Static stuttered in my ear. "God, this is a bad connection," Sophie said.

I walked a bit farther from the building. "I'm at Muffinz, that strip joint where Dawn Rapture works."

"What do you want now?"

"When we were talking yesterday, you said the evidence consisted of fingerprints and cigarette butts, right?"

"Yeah."

"What about the note?"

"Note? There wasn't any…"

A large figure dressed in black charged at me from the doorway of the club. I cried out as strong hands pushed me backward into the dark, narrow space between the buildings. The phone clattered to the pavement.

"Help!" I yelled as I landed hard on my tailbone.

A big, gloved hand came down over my face. My assailant straddled me, holding my legs down.

I fumbled at my purse, but it was jerked off my shoulder and dumped onto the asphalt. The contents scattered.

My captor picked up the little canister of pepper spray. The face slowly lowered toward mine, the pepper spray held between us.

"Is this what you were looking for?" Amanda Chicago asked. She was dressed in black motorcycle leathers with a fuzzy mustache decorating her upper lip.

"Maybe I should use it on you." She pointed the canister at me.

Clamping my eyes shut, I held my breath.

She laughed. "Relax."

The hand lifted off my face, and I let my breath out in a whoosh.

"You have something that I want." She settled more heavily on me. "I think you know what it is."

My respirations were reduced to grunts. "The tape."

"Smart, smart, smart." She tapped my forehead with the pepper spray canister.

"It was in my purse. It's on the ground somewhere."

She reached into a pocket and pulled out a small, black revolver. Standing up, she said, "Then I guess you'd better find it."

On my hands and knees, I sifted through the detritus of

city life and quick, fevered love. I felt nauseous. "Why did you kill him, Mandy? That's what he called you, wasn't it? His little Mandy."

"Shut up."

I sat back on my heels and looked at her. My heart pounded at the back of my throat. "You could have killed her instead. She's just a stripper. Who would care?"

"Keep looking!"

I continued moving garbage back and forth.

"You have no idea what it was like to watch my father turn into a simpering fool. Over a stripper! He belonged to me!"

"Maybe he loved her," I said.

"He did not love her! He loved me! Not her." Amanda kicked me in the ribs. I lay on my side, gasping.

She kicked me again. "Get up! Keep looking."

It was all beginning to make sense. The little mustache. I hadn't recognized her until she'd spoken. Anyone could be forgiven for mistaking her for a man. I wondered if she made a habit of visiting the club.

"Really clever with the cigarette butts."

She smiled. "Weeks ago, I came here to kill her. Then I saw the way the old men drooled over the dancers, and I realized he'd come back. I couldn't kill them all."

"Did you talk to her that night?" I asked.

"I bought her a drink. She was flirting with me. Unbelievable. I helped myself to a few cigarette butts on the way out. Now all will be well," Amanda continued. "She'll be in jail. You'll be dead. Daddy will never give his love to anyone else again."

I shifted a little farther down the alley.

Amanda's toe touched something. She picked up my tape recorder and held it up for me to see. "Look what I found." She played back the last few seconds of the tape, popped it out and tucked it into a pocket.

She smiled at me. "I guess this is it. Too bad for you."

"Wait," I said. "I need to know one thing. How did you get him to the hotel room."

"I suggested to Sal Bolino that my father needed a little bonus. Something special to make him relax. He'd been under too much stress lately. So it was arranged."

"Were you there? Did you watch?"

"I waited in the closet. I just kept telling myself it would be over soon. After the girl left, he went into the bathroom to clean up. I walked over and said 'Hi, Daddy', and shot him."

"In the heart because he broke yours."

She stared at me.

I inched away from her and felt around for something to use as a weapon. "Then you wrote the note to Dawn Rapture? So that she'd come to the room and leave evidence?"

She laughed. "You're just too damn smart. For all the good it's going to do you."

"Where is that note? Dawn's note?"

"She leaves her car windows open. How stupid is that?"

She crouched down directly in front of me. "I want to watch your face when it happens. My dad looked so surprised."

She raised the gun.

I glanced down as my hand touched a cool cylinder. The dark blue hairspray can was nearly invisible in the poor light.

"Bye, bye," she said.

I twisted to the left. There was a sharp "crack", and the breeze of the bullet buffeted my cheek. I jerked the little bottle up and pressed the button.

Amanda yelped and staggered backwards, wiping at her eyes. I launched myself at her. She waved the gun wildly as we bounced back and forth between the walls of the buildings. I grabbed her hand and scraped it along the brick, pressing with all my strength, leaving skin behind.

The gun hit me on the shoulder, and we both dived for it, elbowing each other. She kicked it, then threw herself forward. I fell on top of her. Digging a knee into her kidneys, I lunged past her and snatched it, leaving her empty-handed.

She howled and arched back, scrambling toward the end of the alley. She never made it. Her feet tangled in the straps of my purse, and she went down with a bone-rattling crash. The alley filled with flashing lights and blue uniforms poured in.

Questions came from every direction.

When the furor died down, I picked up the phone and dialled Sophie.

"Oh, my God!" she screamed into my ear. "Are you all right?"

"Thanks for calling the cops."

"I didn't know whether to hang up and call them or keep listening."

"You made the right choice."

"I guess we're even now?" she asked.

I hung up without commenting.

I was hot and dirty, and my ribs ached. I needed a change of scenery. At least until the heat wave was over.

I headed into the club. Dawn Rapture owed me some money, and I wanted to collect before leaving town.

Bev Panasky, *thanks to repressed criminal tendencies, placed second in the 2001 Capital Crime Writers Mystery Short Story Contest. Unable to afford therapy, she spends her free time cruising the airwaves and plotting nasty ends for old enemies. "The Night Chicago Died" is her first published short story.*

Wake Up Little Suzie

Mary Jane Maffini

Now that Pops wasn't there to keep an eye on things, it was all up to Suze. Someone had to make sure Mike Jr. learned his times tables and saved his paper route money for a winter jacket. Someone had to check Mom didn't fall asleep with her cigarette still burning and get them booted out of another apartment. Suze didn't mind. She taught Mike Jr. her best arithmetic tricks and showed him how to tie knots and read maps so he could get his Cub badges. She was a light sleeper, so it wasn't so hard to get up and check the sofa for smouldering butts. Pops always said you do what you have to.

She kept the calendar with the due dates for the rent and the electricity and picked up the money from the trust account at the bank and delivered the envelopes with the exact amount in them to the right places at the right time. Every two weeks she paid the bills for their grocery orders at Morrison's.

Suze made sure she led her Grade Five class (average 98.2 %) because, like Pops used to say, you don't ever give the nuns one more thing to look down their long noses at you over.

She'd had her troubles with the nuns, especially Mother St. Basil, who used to say rotten things to her in front of the class and make mean hints about Mom and her boyfriends. Especially after the time Officer Collins came to the school to ask Suze and Mike Jr. about Arvie. Mother St. Basil was always making a big show of sending Suze to wash her hands and saying things like "dirt attracts dirt." Suze knew what she meant, and so did everyone else in the class.

But now she had Miss deLorentis for Grade Six. Miss deLorentis never said a whisper about how Suze was dressed or what was in her lunch pail. She only cared about what kind of person you were, and not who your mother was. Suze hoped Miss deLorentis never found out that she signed all her own report cards. Miss deLorentis was perfect, with her shiny black hair, huge dark eyes, plaid skirts, tiny ankles and polished leather pumps. She wished Pops could have met Miss deLorentis.

But Pops was pushing up the daisies, as Arvie had just reminded her. "You can't go snivelling to your grandfather now that he's six feet under," Arvie would say with a smirk. Suze bit her tongue so she wouldn't tell Arvie that if Pops was alive, there'd be no way a bum like you could have moved in with Mom. Mom would have slapped her right across the face if Suze talked to Arvie like that. Mom thought Arvie was fun and full of surprises. Suze didn't like those surprises.

Like now, Arvie sneaking up on her while she was frying up baloney and heating a can of peas for supper.

"You're sitting on a fortune, Suze? Know what that means?"

Suze didn't have to know what it meant. If it came out of Arvie's mouth, there was something dirty about it. "That's disgusting. I hope Mom hears you."

But Mom couldn't hear anything. She was playing her three new forty-fives, and she just kept dancing in the front room while Arvie supposedly got her a Captain Morgan's Dark with Coke. She loved the Everly Brothers and so had Suze, until Arvie had started singing "Wake Up Little Suzie" in that creepy way and ruined it for her.

Mom called out from the front room. "Get in here, Arvie, I'm putting on 'Little Darlin'." It would have felt good to hear Mom laugh, except Arvie was getting too close again. Buckingham cigarettes and beer on his breath, and the smell of grease to keep his hair in the duck's ass. Sweat from his open shirt. Suze was stuck by the stove, with him pressing in, stuck feeling his belly on her back. One of these days, she was going to throw up.

"Hey, Mike Jr.," she said, whipping the frying pan off the burner, "what are you doing back so soon?" Arvie whirled just long enough for Suze to duck by him and park herself in the front room. "Mom, I got two really big tests coming up, and I'll be studying tonight, so don't anybody bother me. Okay? Fathers of Confederation. Middle names and everything. And provincial capitals, including the Northwest Territories and the Yukon. So I won't open my door, even if you knock on it. Anyway, I'll have the Hit Parade on, I won't even hear you."

Mom kept dancing all by herself. "Get that stinking baloney out of here. And make sure Mike Jr. goes to bed all right."

Suze tried to lean close and whisper so Arvie couldn't hear. It wasn't such a great idea for Arvie to know everything. It wouldn't be the first time he'd been through Mike's stuff when Mom got past her third dark and dirty. Suze was pretty sure that's when Pop's war medals went missing. "He's at the Cub sleep-out tonight. You know that. I'm doing his paper route for him tomorrow."

Mom gave her a small shove. "Watch your feet, Suze."

Pops always said that Mom used to be fine. It was only after Mike Sr. passed away she went a bit foolish. He could hardly blame her, no husband and two kids. What would Pops say if he saw Mom the way she was now, with her hair bleached nearly white and her red lipstick, wearing tight Capris and her banlon sweater opened to the third button? She used to have mouse-coloured hair like Suze, and she used to be just as skinny. They both had freckles, but now Mom's were buried in pancake makeup.

Suze ate her supper at the dinette set with her back to the wall and her eye on the door in case Arvie came back. That was the reason Suze didn't have much stomach for the fried baloney and peas, even with tons of Heinz.

She ducked into Mike Jr.'s bedroom, which was really a storage closet, and felt around under the lumpy mattress, but no luck. It took a while for her to find the purple Crown Royal bag full of quarters, dimes and nickels stuffed into Mike Jr.'s Davy Crockett hat. She shoved the bag under her blouse. It wasn't fair that Mike Jr. got stuck without a window and had to do his homework at the kitchen table when Suze had a desk. Pops had built it himself. It had gotten a bit beat up in the last three moves, but it was still good once she put a pile of books where the leg had broken off.

Outside Mike Jr.'s room, she spotted Arvie leaning against the wall in the dark end of the hallway. "You going out tonight, Suze? You got someplace special in mind?"

Her heart jumped. She didn't see how he could know anything, but he did have that slippery grin on his lips, and she often caught him following her. Of course, she always gave him the slip, but it wasn't that easy. Pops used to say, keep your head up and don't let them see you sweat. She made sure she didn't run, just moved normally, until she closed her own door behind her and clicked the lock. She could still smell Arvie, even though he wasn't there. That was bad, having his smell in her head.

She listened, just in case Arvie was going to pull something tricky. After three dark and dirties, Mom could be passed out any minute. But it was quiet. And she had a Yale lock, bought with her summer baby walking money. She turned on the radio, Top 100, nice and loud. She slipped on her Mary Maxim sweater and hooked the rope on the radiator and opened the window. She hung on tight and shinnied down to the shed roof below. The rope always burnt her hands. She grabbed the rainspout on the side of the back porch and made it to the ground in two jumps, just missing Mike Jr.'s Red Rider wagon ready for the papers in the morning. Carrying all of Mike Jr.'s paper route money unbalanced her a bit. Maybe someday they'd move to a first floor apartment where you didn't have to practically break your neck to sneak out

Suze loved this kind of night. The wind whipped the trees. The leaves whispered. The ones that had fallen crunched underfoot. Someone had been burning leaves in their yard. A couple of times she thought she heard something scurrying in the bushes. Just in case, she picked up a brick from the side of the Thompsons' house, where they were building a garage. They could afford to build a garage, but they never gave Mike Jr. so much as a nickel tip for the paper, and they cheated Suze when she walked the baby.

Sometimes it was good to have a brick on you. She kept away from the streetlights as she headed down the street. She stepped out of the way of the sandwich board sign on the sidewalk outside Viger's Variety Store. Mr. Viger was always yelling at kids when they bumped into it. She didn't mind being in the shadows. It was only a half moon, but she knew the way, could have found where she was headed in the pitch dark. Even though it was October, a bunch of Protestant kids were still slamming balls around as she passed the Tennis Club. In spite of the bright lights on the court, no one turned to watch her hurry by on the path behind. She checked twice over her shoulder then slid down the ravine and got herself over the brook and up the hill. You had to watch out on that path. If you weren't careful, you could bump into a rubbydub or find your way blocked by some older boys with that look in their eyes. Just in case, Suze kept the brick in her hand. And she could disappear through the trees like a puff of fog if she had to. Tonight the path was clear. She scrambled over the rocks, jumped the five-foot wrought iron fence and landed on the soft lawn.

The cemetery. It made a lot of people nervous, but Suze had always liked it, even more so now that Pops was there. Normally Suze would have stopped to check out the freshly dug grave in the next plot. But tonight she needed to get to Pops first. She cleared a few crunchy oak leaves from the front of Pop's gravestone. She checked that the little chrysanthemum she'd planted was still alive. They were supposed to bloom right through until November. Suze didn't have a lot of luck with the plants she brought to Pops, but she was working hard to get the hang of taking care of them. Next maybe she'd try to find some holly or something nice for Christmas. She didn't think the gardener at St. Francis of Assisi would miss one more plant.

She plunked herself down and leaned back onto the smooth slab of the monument and closed her eyes. It felt good, and no wonder. One hundred percent imported Italian granite. Soft grey with peach streaks running through it. Pops had told her all about the granite when they buried Mike Sr. The details made the difference. Dimensions. Shape. Choice of stone. Lettering. Pops favoured Gothic.

Cost more than his Desoto, he used to say, but his boy was worth it. The plot too cost a bomb, but Pops said you can't take it with you, but you sure can lie in it. Gramma's name was there first. Greta Mabel Hagan, beloved wife of Joseph, 1906-1950. Suze didn't really remember much about Gramma.

Then, of course, Michael Gerard Hagan, 1932-1955. Every time Pops took them to visit, he'd make her and Mike Jr. swear on that grave they were never going to park their sorry butts within fifteen feet of a motorcycle. And last there was Pops himself, Joseph Alexander Hagan 1902-1957. Suze was saving up to have "beloved grandfather" added, in Gothic.

The week after they buried Pops, Suze had spent a lot of time checking out the surfaces of every headstone in the cemetery, running her hands along their satin surfaces, comparing their thickness, design, tracing the different kind of lettering, admiring the sculptures on the fancy ones. This was the best by far. Pops had done a good job. He had classy neighbours too. The McCurdys on the left and the Hetheringtons on the right, even though Pops never had much use for the Hetheringtons. Still, they were important people.

Pop had always kept up with the news, and Suze made sure he got it. And she asked for advice too. Pops loved giving advice.

"Half moon tonight, Pops. You can see the big dipper. Nice weather, a bit cool. Things are good at school, and Mike Jr. got a ninety on his spelling test. But I got a problem with Arvie. He took Mom's cigarette money twice this month, and she's drinking a lot more with him around, and I caught him snooping through Mike Jr.'s room so many times already. He even follows me when I've got the rent. I had to duck through Chapman's lumberyard to get away from him. So I figured you wouldn't mind if I stashed Mike Jr.'s jacket money here under your chrysanthemum so that Arvie doesn't get his mitts on it."

Of course, Pops wouldn't mind something like that. She didn't mention Arvie rubbing up against her all the time and barging into the bathroom when she was in the tub. There wasn't anything Pops could do about it, and there was no point in worrying him.

Learn to pick your battles, Pops always said.

"Good news, Pops. You're going to have more company next door. Mrs. Hetherington from down Parker Street. You know her, she always went to the seven o'clock mass with that black hat on with the feather. You always said she thought she was Mrs. God. Her funeral's tomorrow at eleven. I heard the Monsignor saying the Mass. I imagine it will be a big deal, not as big as yours, of course." The Bishop himself had said Pop's funeral mass, since Pops had been big in the Knights of Columbus, so he wouldn't begrudge Mrs. Hetherington her Monsignor, even if he never could stand her when she was alive.

After Suze had filled him in on the news in the neighbourhood, usually she just sat there, relaxing, enjoying the quiet, leaning against the granite. Sometimes, if it had been a long day, she fell asleep. This time she jerked awake when she heard a soft thud from behind the headstone. She sat up. The wind? A raccoon? Gravediggers?

She smelled him before she saw him.

"Wake up, Little Suzie," Arvie said.

"I'm not asleep." Suze tried to keep her own voice calm, because she hadn't planted Mike Jr.'s money yet.

"How come you're playing hard to get?"

Suze thought fast. Arvie sounded drunk. Drunk enough to be mean, but not drunk enough to stumble over his own feet.

"You heard me," Arvie slithered around to the front of the gravestone. "Are you some kind of tease? There's a name for girls like you." His eyes glittered in the dark.

"Who's that behind you?" Suze said.

"You little slut, I'm not falling for that again," Arvie said.

Suze grabbed Mike Jr.'s money and scrambled behind the gravestone. She got to her feet and ran like hell. She zigged and zagged the way the boys did on the football field. Arvie was breathing hard and swearing. Suze was used to running, and she got as far as the McCurdy's plot, then she jumped over three small crosses of the Clancy babies, hoping Arvie would injure himself on them. But Arvie must have played football, because he seemed to catch on to her tricks. Her lungs were bursting, and she tried to think—if she got to the path and close enough to the tennis court, maybe some of the Protestant kids would hear her if she could scream loud enough. Even a rubbydub would have looked good at that moment. Arvie couldn't do anything with anyone watching. She doubled back and headed towards the fence with the path on the other side of it, coming up close to Pop's grave, when Arvie launched himself. He slammed her behind the knees. She got a mouthful of damp earth from Mrs. Hetherington's freshly dug grave when she hit the ground.

He was heavy and strong. Suze couldn't move out from under him, couldn't breathe. Arvie lifted himself long enough to flip her over.

"You know you've been asking for it," he said.

You do what you have to, Pops would have said.

It seemed like Suze's arm had a mind of its own, like it belonged to someone else. It seemed like slow motion watching the arm arc and the old Crown Royal bag with Mike Jr.'s paper route money make a perfect half circle before it slammed into Arvie's temple. Slow motion as the bag opened and nickels, dimes and quarters scattered around the open grave, clinking. Suze was floating somewhere else, watching.

She lay still for a long time with him on top of her, twitching. He made a noise like a gurgling drain. It seemed like an hour before she was able to push him off.

Suze crawled a few feet and was sick in the McCurdy's rose bushes. When she finally got her legs to stop shaking and forced herself to look, Arvie had stopped gurgling. He lay there, the side of his head a new shape. Suze gathered up what she could find of Mike Jr.'s scattered collection of quarters, nickels and dimes and tried to think. What would Pops do?

*　　*　　*

Miss deLorentis understood about the funeral. She squeezed Suze's hand. Her black eyes shone.

"Of course, you must go. Especially an old family friend. And no, you won't need to make up anything you miss afterwards. You're so far ahead. Your detailed map of the provinces was magnificent. You really have what it takes."

Suze put on her navy sweater and her Black Watch kilt. She borrowed Mom's little black veil with the bow on it. Mom was passed out on the sofa, so she didn't need to make up a lie.

The funeral went all right. Suze didn't think the Monsignor had nearly as much class as the Bishop. The Hetheringtons didn't seem all that upset. Pops would enjoy hearing about that. He once said that Mrs. Hetherington had the temperament of a wasp and the face of a basset hound and the mind of a cesspool. Suze arrived at the cemetery shortly after the hearse and watched the six pall bearers slowly lower the mahogany coffin with the shiny brass handles into the open hole. When it settled in, each member of the Hetherington family threw a handful of earth onto the coffin. Five grown-up sons, each with the same sloping shoulders and unhappy eyes as the father. None of the Hetheringtons had started to cry at that point, and it didn't look like they were about to. They were not people who looked good in black. No one put a flower on the coffin like Suze and Mike Jr. had with Pops. Suze didn't expect they would engrave "beloved" on Mrs. Heatherington's stone. Suze shook Mr. Hetherington's small dry hand before she left. "I'm sorry for your loss," she said.

*   *   *

At the desk, Officer Collins looked up with surprise. "Look what the cat dragged in, will ya, Reg."

"Here comes trouble," said the other cop, who had a pockmarked face.

They were both grinning, but Suze managed not to grin back at them.

"Something wrong, Suze?" Officer Collins said.

"My Mom's boyfriend has gone off, and she's real worried about him. I wondered if you can do something to find him."

"You mean that Arvie Penny?"

"A bad penny always turns up," Officer Collins said.

Suze waited until they stopped laughing. "She's scared something bad might have happened to him."

The other cop said, "I imagine it did. But I'll tell you, she's better off without Arvie Penny. And so are you kids. Trust me."

"Can you put out a bulletin? On the radio?"

"Get a load of that, will you, Reg. A bulletin."

"That's a laugh and a half. Look, that bum is probably stepping off the bus in Toronto now, planning to hole up with some little piece of jailbait."

"Watch your language, Reg. There's not much we can do about it, Suze. Remember I warned you about him? We don't have him in the cell. Tell her to call us if he comes back."

"Okay," said Suze.

"Maybe we can toss him behind bars for her," Officer Collins said.

215

"I know he's not the greatest guy but, even so, can you do a search or something?"

"I wish we could help you, Suze, but we're having a busy time of it here. We got a lot of petty theft and vandalism going on. Things disappearing, building materials, flowers, shrubs, lots of crazy things. Someone dumped a load of dirt in the nuns' station wagon over at the convent."

"Well, whatever you could do to find him would be appreciated," Suze said.

"Never gives up. God, you're just like the old man. Ain't she, Reg?"

"Your grandfather all over. Same eyes, same attitude. Too bad you're not a boy, you'd make a hell of an officer when you grow up, just like Joe."

"So listen, Suze," Officer Collins said. "If he never shows up, your mom's lucky and so are you. Good riddance to bad rubbish."

"Thanks anyway," said Suze. You gotta get your ducks in a row, Pops always said.

*   *   *

"Quarter moon tonight, Pops. You can see both the dippers. There's a bit of frost in the air. The Protestant kids finally quit playing tennis. I'm sorry for the inconvenience about your new neighbour. I did what I had to, and I hope it doesn't bother you too much." Suze was leaning up against the cool front of the gravestone, bringing Pops up to date. "They say eternity's a long time, and it's bad enough you got to put up with Mrs. Hetherington right next door, let alone Arvie buried right underneath her. I was pretty worried they'd find him before they buried her. I did a good job covering him up.

I used the sign from Viger's Variety, it was just the right size and heavy enough in case he stiffened up. I levelled the space around him with some bricks from the Thompson's and put enough dirt on top to hide everything. The hardest part was getting rid of the extra soil so the mound wasn't too high after they covered the coffin. I'm glad I had Mike Jr.'s wagon. You always told me to watch out for the details. Lucky not everyone's good with details like you. No one noticed the hole was only about five feet. I know you wouldn't approve of some of what I did, but remember what you told me about making tough choices when you have to.

"Mom's still drinking too much and crying most of the time. She says she's going to leave us here for a while and go to Toronto looking for him. That might be good. We won't have to worry about fires in the sofa. Mike Jr. got his citizenship badge and his winter jacket. I got a hundred per cent on the Great Lakes and Canada's exports. You would like Miss deLorentis a lot. She says I've got what it takes. I think she's right. I think I'll have what it takes to be a cop like you when I grow up."

Mary Jane Maffini *is author of the Camilla MacPhee novels:* Speak Ill of the Dead, The Icing on the Corpse *and* Little Boy Blues *with RendezVous Press. She introduced the Fiona Silk series with* Lament for a Lounge Lizard *in 2003. A five-time nominee for Crime Writers of Canada Author Ellis awards, she won "Arthurs" for Best Short Story of 1995 and 2001.*

Unchained Melody

A tisket, a tasket
A red and purple basket
I sent some poison to my ex
And on the way they lost it
They lost it, they lost it!
They lost it, they lost it,
The postal service lost it.
And if someone should pck it up
I know that they will die.

Joy Hewitt Mann

From This Wicked Fall

Kathryne Finn

Wat, who had once been the Schoolmaster Printer, but was now no more than a legless cripple, sat high on the back of Shadow, who was once a magnificent black war horse, but was now no more than an elderly beast of burden. Together they endured gaping stares from the folk of Saint Albans town. While Wat did not care for being an object of public scrutiny, at least he was not alone. At the horse's head walked Gorta, who gathered a few stares of her own, being a woman of great size, as tall as Shadow, and in whose footsteps padded the largest dog most people had ever seen.

It was the year of Our Lord 1488, the twenty-second day of June, the Feast of Saint Alban, and, like everyone else, Wat and Gorta were on their way to the Market Cross. There they would watch the eponymous statue of abbey and town roll his eyes and nod his head when the Abbot called, "Arise, arise, Saint Alban, and get thee home to thy sanctuary." All around, people were singing a curious song: "From this wicked fall, rose a martyr brave and tall/ Give us back our eyes, Saint Alban, strong and wise/ Then from this wicked fall, you will save us all." That refrain would continue as the crowd followed the plaster saint back across the square and into his home, the abbey cathedral. For every year on this day, the huge, unwieldy figure did indeed obey the Abbot's bidding.

It was not exactly a miracle. The statue, on wheels, was pushed by four monks, and its hollow interior was fixed with a set of pulleys so one monk could control both the nodding head and the rolling eyes. Still, no matter how many times the people of Saint Albans had seen the yearly show, it never ceased to fascinate and delight them. Once the saint was back in his chapel behind the high altar, they stayed for Mass, then passed the afternoon celebrating at the fair booths set up around the Market Cross. But this year they were in for a surprise.

The customary pronouncement was issued in a rich, clear voice: "Arise, arise, Saint Alban, and get thee home to thy sanctuary." There was no response. The statue was stone still, no nodding head, no rolling eyes. The Abbot repeated his command in a louder voice. When this second charge was also ignored, the door in the base of the statue was opened. And there, revealed for all to see, was not—as the people half-expected—a monk sleeping off early celebrations, but the body of a townsman. Indeed, he might not have been dead at all, for there was no blood, no mark of violence, but beside him, staring vacantly out at the crowd, lay both his eyes. This year, there was surely a miracle.

*   *   *

When England was still the Roman province of Britannia, Saint Alban was its first Christian martyr. A well-respected citizen of the town then called Verulamium, he gave sanctuary to a holy man who preached the new religion and became a convert himself. When Alban's crime against the laws of Rome was discovered, and he refused to repudiate his faith, the future saint was led to a place outside the town walls and his head was struck from his shoulders. No sooner was the deed done than the executioner's eyes fell from their sockets to the ground, now wet with sacred blood. All this took place in the year 209, and on the hill where the martyr met his fate, an abbey was founded. By 1488, it was one of the most powerful monastic houses in all of England, and its abbot was a peer of the realm called William Wallingford, a sophisticated man who believed in the intellect as much as the spirit and had somewhat cynical ideas about the validity of miracles.

With his first glimpse of the eyeless corpse, the Abbot's own eyes hardened, while all around him were excited whispers of what the saint had wrought. "A terrible sin...to be so punished...defiled something sacred...a wicked fall from grace...it is a sign...Saint Alban is warning us." Then there were the practical questions. "Who is it? Can you see?... Do you know him? A stranger?" But the dead man was not a stranger to Abbot Wallingford, nor to at least one other present that day. The Abbot saw Wat, the former schoolmaster and printer, perched high above the rest of the crowd. Indeed, it was hard to miss him. So, turning to Brother Phillip, his secretary, Wallingford gave orders to remove the body to the great gatehouse of the abbey and to summon the man on the black horse.

*   *   *

It was Wat and Gorta's first outing since she had arrived at his tumble-down cottage on the end of Fishpool Street half a year and more ago and found him in seriously sorry straits. If Wat was never a man of stature with enough faith or ambition to take final vows and become a monk, at one time he had thought himself useful. He saw innumerable boys at the abbey school through the complexities of arithmetic and grammar, herding them to Mass every morning, insuring they said their Hail Marys before retiring each night. And in his single shining hour, he convinced the Abbot to import one of the new printing presses from London. By candlelight, during the long hours of night after his teaching duties were done, working from a manuscript he found in the abbey library, Wat took up the exacting, yet satisfying, task of setting type. Then, at last, with the help of a part-time apprentice called Thomas, he printed a singular book.

It was a surprising success, surprising to everyone but Wat, and the first edition of some two hundred copies sold out in weeks. But on the very day when he received permission from the Abbot to do another printing, he was struck down. Perhaps it was punishment for his sin of pride, perhaps it was only that he had worked too long and too hard, but a blood bubble burst in his head. Though he did not die, he could no longer use his right arm or his legs. His teaching duties were assigned to a younger man, his printing press was taken over by his apprentice, and he was reduced to bare existence in a hovel, haphazardly cared for by a neighbourhood slattern. He endured filth and despair for nearly a year. Then one day, when he scarcely had any desire left to live, he looked up and saw the apparition of a large woman, a black horse and a white dog standing in his open doorway.

Gorta's story was both more complex and more mysterious. She was born, and had lived for fifty years, amongst the ruins of a manor that had belonged to her ancestors since the Norman Conquest. But her mother and father had not partaken of the benefits of matrimony—nor, for that matter, had her grandmother and grandfather—so she had no legal claim when a far distant cousin had inherited the manor and simply turfed her out. Until that day, she had enjoyed peace and a certain level of security, practicing the craft of herbs and simples taught her by her mother, healing one and all who came to her for help. When she suddenly found herself homeless, she was not entirely alone. She had the great horse left her by her father and Dagda, the white dog, who was her intimidating guardian. Nor was she entirely without resources. Her highly regarded skill had provided her with life's necessities and even an occasional handful of coins. In addition, she possessed two family treasures—a book written by her grandmother, a copy of the very one printed so painstakingly by Wat; and an old leather satchel filled with inscribed parchment. There was only one trouble. Gorta could not read. And that had brought her to Wat's door.

She nursed the former schoolmaster and cleaned the cottage. Then, since she had no place else to go, she simply moved in. In return, feeling blessed by her presence, he read to her. Just so, they passed a contented winter and spring enclosed by the old walls, but when summer came round again, she decided it was time for them to venture forth. Ignoring Wat's resistance, she picked him up like a sack of potatoes, settled him on Shadow's back, gathered the reins, whistled to the dog, and off they went. Because Wat was so much higher than the rest of the crowd, when the door in the statue opened, he had a good view of the body. He gasped, as dumbfounded as everyone else—not by thoughts of miracles, but because he knew the dead man. It was his one-time apprentice, Thomas.

*   *   *

Wat looked around the large room he had once occupied with such pleasure. It was on the second floor of the great gatehouse, above the vaulted entrance. Gorta had carried him up the circular stairs he once had taken two at a time, eager for his evening's work. It was still the same, the fireplaces at either end, the deep ceiling beams resting on their stone corbels, and in the center his printing press. Wat's fingers itched to touch the type again, to select each perfect letter from the racks, to form words and sentences and paragraphs until he had created a whole page that would then be inked and printed. Even his useless hand could remember how it felt to hold a finished book.

But if the room was generally the same, there were also disturbing differences. The press had not been properly "put to bed." Wat had never left the room, no matter how late it was nor how tired he might be without tidying it, but now there were large inkblots on the floor, and torn, smudged paper. One or two racks containing the precious type had been overturned, and individual letters spilled out. Worst of all, the body of Thomas was laid out on a table beneath the eastern windows.

Then there was Abbot Wallingford who, as far as Wat knew, had never before set foot in this place. He sat with aplomb in a high-backed chair, apparently undaunted by the day's events, while his secretary hovered nearby like an anxious crow. Wat sighed. Whatever difficulties were in store would only be made worse by the presence of Brother Phillip. The monk had always been a source of both secret laughter and irritation at the abbey. He had been elevated from a desk in the scriptorium—where he had laboured year after unimaginative year producing precise manuscript copies—to his present position at the right hand of the Abbot.

Indeed, they seemed an odd pair, but it was Brother Phillip's very precision and lack of imagination that made him useful to the man whose adventurous mind and philosophical bent often carried him into far-flung realms of new thought.

To give credit where it was due, the secretary offered his master both organization and devotion, following the Abbot everywhere with a pouch containing ink, quills, a quill knife and parchment—the tools of a born scribe—tied round his waist. But the man was also obsessive and dogmatic to a fault. Today, for instance, Abbot Wallingford would be disinclined to accept the "miracle" without question, while Brother Phillip would be ravenous in his belief. Wat steeled himself for what lay ahead.

"Ah, Schoolmaster," the Abbot's tone was welcoming, and Wat remembered he had always used his voice to great effect. "It seems we meet under strange circumstances. But tell me, who—and what—is that you have there?"

Wat hesitated. It was always difficult to explain Gorta, particularly when she was accompanied by Dagda, who had followed them up the stone stairs and now lay quietly at their feet. Finally he fell back on the story he used for his neighbours in Fishpool Street. "She is my cousin, your Grace, come from Essexshire to care for me, and this is her dog. I had to bring her with me. You see, Gorta is my legs."

Unperturbed, Wallingford nodded. "Good, then. Bring him over here, woman. Brother, get a stool so he may sit while we confer. You had best leave that great beast where he is, though. I am partial to dogs myself, but my secretary is terrified of them. Now, Schoolmaster, tell me what you can about the dead man."

"Not much, I am afraid. He wasn't one to let people know him. I was told he lived in the English community at Bruges, where he was apprenticed as a lad to a typefounder. He travelled to London in the wake of Caxton when my friend set up his press at Westminster. Caxton, in turn, occasionally lent Thomas to me when I needed help. By the time I had my—

uh, accident—he was ready to take over full responsibility here."

"How can you say 'accident'?" Brother Phillip murmured darkly.

The Abbot ignored him. "Almost no one else knew him either. I myself saw him but once or twice. Certainly not as much as I saw you in the days when you convinced me to import this infernal contraption."

He smiled at his little joke and waved a languid hand at the printing press, but his secretary muttered, "Just so."

Again Wallingford continued as if no one else had spoken. "Brother Phillip carried any necessary messages back and forth between us. It seems the printer kept much to himself and was deeply involved with his work."

"Aye, that would be very like him," Wat agreed. "One thing I do know, he had a passion for the art of printing. He claimed it would carry us into a future where all men might own a book and read it themselves."

"And all women," Gorta said.

They turned to stare at her. Then the Abbot laughed. "You must believe the same, Schoolmaster, since your best known book was written by a woman."

Still watching Gorta, Wat blushed. "I suppose I do."

Brother Phillip, no longer able to contain himself, began to spit words. "And that is why you were sore afflicted...why we have witnessed this very day a miracle. While the people were singing the song to Saint Alban, this man, too, was struck down. You see him before you with not a mark upon him. Yet he is dead, and his wicked eyes have fallen from his head."

Wallingford held up a silencing hand. "Calm yourself, Brother."

"You must forgive me, I cannot be silent. I had not told

you yet, but Thomas was going to ask your permission to make another edition of that woman's book. All those years it rested in our library, and no one set eyes upon it until this man printed it for all the world to see." The monk pointed an accusatory finger at Wat.

"Ah, my dear Phillip, perhaps you do not know the very song you mention, the song you yourself sang today, is by a woman." The Abbot responded to his secretary's stricken look with derisive malice. "Aye, quite so. A nun in the Rhineland was its authoress long, long ago. It was but adapted by the folk in our town. So, if the printer's sin was disseminating the work of a woman, it seems you too are guilty, and I must order your eyes cut out. What say you to that?"

Wat was shocked by a side of the Abbot he had never seen, and then surprised by Brother Phillip's courage, for the monk answered, albeit meekly, "I say it was a miracle."

Wallingford sighed impatiently. "You are very tiresome. Yet, I suspect most of the town also would like it to be so. And a miracle we may well have, but we must seek some answers before it is proven. Schoolmaster, what questions might you have if you were serving as the devil's advocate?"

"Oh, your Grace, I would not presume." Wat had an uneasy feeling he was being used for some end he could not see.

"Come now, humility is not helpful here. You knew the man, you knew his work. What would you ask?"

Wat was still uncomfortable, but he could not deny the state of the room made him curious. "First, what happened here? Thomas had too much reverence for his work to leave it in this disarray."

Wallingford nodded. "Do you have an explanation for that, Brother?"

"A wind of Heaven swept through and scattered the tools of the Devil."

"How picturesque. Well then, Schoolmaster, are there other questions?" The Abbot was obviously amused by the debate he had instigated between reason and emotion.

"What was Thomas doing in the statue? How did he get there? Is there not usually a monk who pulls the strings?" Wat was beginning to enjoy himself after all. "Why was there no blood anywhere? Granted, he seems unmarked, but his eyes..."

Brother Phillip crowed triumphantly, "This is the greatest proof of all! Did not the eyes of Saint Alban's executioner fall from his head? Is it not the same here? It was surely accomplished by the hand of God."

"There could be another reason." The three men looked around as if they could not imagine who had spoken, but Gorta was undeterred. "If he was already dead when his eyes were taken out, he would not bleed." Then, indicating the body, she addressed the Abbot. "May it please you, sir, I should like a closer look."

He gave his now speechless debaters a wry glance "It seems all questions—even all answers—have ceased for the moment, so please do what you will. Perhaps you can provide us with further information."

While Gorta went quietly about her quest, Wallingford continued. "Allow me now, as a matter of form, to suggest other alternatives. To the question of what happened in this room, may I suggest some physical upset, either in the person of the printer or in another who might have confronted him here. Why was he in the statue? If, in fact, he was killed by human hands, perhaps it was simply a place to hide the body or a way to direct suspicion toward a desired end. How did it get there? Quite easy. The statue is removed from the cathedral to the

Market Cross at sundown on the eve of the feast day and then left alone there until our quaint procession begins. But harder to understand, and perhaps more important, is the question of the monk who usually pulls the strings. That is Brother Aengus, and it occurs to me I have not seen him today. Phillip, send a message to find him and have him come here to us."

Wat watched the monk make his way across the room, giving the still-quiet dog a wide berth, and start slowly down the stairs. Poor fellow, Wat thought, he really wants nothing to come between him and his miracle. Then he turned his attention to Gorta, who held a small wooden box into which she gazed intently. When she put it down, Wat realized with a start it contained Thomas's eyes. Next she concentrated on the dead man's hands. "Wat," she said, "he has nicks and little cuts on his fingers. Would that be a normal thing?"

"I had them all the time. The type can be sharp, and it is easy to get pinched when you are working with the press."

She called softly, "Dagda, come to me." Then, while Wat and Abbot Wallingford looked on in quizzical silence, she held one of the stiff, dead hands out to the dog and said, "Smell. Good boy. Now, go. Find."

By the time Brother Phillip returned, Dagda was moving intently around the room, poking his nose into corners and under stools, snuffling through ashes in the fireplaces. With increasing anxiety, the monk attempted to keep the Abbot's tall chair between himself and the big white animal, at the same time whispering: "I left word we have need of Brother Aengus. But what is happening here?"

"Watch this. It is quite interesting, really. The dog is looking for something he smelled on the printer's hand." Wallingford looked up at his secretary. "Oh, for pity's sake, do not fret so. He will not harm you. He is under perfect control."

Dagda completed his circumference of the room. There was nothing left to investigate but the printing press. As he approached it, his nose went up into the air, twitching with excitement. When he reached the spilled type, he stopped and began to whine. "Good, Dagda," Gorta said. "What is it?" The dog barked two times. She nodded. "Just as I thought."

The Abbot, caught halfway between irony and curiosity, struggled to reassert himself. "Well, woman," he began, then stopped, and started again, his voice ingratiating. "Gorta, I believe you are called. Please, do not keep us in the dark. What have you learned? What has the dog—uh, told you?"

"The printing press killed him, sir."

"Ah, you see!" Before anyone could say a word, Brother Phillip began to rave. "He was destroyed by his own evil, and the saint who watches over us set him before the people so they might be warned what happens when..."

"Hold your tongue!" The Abbot came abruptly to his feet, shook his secretary like a terrier with a rat and added viciously, "You could lose it as easily as the printer lost his eyes." Then, brushing off his robes, he grandly reseated himself and turned back to Gorta. "Explain what you mean."

Wat tried to signal her to be careful, but Gorta, ever unafraid, was caught up in helping solve the mystery.

"There was poison on the type. Nightshade, it was. Some give it the name 'dwale' or 'Devil's cherries'. But whatever it's called, it's deadly."

"How do you know what it was?"

"As you said, sir, Dagda told me. He can nose out poisons when we humans can't even get a whiff of them, and I've trained him to tell me what he smells. One bark is for Monkshood, two for Nightshade. There are others, but I don't suppose you want to know them all."

"You amaze me, Gorta." Did Wat hear menace in the Abbot's voice? "However, I think you suspected something before you sent the dog on his search."

"Aye, that I did. The eyes, you see, were so dilated I could hardly tell what colour they might have been in life. Nightshade does that. And Wat's question about the state of the room made me wonder. A man who has taken Nightshade becomes wildly agitated before he dies. In his delirium, he might have caused just such disorder as we see here."

Wat broke in, hoping to deflect the Abbot's fierce focus from Gorta. "How could he be poisoned by what was on the type?"

"It would take time, but the juice from the roots can enter the body through even the smallest opening in the skin. Poor Thomas's hands were covered with cuts."

For perhaps the first time since the body was discovered, they looked at it and remembered it was once a man. "But he was such a quiet, gentle fellow," Wat said. "Who, why—"

Their individual thoughts were interrupted by the sound of footsteps coming up the stairs, laboured footsteps. Then a bleary-eyed monk appeared in the doorway.

"Ah, Brother Aengus, come in," said Wallingford.

"My lord Abbot, pray forgive me. I took a sleeping draught yestereve. I have only just been wakened."

"How interesting. Have you been unwell?"

"Nay, but barely able to close my eyes of late. Brother Phillip heard of my trouble and made a wee dram for me. I thank you, Brother, but I am afraid it worked over-well."

"How kind of you to succour your fellow monk, Phillip. It seems your scant knowledge of potions is occasionally useful."

The Abbot's voice had changed again. It was sly and speculative, his gaze piercing as he looked at them all. We are like chess pieces about to be moved around a board, Wat thought,

"So," said Wallingford, "let us return to the schoolmaster's last questions. Who? And why? Supposing, as perhaps we now must, the act was a human one, why would a person—or persons—want the printer dead? What do you think, Phillip?"

The monk was clearly loathe to give up his miracle and follow this line of thought. "Revenge?"

"Ah yes, revenge. Always a good reason. But for what? Can you shed light on this, Schoolmaster?"

"As far as I know, Thomas never did anything, nor wanted to do anything, but practice his craft," Wat began cautiously. Then he took a deep breath and went on with more courage. "But I cannot see a cause for vengeance in that. Nor could it have been some sudden anger. Not only would he not elicit that, but poisoning doesn't take place in a moment of passion. It requires planning. Perhaps then he had come by knowledge that was dangerous, or someone wanted to stop him from doing something. Not this new edition of my book, for his decision regarding that was recent, but something over the long term."

"Clever thinking, but perhaps all are true. Perhaps it was a matter of stopping him from spreading this knowledge and of revenge. So now we must ask, whom did he damage by knowing what he knew, being what he was, and doing what he did?"

"All of us! The town, the abbey, even Saint Alban himself." Brother Phillip was so agitated he could scarcely get his words out. "This printing...this thing he did here...with this...this Devil's apparatus? This is the wicked fall!" He started wildly across the room. "I will not stay here any longer. I will put an end to this. I will tell everyone the miracle is being defiled!"

"Wait, Phillip. Stop!" The Abbot was on his feet again. Gorta started after the fleeing monk. But Dagda was faster than either of them. He planted himself in the narrow doorway that led to the stairs. Brother Phillip halted on the spot, edged away from the looming creature that blocked his escape, and turned to face the others: Brother Aengus, still dazed; Wat, helpless on his stool; Gorta, terrifying as her dog; and the Abbot, all pretence, all urbanity gone.

Imagining pity in his master's face, the overwrought monk pleaded: "Father, dear Father, can you not see? Our blessed saint was trying to save us all. He needed a messenger, someone to be his hands. And his eyes."

Seeing no nodding head, no responding light of understanding, he became more frenzied. "How can you take the word of this ignorant woman, this witch with her hell-hound at her heels, over that of your faithful servant? Aye, your servant who laboured in the very storehouse of learning, the scriptorium where we kept knowledge safe. Then there came this wretched Thomas, and all those like him." He directed a strange wide-eyed glare at Wat.

"They destroyed what we had there. They stole our precious knowledge and dispersed it far and wide. Like Eve offering the apple. This man," he pointed erratically at the body, "this instrument of evil, had to be stopped. They must all be stopped!" His voice rose to a mad shriek. Maniacally, he began to sing: "From this wicked fall, rose a martyr brave and tall." Suddenly he reached into his pouch, the sharp glint of his quill knife flashed in his hand, and he rushed at Wat.

The moment was frozen in time. Brother Phillip raised his stabbing arm high. Brother Aengus stumbled stupidly aside. Gorta turned in horror. Abbot Wallingford made a gesture of futility. Dagda leapt from his place by the door. And Wat held up his one good hand to defend himself. Then the monk fell dead at his feet.

They knew he was dead because he convulsed violently, his eyes rolled back in his head, though they did not fall out, and then he was still. Gorta stooped to feel the life point under his jaw, but there was no pulsing in his neck. The shocked silence grew until at last Abbot Wallingford asked, "Is this then our miracle?"

"Nay, it was the Nightshade. He, too, has a cut on his hand."

Wallingford's voice was kindly now, perhaps even a little sad. "It is a common mishap with scribes as well as printers. Poor Phillip, he did not even know enough to protect himself."

Gorta got slowly to her feet. "Perhaps he did not want to."

"You are, indeed, a wise woman." The Abbot reached down and closed the eyes of his former secretary. "He did not understand that printing may be its own kind of miracle. And he truly feared a future where all men might own a book and read it themselves."

"And all women," said Wat.

Kathryne Finn *has turned her sharpened quill to ad copy, novels and practically everything in between, though this is her first published short story. She escaped from Toronto to New York for many years but now is back in Nova Scotia. Though truthfully, through the medium of imagination, she lives mostly in the Middle Ages. Wat, Gorta and Dagda will reappear in her trilogy,* The Julyana Chronicles, *which is presently searching for "its own kind of miracle".*

Hokey Pokey

Vicki Cameron

Rayette tapped on the glass. "Are you open yet?" She was wearing the outfit she had bought yesterday, a mauve blouse with a rhinestone yoke and orange track pants with a sports logo written down one leg.

"No, not yet. Five more minutes." Always the same routine, every morning. Zen wondered why Rayette never left home five minutes later.

"Can I come in? I won't be in your way."

"Sorry, it's against regulations." As if there were regulations governing the opening hours of the Good Neighbours Second Hand store at the corner of Main and Mill.

"I won't tell."

"I've got this one more bag to open. Then you can come in." Zen lifted her hand, to show she'd just brought in a green garbage bag, abandoned at her door overnight by a zealous spring cleaner. She could tell by the heft it was full of boots and shrunken woollen sweaters.

Rayette's eyes lit up, as usual, at the thought of one more bag of delights, and her the first to see it. Zen could see the drool forming. If Rayette knew how many unopened bags there were in the storeroom, she'd go mad.

Moving to the back of the store, Zen ambled down the

aisles, tossing errant items back in their home bins as she went. Customers were so careless, poking around in the merchandise indiscriminately.

Someone rapped on the glass. Zen turned to shake her head at Rayette, but Rayette's place had been taken by Constable Fray. Six foot four and looming. Built like a marathon runner spread out over too much length. He had something in his hand, a skinny pale arm attached to a girl who looked like she needed an escape route. A vandal, no doubt, but Zen hadn't noticed any of her windows broken this morning.

She opened the door, stepped aside to let Fray and the vandal in, then blocked Rayette with a firm hand on the rhinestones. "Sorry, looks like official police business. I won't be open for another fifteen minutes, I'm afraid. Can't flout the regulations when the law is on the premises."

"That's not fair." Rayette stamped her running shoes. Comfortable shoes for a long day at the bins. Bought last Thursday for fifty cents because they had no tread left.

"It can't be helped. Why don't you go down to the Wiggly Finger for coffee? Come back in half an hour."

"Oh, yeah, sure. And who'll get in ahead of me?"

"Tell you what, you take a break, and I'll stay closed until you come back."

Rayette's face lit up. "Deal."

Zen turned her attention back to Constable Fray. He was standing beside the bin of ladies' undergarments. "What can I do for you, Jeremy?"

"Allow me to introduce," he swung his charge in front of him like a curling broom, "Sasha Dempster. Sasha's been found guilty of shoplifting and sentenced to fifty hours community service. I thought she could work it off in your store."

Sasha's gaze drifted over the cash register, trickled across the used shoe rack and landed on the hat tree. Sasha was wearing stained blue jeans and a Gap T-shirt with a little plastic sticker on the chest stating S/P.

"You're bringing a shoplifter to work in a store? Would you send a chocoholic to work at the chocolate factory?"

"Sasha specializes in Gap. She won't lift this used stuff. Look at her."

Zen looked. Sasha's nose was wrinkled in disgust at the sights in the baby clothes bin.

"What about my cash register?"

"What'dya got in there, dimes and quarters? She's not a thief, she's a shoplifter. I'm supposed to find her a placement, and there aren't a lot of options in town."

"Jeremy Fray, this won't work. I don't need any help."

"Oh, yeah? I happen to know that your Aunt Maude is off on a theatre tour in New York with my Aunt Helen, so you'll be short staffed until Maude gets back."

Zen sighed. He had her on a technicality.

* * *

Maude swirled around, singing in the hotel room bathroom. "…shake it…do the hokey pokey…yourself around…all about. Boom!" Red, white and blue reflections sparked off the chrome fixtures. "How do I look?"

"Like a patriotic sausage in a sequined casing. Honest to God, Maude, you should have thrown that thing out thirty years ago. Or thirty pounds ago. Whichever came first."

"You're just jealous. This is my lucky dress. And my lucky purse." She held up a beaded green and yellow bag shaped like an elephant with tassels and fringe. "I always get lucky in this outfit. Always get to do the hokey pokey."

"Maude, you're over sixty. Give it up. Your pokey is getting pretty hokey."

"You're just jealous of my figure, Helen Fray."

"Your figure is as sagged as mine, and we have tickets to *Same Time Next Year.* I can't believe you'd skip it for a night in a bar." Helen went back to the row of cardboard boxes on the small writing desk. "You want any more of this chop suey? Because if you don't, I'm eating it. It's really good."

"Nope, it would spoil my makeup. Don't wait up."

* * *

Day Two. Seven and a half hours down, forty-two and a half hours to go. Zen walked through it one more time. Sasha was dumber than a toasted marshmallow.

"In the morning, you bring in any bags that have been dropped off overnight and heave them onto the pile."

"What if there aren't any?"

"There usually are."

"If there aren't, do I wait for them?"

"No, you thank whoever stole them and carry on. Our first task is to tidy up. People leave things in the wrong bins all day. They change their minds half way across the store and toss the thing, whatever it is, into the closest bin. You go around the bins and sort them out."

"What if I don't know what the item is or where it belongs?"

"Hold it up. Read the signs."

"Oh. I didn't think I'd have to work that hard."

Zen tried not to sigh, or scream, or whap the kid upside the head. Remain calm. Move on to the next issue.

"If there's no one in the store, you can open a new bag and

sort it into the correct bins. If the doorbell chimes, you leave the storeroom and come back onto the floor. You always stay on the floor when there are customers."

"Why?"

"Shoplifters."

"You're kidding, right?" Sasha's little pierced nose wrinkled.

"What, you don't think people would tuck a torn windbreaker under their shirt, or jam some used undies up their sleeve? They would, and they do. So keep your eyes peeled. I'm sure you'll recognize the signs."

"Okay."

"See that woman at the door? That's Rayette. She always tries to get in early. Don't open the door until ten o'clock sharp." This morning, Rayette wore a pink satin kimono over biking shorts and a tube top.

Rayette tapped on the glass and held up her wrist, showing her watch.

Zen pointed to the back room and held up one finger.

Rayette grinned and nodded.

"Come on, we have to go to the back room now and open a bag so we have some new things to put in the bins before we open the door. Rayette likes that. Makes her feel special."

Sasha blinked. "Special?"

"Yes. If you do something nice for a customer, she keeps coming back."

Zen led the way to the mountain of green bags.

"Wow, there sure are a lot."

"It's spring. Lots of people cleaning out the closets. Mrs. Witherspoon died this winter, and now her family is clearing out the stuff so they can sell the house. We'll get a lot of bags and boxes in the next few weeks. So it's important you learn this next step. What we don't want in the store this week are more snowsuits. What we do want is summer clothing. So before you open the bags, you feel them."

Sasha stuck out tentative fingers and prodded the closest bag.

"What do you feel?"

"Boots. Big ones."

"Good, and where there's boots, there'll be mittens and scarves, so we don't want that bag. Toss it over against the far wall. Pick another."

"Cool. This is like a game." Sasha smiled for the first time since she had begun serving her sentence. She poked a couple more bags, and in a moment her fingers were tickling the bags like Jelly Roll Morton tickled the ivories. "This one," she said, "has dresses and skirts."

Sasha tore the twist tie off the bag. Dresses and skirts tumbled out.

"Good call, Sasha," Zen said with a grin. "You may have a latent talent."

Sasha did a little dance like a football player who has just scored a touchdown. Together they carried the booty out to the store and tossed it in the appropriate bins.

Zen nodded toward the door. "Let the games begin," she said. Sasha crossed to the front of the store and unlocked the door.

Rayette exploded through the door like a sprinter out of the blocks.

*   *   *

"Helen? Helen, wake up, please wake up. We got trouble."

Helen rolled over and opened one eye. "Wha? Maude? What time it is?"

"Five."

"Five in the morning? Are you crazy?"

"Shift over. I gotta sit down. This is too awful."

"You're not kidding. I need about two more hours sleep."

"Shut up and listen. We gotta get out of here. We got big trouble."

"What, you got yourself pregnant?"

"No, silly. Worse than that."

"Your hokey failed to pokey?"

"No, I met this man."

"Jeez, Maude, are you getting married? Do you need me as a witness?"

"Will you stop jabbering and listen? I met this man. My age, about fifty, and handsome and rich."

"Your age or fifty? Which is it? You're older than I am, and I'm sixty-one."

"Do you mind? I'm trying to tell you something important here. So he said he'd never met anyone quite like me, and he pulled out a diamond ring, honest he did, and I don't want to hear any of your wisecracks. He says let's get married tomorrow."

"And you fell for it."

"There was no falling, oh, I guess there was once we got to his hotel room. Didn't I tell you this dress works every time?"

"Yeah, the hokey gets pokeyed. Sometimes I wonder why I bother going on bus trips with you."

"Just listen, will you? So anyway, we get to his hotel room, and he wasn't too bad, considering…"

"Considering he had to leave his teeth in a glass?"

"…but about an hour ago, I rolled over…"

"And crushed him?"

"…and he's dead."

Zen stood in the back room doorway watching Sasha choose the bags. Constable Fray wandered in and hovered beside the fish tank in the front window. Zen joined him.

"Looking for an aquarium, Jeremy? Something to help focus your thoughts so you can come up with more brilliant ideas?"

"How's my protégée doing?" he asked, tapping on the aquarium glass.

"Dumber than toothpaste, thanks a bunch."

"Hey, no, she has to be smarter than that. She's a Dempster. They've been off welfare for four or five months now."

"Okay, smartie. Try asking her about the merchandise."

Zen called Sasha out of the back room. She came carrying a heap of clothes. "Sasha, come here. Tell Constable Fray what you're going to do with those."

"Put them in the bins?"

"Which bins?"

"The empty bins?"

"What's the top thing on the pile?"

"Man's shirt?"

"So where will you put it?"

"Maternity wear? My mom always wears Dad's shirts when she's pregnant. For a long time afterwards, too."

"Let's put it in men's shirts today. What's next?"

"Bag of gravel. I know, I pour it on the doorstep so people won't slip on the ice."

"Sasha, it's summer."

"Oh."

Fray smiled and picked up the bag of gravel from her armload. "This is aquarium gravel. You could pour it in this fish tank, maybe find a little castle and a miniature diver. Give this fish tank curb appeal. I might want to buy it. How much is it?"

"I don't know."

"There's a sticker on it, says $5."

"Oh."

Fray smiled at Zen.

"So how much is the fish tank, Sasha?" Zen asked.

"I don't know. But if I put the gravel in, it will make you feel special so you'll come back tomorrow." She dropped her armload in the closest bin and tore open the bag. Gravel spewed all over the floor.

Fray shook his head as he inched toward to door. "Sorry, Zen, I didn't know. I guess I owe you one. I'll, um, shop here more often."

"I'll say this, she has a gift for opening the right bags. Two days and not a single snowsuit. She might have a calling."

Fray slunk away with a shrug.

Half an hour later, the door jingled and two men came in. Tourists, had to be. No one in a black silk suit shopped in a used clothing store. The men were identical in height and had the body build of body builders. Both wore sunglasses. She could only tell them apart by their hair. One had soft black hair slicked back and styled, and a tiny goatee. The other had coarser hair shellacked into an unruly helmet threatening to turn woolly if the wind changed.

They stopped at the cash register. Zen wished she had a silent alarm.

"I am Sharif," the goatee one said. "This is my associate, Rafael. We are looking for a woman named Maude Crombie. We were directed to this establishment by the esteemed owner of the fanciful café."

"Sorry, Maude isn't in today. She went on holiday."

"Yes. To New York. She is home now."

"No, she won't be home for another three days."

"I would beg to differ. She is home. Please tell her we are seeking her to discuss a delicate matter. Shall we say, tomorrow, then, here, at eleven of the morning?"

*   *   *

Zen pushed the empty pizza box to the far end of the kitchen table. "You're not telling me the whole story."

Aunt Maude looked nervous with her protective pizza wall removed. "Sure I am. Helen wasn't feeling well, so we came home early."

"That is not true. I can tell by the way your fingers are twitching that paper napkin into a swan. What happened? Is there a red, white and blue sequined dress involved?"

"Well, yes, I did go out on the town. But nothing happened. When I got home, Helen wasn't feeling well, so we decided to pack it in."

"Really? Guess it's time for that dress to be delivered to my store. Some kid will love it to dress up in."

"No, you can't take my lucky dress. It never fails, my hokey pokey dress. Not one failure in thirty years."

"You just said nothing happened to you in your lucky dress in New York. So you must be lying."

"Well, okay, the dress worked. But when I came home, Helen—"

"—wasn't feeling well, yada yada yada. There's something else. You're wearing a new ring."

Aunt Maude flashed her left hand. "Diamond and ruby. Isn't it wonderful?"

"See how happy you are with it when your finger turns green."

Aunt Maude's face crumpled. "You don't think it's real?"

"I'd need to take a closer look."

Aunt Maude handed the ring over. Zen held it up to the light. The diamond blazed a rainbow at her. She looked inside the band. 14k. A designer's signature. She passed it back. "It came out of a Cracker Jack box. But it's pretty. Don't wear it in the shower, or there'll be nothing left by the time you're dry."

Aunt Maude looked disappointed. She slipped the ring back on and went to watch Jeopardy.

Zen crushed the pizza box and tossed it in the recycle bin. Aunt Maude had come home early from New York wearing an expensive diamond ring, and two goons from New York were looking for her. She'd better call Jeremy.

His machine said all our constables are busy, but if she'd leave her name and number, one would get right back to her.

*   *   *

"So I put the gravel in the fish tank, and those two little people, and the little house. I couldn't find a diver." Sasha smiled again. "And I found this in the Christmas section. Can I put it in too?" She held up a gold plastic snowflake. "It's pretty."

Zen stared down at the little tableau. Well, it was unlikely anyone would ever want to put salt and pepper in them anyway. "That's good work, Sasha. You're getting the hang of things."

"And I made some new signs for the bins."

Zen studied the notebook pages taped to the bins. They were drawings to indicate the contents. No words. That explained a lot. "I like the signs. We'll get some coloured markers and decent paper, and you can make big signs. And if you ever find a Gap shirt in the bags, you can have it."

Sasha's eyes danced, and she fled to the backroom.

The doorbell jingled. Rayette, in a fifties housedress from the Witherspoon collection, glanced up from the bins to see if it was competition.

"Feeling better, Helen?"

"Better?"

"After your touch of Fibster flu."

"Oh, yes, better, thanks."

"You wouldn't know anything about a diamond and ruby ring?"

"She didn't tell you what happened, did she? All right, I will. I'm sick of covering up for her indiscretions."

Helen came behind the cash counter and lowered her voice. "You know what she does in that wretched dress, don't you? Goes to a bar in search of some hokey pokey. So she got lucky, and by morning the guy was dead. Heart attack, by the way she described it. I can't stand this any more, Zen. I missed *Hair* because of her. Either you talk sense into her, or I'm going to take that dress and burn it."

The doorbell jingled. The two well-groomed men in silk suits entered, keeping their arms close at their sides so they wouldn't touch anything that might contaminate them. Zen glanced at the clock. Rif and Raf, right on time, as promised.

Helen backed away to the children's games bin.

"We arranged to meet with Maude Crombie here today," Sharif said. His eyes swung over to Helen. "Please produce Maude."

"Maude is sick today. Old ladies, you know. Can't take the excitement of a big trip. I am her representative. What can I do for you?"

Sharif and Rafael exchanged glances and nods. "Our

employer had occasion to meet Maude in New York," Sharif said. "He had something of value. We believe Maude is now in possession of this valuable commodity. We request its return." He showed her a glimmer of white teeth, but she wouldn't have called it a smile.

"I understand. Your employer, is he well?"

Sharif shrugged. "Old people."

*   *   *

"Maude, you are giving that ring back right now. I saw those men. They were scary. Zen stood up to them fine, but she won't last long when they start breaking her fingers."

"No way. It must be worth something if two guys drive up from New York in a Crown Victoria to get it back."

"How do you know what they drive?"

"I saw it cruising the neighbourhood. Are they after me?"

"You bet."

"I gotta get out of here. Let's go to Niagara on the Lake and catch a couple of plays. Go home and pack. I'll be ready in an hour." Maude hurried to the bathroom.

Helen heard the shower. Every year, the same fiasco. If she didn't do something right now, it would be the same next year. That damned dress.

*   *   *

Zen looked up from the rows of shoes she was straightening. Helen was sneaking in through the back entrance, through the storeroom. She sidled up to Zen and furtively passed her a crunched up plastic bag.

"Here. I took it off the sink while she was in the shower.

Give it back to them." She slipped back the way she came. Zen went to the window and watched.

A moment later, Helen scurried out of the alley and across the street, headed for the Wiggly Finger. The sign hanging outside the establishment said Marybeth's Wieners & Fries, and below it hung a sheet metal hand pointing to the door, with the jointed finger wiggling in the breeze. Spy headquarters. Helen had something else to hide.

In the store, Rayette, in a trench coat, was poking through the miscellaneous bin. Sasha emerged from the back room bearing another armload of ladies' dresses, which she managed to deliver to the dresses-on-hangers section.

The door opened, and Sharif and Rafael loomed in front of her again. "We have tired of being patient. This town is very small. You will deliver the commodity."

Zen hoped someone wasn't hiding a pair of matching earrings. She unclenched the plastic bag. "I believe this is the commodity?" She tumbled the diamond and ruby ring onto her palm.

Rafael picked it up, held it up to the light and muttered something in another language. He slipped the ring into his pocket.

Sharif sneered. "This is not the commodity we seek. However, it is proof Maude is the correct person. Come with us."

Zen found herself clamped between two silk suits, nearly suspended by strong fingers around her upper arms. A moment later she was pushed into the back seat of the Crown Victoria with Rafael, while Sharif drove. They knew exactly where she lived. She considered her options. "Do as she was told" seemed to be the best one.

Inside her living room, Sharif nodded to Rafael, who let go

of her arm. "Very well. Where is this Maude's bedroom?"

Zen pointed at the door to the left of the bathroom. Rafael disappeared down the hall. Zen heard the sounds of drawers yanked open, shoes tossed against a wall. It sounded like Buck a Bag day at the store.

Rafael stepped into the hall and glared at her. His hair was springing out of its gel prison in wiry tufts. He crossed the hall and entered her room. She heard the same sounds again. Rafael reappeared in five minutes, shaking his head and muttered something to Sharif.

"We will reconsider our options," Sharif said. "We'll be back."

They left the house, and the Crown Victoria steamed out of its berth.

Zen surveyed the disaster formerly known as tidy bedrooms. Aunt Maude's had been hit hardest, with nothing left hanging in her closet. If Rafael had taken anything, it would be difficult to itemize the loss. He appeared to have come out empty-handed. What would he have been hoping to find? Aunt Maude's credit cards? She sat down on the edge of the mattress, stripped clean in the search. The aunts had gone to New York for some theatre and fun. Aunt Maude had been up to her usual tricks, which Helen routinely ignored, but this time they came home early with their tails between their legs and a diamond ring on Aunt Maude's finger. Now a couple of guys from New York had tossed her home. How had they tracked Maude down? How many ladies on bus tours of the theatre district wander the bars in Seventies sequins?

Zen took her own turn at tossing Aunt Maude's room. The sequined dress was missing. Rafael had nothing lumpy up his sleeve when he left.

Helen.

Zen hurried back to the store. A Crown Victoria with New York plates was parked in the loading zone. Inside, Sasha stood by the window, looking like she was hoping a transporter would beam her up.

"Honest, I couldn't stop them," she said, clinging to a set of matching china dogs. "I told them I was the only one who could open the bags. They didn't listen."

"Who, Sasha?"

"Those two fancy men. And Helen."

"Is there anyone else here?"

"Someone called Maude. And Rayette."

"Where?"

"Rayette's trying on a dress. Maude is with Helen and the men in the back room. They were sure mad. Shook Helen until her false teeth fell out."

"Why Helen?"

"She was the one who brought in the bag of clothes. They said Maude had something that belonged to them, and Helen had put it in the bag of clothes."

Zen sprinted to the back room and was rained on by snow boots and mittens. Sharif and Rafael were ripping bags apart, scattering the contents indiscriminately. Rafael flung a pile of white at her that could only be Mrs. Witherspoon's flannel nightie collection. Helen and Aunt Maude clung to each other in the corner.

Zen hauled them out of the way. She lined them up next to the cash register. "Aunt Maude, you'd better confess. Helen says the guy died."

"It was natural causes." Aunt Maude thrust her hands on her hips. "Then SHE, who is supposed to be my best friend, takes my ring and my dress. My designer dress, that I bought in the seventies, and it still fits like a glove."

"Like a sausage, I keep telling you," Helen said.

"You took my dress and jammed it in a green garbage bag and left it here. My designer dress. I might never speak to you again, Helen Fray."

"It wouldn't be too soon, Maude Crombie. I've had about enough of that stupid dress."

Zen held a hand between them. "Time out. So those men are looking for your dress? That doesn't make sense. I can believe they tracked you down because of the dress, everyone would remember seeing you in it. Ask a few bus drivers, and pretty soon your address pops up. But why do they want the dress? What are you hiding?"

"Nothing. Honest. I don't know why they want the dress."

The dressing room door opened. Rayette stepped out encased in a red, white and blue sequined dress. "How much is this? I love it. Fits me like a second skin."

Aunt Maude sucked in her breath. "That's not for sale. That's mine. Zen, you get my dress back from her or I quit."

"I found it in Housedresses." Rayette said. "Fair game."

Zen stepped between Rayette and Aunt Maude before any ripping happened. "Aunt Maude, you tell me what's going on or I sell this dress to Rayette for two dollars."

Aunt Maude made a strangled sound. "Okay, okay, you win. I got up to pee at three-thirty and found the guy dead beside me. I panicked. Those goons had driven us to the hotel. I knew they'd be back in the morning. I wanted to keep the diamond, so I had to get out of there and get a cab back to our hotel. I didn't have much cash in my elephant purse so I went through his pockets. He had a lot of money. I took it. That's it. End of story."

Zen stared at her. "Rayette, that dress looks nice on you," she said over her shoulder. "You'd be planning to wear it to Bingo?"

"Okay, okay," Maude said, flapping her arms. "He had some stones in one pocket. I took them, too."

"Stones?"

"Pebbly things. Milky white but transparent. Dirty on some edges."

"And you thought they were—?"

"Uncut diamonds. I've heard stories about New York."

Zen glanced back at the storeroom. Clothing billowed out the door. She left Helen and Aunt Maude staring each other down and dragged Sasha over to the window. "Listen, in the bag where you found that dress Rayette is wearing, did you find a beaded elephant purse?"

Sasha nodded.

"Where did you put it?"

Sasha pointed to the hangers in the wedding dress section.

Zen flipped through the hangers until she found the green and yellow beaded elephant. She opened it. It was empty, save for a pebble in one corner. "Was there anything in it?"

"Yeah, some gravel. I'm not so dumb. Make somebody feel special."

Sharif and Rafael emerged from the storeroom. Sharif looked sweaty and uncomfortable. Rafael's hair was spritzed up like candy floss.

Sharif posed like a wrestler in front of Aunt Maude and Helen. "We have been unsuccessful in our search."

Rafael nudged him and pointed at Rayette. Sharif's eyes bugged out.

"I see you were not lying. We have been too late."

"I'll say you're too late, buddy," Rayette said. "I bought this fair and square for two dollars. Finders keepers."

"I think you might be looking for this." Zen held up the elephant purse.

Rafael snatched it from her hand. He looked inside, pulled out the sole stone, and showed it to Sharif.

"Where are the rest?" Sharif shook the bag in Aunt Maude's face.

"I dumped them," Sasha said. "Nobody goes to a wedding with a bag of dirt."

"Tell the nice man where you dumped them," Zen said.

"In the fish tank, with the other gravel."

Helen whipped her head around to the window display so fast Zen heard it crack.

"And where is the fish tank now, Sasha?" Zen asked.

"Constable Fray bought it. He said it would be calming and restful in the police station, when he had to take people in for questioning." She reached in her pocket and pulled out a five-dollar bill. She handed it to Zen.

Zen turned to Sharif. "I believe your work here is done. We won't detain you any longer."

Sharif straightened his jacket and marched out. Rafael followed, tall and strong and carrying the elephant purse.

The door jingled shut. Outside the window, the two men conferenced at the fender of the Crown Victoria, with much pointing at the police station.

The only sound in the store was the tumbling of snowsuits down a slippery slope of slashed green bags.

"Helen, I'm gonna kill you."

"Maude, I'm never going anywhere with you again."

"Oh yes, you are. You're going to the police station with me. You're going to talk your nephew into giving me back my diamonds."

The two women pushed each other out the door.

Zen grabbed the phone to give Jeremy the heads-up while they crossed the street.

Sasha turned to Rayette. "I don't think that's a lucky Bingo dress. I found the one Mrs. Witherspoon wore the night she won a thousand dollars. Come on, I'll show you."

When Zen got off the phone, the sequined dress was hanging in the overcoats section and Rayette primped in front of the mirror in a purple sateen square dance dress with a rhinestone yoke.

Zen smiled. "Sasha, I guess I need a new employee. It's time you learned how to handle the cash register. We're going to put little pictures on it so it will be easier to use. Rayette is going to give you two dollars for that dress. Rayette, you're going to be patient, because Sasha is new and it takes her a little while to catch on. But she's really good at making customers feel special."

Vicki Cameron's *short stories have appeared in the Ladies' Killing Circle anthologies,* Storyteller *magazine, and several German anthologies. Her young adult novel,* That Kind of Money, *was nominated for Edgar and Arthur Ellis awards. After a successful shopping trip to Frenchy's, a popular used clothing chain in Nova Scotia, Vicki felt the desire to capture the bins in a story.*

The Minstrel Boy

Barbara Fradkin

D r. David Browne turned slowly in place, scanning the
devastated street. The occasional moan of pain or frantic
mother's call could still be heard, but in the main a stunned
silence had descended upon the scene. The seriously wounded
had been transported to hospital, and the one dead man had
been removed by the police. The remainder huddled in the lee
of shops, cradling injured limbs and bloodied heads.

Three constables moved among them, taking witness
statements and stilling the last tremors of the deadly rage. City
workmen had already begun to clear away the bricks, tattered
banners and shards of glass that littered the streets, and
shopkeepers were venturing back to assess the damage.

"Haven't seen a riot like this in Ottawa since the 1860s,"
came a voice at David's elbow. He turned to find one of the
constables, breathless and sweaty beneath a patina of dust.
"Used to happen all the time when I were a boy, between the
Frenchmen and the Irish, or the raftsmen and the Bytowners.
But we was all hoping since the government came, folks would
settle down a bit."

As an Anglo-Irishman growing up in working-class
Montreal, David had seen worse, but the thought was no
comfort. The Fenians used to sneak across the Vermont border

every year to foment trouble at Orange Parades, and his older brother Liam, a staunch defender of the Empire, had come home twice nursing broken limbs but crowing about the number of traitorous Papist skulls he had cracked. David had hoped to find the old feuds less entrenched in Canada's fledgling capital city, but the carnage outside Upper Town's newest Catholic church was disheartening.

"It appears to have been the work of a few inflamed youths, however," he ventured with more assurance than he felt. "I haven't encountered many of the leadership from either side."

"Perhaps not," replied the constable. "But it's them leaders stir the lads up, and now a man's been killed, which makes it a very serious matter indeed. I don't suppose any of the lads volunteered any information while you were tending them, did they, Doctor? I've interviewed more than a dozen witnesses with na'ar a useful bit of information between them. They've all turned deaf and blind."

David shook his head. "Who was the dead boy?"

"No one's admitting, and he were beat so bad about the face it's hard to tell. All I found were this truncheon lying nearby." The constable removed a piece of wood from the accumulated debris in his cart. "I'm worried the lads know very well who he is and who did him in, but they've got their own form of justice planned. Know what I mean?"

David knew precisely what he meant, but as he turned the wood over in his hands, his answer died on his lips. It was part of a shaft, carved, oiled and sanded smooth. Although it was splintered and sticky with blood and dirt, he had no trouble recognizing it. With that recognition came a great despair.

Jimmy.

*   *   *

After he had treated the wounded, David urged his horse down Sparks Street towards the crowded tenements of Lebreton Flats, where Jimmy lived. All the while he feared what he would discover. Prayed that he was wrong. It seemed impossible that such a lyrical, lovingly fashioned piece of wood could have found purpose in the carnage of a common street brawl.

The first time David had seen the wood, Jimmy had been cradling it in his rough stableboy's hands, sanding the fine grain of its maple shaft. David had just returned to the boarding house from Dr. Petley's surgery, where he'd been assisting until he had sufficient funds to establish his own practice. His brother was still stubbornly refusing to underwrite what he regarded as David's folly in abandoning civilized Montreal for a dusty, treeless timber town. But David had found Ottawa a lively, if fractious, city with a shortage of doctors to attend to the new Dominion's burgeoning public service. He would prove Liam wrong yet, and for the first time use his own resources to establish himself.

His first move had been to purchase a horse and carriage so that he possessed the means to respond to calls from across the city. Widow Barnaby's boarding house had a generous stable at the rear, and David had first encountered Jimmy when he'd brought his new horse home. She was a small, wiry bay, sway-backed and no longer young, but beautiful nonetheless for being his very own. He scrutinized Jimmy's every move as the boy watered her and rubbed her down, singing a lilting Celtic ballad as he worked.

"My mother used to sing Irish songs when I was a boy," David observed. "But I haven't heard that one."

"Made it up meself," Jimmy mumbled, picking up a currying brush. Despite the boy's broad hands and ungainly limbs, something about his touch seemed tender.

"You use words well. Can you read?"

Jimmy reddened beneath his freckles. "Some. Not much call to."

"Jimmy!" a man bellowed from the adjacent room. "What're you yammering about out there! Get on with—" The head groom thrust his balding head through the door and snapped to attention at the sight of David. Deference erased the sneer of contempt from his face. "Dr. Browne! Jimmy ought to be fetching your carriage out the front entrance, sir."

"Thank you, Mr. Regan. In future he will, but today I wanted to oversee her care myself."

Hands clasped behind him, Mr. Regan inspected the horse with military solemnity. "If you have any concerns or complaints, doctor, please inform me immediately." He gave Jimmy a meaningful stare before taking his leave.

Jimmy bowed his tousled head as he resumed his chores, but the joy was gone from his step and the song from his lips. The following afternoon David stopped by the bookstore on a whim, and as Jimmy loosened Lady's traces, David laid his purchase down on the boy's favourite straw bale.

"This just came into the bookshop, and I thought you might enjoy it. It's the adventures of a young lad named Tom Sawyer."

Jimmy averted his gaze shyly without response, but the next morning the book had disappeared. When it reappeared on the straw bale a week later, David replaced it with *Gulliver's Travels* and then with a tale by the popular British author Charles Dickens. Over the spring, this informal tutelage slowly grew, away from the critical eye of the head groom. One morning when David arrived to fetch his trap, he found a notebook sitting on the bale. Jimmy was bent over a maple log, painstakingly whittling. David picked up the notebook, which was filled with a sprawling, clumsy hand. Jimmy focussed even more intently on his whittling.

"May I borrow this?" David asked. "The nights are long, and the company of my fellow boarders is sometimes wanting."

David interpreted Jimmy's buck tooth grin as acquiescence, and no more was said. When David settled into bed with the notebook, he found his intuition confirmed. The writing was ragged and the language rough, but the long rambling ballad itself was fascinating. Adventures on the high seas, discoveries of distant lands; a journey into a young man's dreams as he gazed out through the bars of the life to which he was born.

The ballad would not leave him. The next day David went to view a modest house on Daly Street. Houses in Sandy Hill were being bought by Ottawa's new professional families as quickly as tradesmen could erect them, and with its proximity to the hospital on Rideau Street, it seemed the perfect neighbourhood for a young physician to establish himself. The red brick house had room on the main floor for both a consulting room and a modest surgery, as well as ample quarters for himself upstairs. A third floor held sufficient space for domestic staff once he was able to afford them.

That latter qualification troubled him all the way back to the boarding house until he spied Jimmy hard at work at his carving. From the chunk of maple, the curved frame of a harp had emerged. A brilliant idea set David's hopes soaring.

"Jimmy." He tried to make his words sound casual. "I will be moving to my own house soon, and I will need someone to care for Lady, and perhaps to tend to some of the domestic affairs whilst I'm in surgery."

Jimmy barely paused, but his fingers fumbled over Lady's bridle.

"On the third floor, there's a room with space for a bed,

desk and gas lamp by which to write. I can't pay you much yet, but I can offer you room and board in exchange for your services. On one condition."

"Me ma needs me at home," Jimmy interjected, but David paid scant attention, for he had attended at Jimmy's mother's last confinement himself, and he knew there wasn't a square inch to spare in their cottage.

"On one condition," he repeated. "There's a small school two blocks from my home. I've spoken to the headmaster, and you may begin classes in September. There you will read not only Mark Twain and Charles Dickens, but Shakespeare, Thomas More, and all the great writers of history."

Jimmy flushed a mottled red, and David caught a momentary glint of moisture in his eyes. Briskly, David reached into his black bag. "There's no hurry to decide. Meanwhile try this cat gut on the harp; it should produce a better sound than horsehair on the lower strings."

Jimmy didn't meet his gaze nor reach for the suture thread, which David laid on his straw bale, while Jimmy busied himself rubbing down the tack. To save the boy further embarrassment, David retrieved his black bag and headed for the house.

"It's a long way," Jimmy murmured, almost out of earshot. "From me kin and me mates. I wouldn't know a soul."

David paused to reconsider the wisdom of his idea. Jimmy was a mere boy, fourteen at the most, rough-hewn and lacking the easy confidence that comes from breeding. David knew better than most how it felt to walk into a classroom of fashionably dressed and impeccably bred young men, not daring to speak lest his peasant grammar make him the laughingstock. In his shame, he'd even invented a father who had been a brave ship's captain lost at sea rather than own up to the drunken, penniless candlestick maker who'd blighted his youth.

By what perverse missionary zeal did he presume to drag this shy, reluctant boy along this same path? He retraced his steps to the stable, where he surprised the boy bent over his harp with the new cat gut. Jimmy thrust it aside and returned to cleaning the bridle.

"Jimmy, I know I'm Protestant, but I was a boy like yourself once, living in a shanty and apprenticed to a bootmaker. But I had a dream, and in this new country our fathers chose, we are all entitled to dreams. The Lord has given you a great talent and the means to fulfil whatever dream you will. But it must be your dream, not mine."

"Me Da's already worked hard to get me this position here. He won't accept charity."

David intended to arrange payment of Jimmy's tuition, so that he would not experience the derision heaped on the charity cases. "I'd expect you to work hard. I need a man I can rely on. Why don't I call on your father after church on Sunday, and discuss the arrangement with him?"

The boy's eyes widened. "He's a bit old-fashioned, is me da. Just so you know, he don't like words the way I do."

*   *   *

David had occasion to recall Jimmy's warning during his encounter with the boy's father that Sunday afternoon, for more apt words were never spoken. In the sweltering noon-day heat of June, he had been ushered to the only easy chair in the front room to face the man's stubborn, hard-bitten stare. A massive wooden crucifix dominated the tiny room, a palpable symbol of the divide between them.

"'Preciate the offer, Doctor," Mr. Donahue said. "But I got Jimmy a good position at Widow Barnaby's, with tolerable pay and a chance for advancement. What would he be learning from books at school?"

"He's bright, Mr. Donahue, and he's good with words."

"Oh, aye? Lot of good that is to the likes of us. I's a mill worker, and I'll not say I's ashamed of it, but I wants better for me sons. Jimmy's good with his hands, and he's got a way with animals. Widow Barnaby is right pleased with him."

"The head groom doesn't seem as enthusiastic."

Mr. Donahue was unperturbed. "Mr. Regan wants the job for his own brother's boy. A no-good layabout never done an honest day's work in his life."

"Nonetheless, it's not the happiest arrangement for the boy. I'm offering him a chance to tend my horse and go to school at the same time. Perhaps later to college so he can procure a position with the government."

Mr. Donahue said nothing, but his clamped jaw betrayed his contempt for that idea. David searched for a currency the man might value.

"I'll pay him, naturally. The same wage he earns at the stable, minus a modest room and board. Let him try it for the school term, after which, if he prefers, I'll ensure he's reinstated at Widow Barnaby's."

The father folded his thin, sinewy arms across his chest as if to bolster his defiance. "But he'll be no better than a servant boy, doing whatever chores you've a mind to ask him."

"I could teach him a great deal that could prove useful to him in later life, to help prepare him for..." Seeing a scowl of protest forming on Mr. Donahue's brow, David let his voice trail off. Assistance arrived from an unexpected direction.

"It would have to be a Catholic school," a sharp voice interrupted, and David turned to see an extremely stout woman filling the doorway to the back room. She was perspiring profusely as she mopped a stained dishrag over her brow.

Her husband glowered. "He's not going to no school."

"But he'd still get his wage, Jem, and we could use the room here. And you know how he is, writing his poems. Not much for man's work anyhow."

"My point. School's no place to toughen him up."

David debated the wisdom of intruding on the domestic discord and costing the father further loss of face. He sensed, however, that the mother was the force to be reckoned with in the family.

"It would be a Catholic school," he assured her.

"Not them Christian Brothers!" Effecting a strategic retreat, the father found another position to defend. "I don't want no French."

"It's an Irish school a mere two blocks from my new home in Sandy Hill."

"That's a long way off," the father countered. "When would he ever get time to come see his ma?"

"Every Sunday, so he can go to church and have Sunday dinner with the family."

Outmanoeuvred, the father cast about for a fresh avenue of protest, and into the breach leaped Mrs. Donahue, who bustled forward with surprising speed to usher David to the door. "Thank you for your interest, Dr. Browne. We'll think on it, and you'll have our answer within the week."

*   *   *

The first rumblings of trouble came on Dominion Day two days later. Half a dozen youthful revellers imbued with more spirits than common sense took to the streets from Darcy's Tavern in the wee hours of the morning, singing Irish freedom songs and setting the Union Jack ablaze outside the Bank of British North America. The following evening, when David returned from his hospital rounds, he found Jimmy seated on his customary straw bale, but his harp lay forgotten at his side, and he was immersed in a newspaper. When he glanced up, David beheld a resolute sorrow in the boy's gaze that quite took his youth away.

Jimmy shoved the newspaper behind the bale and jumped up to take David's horse. David leaned over to retrieve the paper, which he observed with distaste to be *The Sentinel,* the latest publication of the Loyal Orange Order. Based on the Dominion Day skirmish and a similar one in Toronto, the editor was making dire predictions about the resurgence of Fenianism and exhorting all loyal Canadians to march in the Orange Parade on July 12th in defence of the empire.

Jimmy watched him nervously. "It's Mr. Regan's, sir. I was just looking."

To David, it felt like a pestilence that refused to die. "Is there usually trouble at the Orange Parade up here in Ottawa?"

"Me da says there used to be fearsome fights back when he were a boy. There's not been much to it lately, but... There's talk of them marching up Kent Street past St. Patrick's Church."

"Most of it is just youthful ebullience fuelled by a drop too many, Jimmy. Best to just let them march to their hearts' content. Stay out of their way, and no trouble will come of it."

Jimmy merely averted his gaze and bent over Lady's hoof with exaggerated scrutiny. Sensing his doubt, David sought words to reinforce his point. "My own brother suffered a few broken bones in his youth before he learned that lesson."

"And me da's brother got his throat slit by an Orange farmer 'afore he had a chance to learn it," Jimmy replied quietly.

Shocked into silence, David took a moment to recover

before pointing out that was all the more reason not to perpetuate such ignorant, uncharitable attitudes. Jimmy shook his head.

"It's the Prods as is ignorant, Dr. Browne. Saying we're lazy and good for nothing but fighting, cheating and making babies. And July 12th—what is that anyway? They're celebrating the day their Protestant king defeated our Catholic one and took over our land. It's a day to rub our noses in it, that's what it is."

Jimmy's vehemence took David aback, but the truth of the boy's analysis could not be denied. It was an analysis shared by the Governor General and by many of the Orange leaders, who in the interests of reconciliation had recently called for an end to the parades. Regrettably, the bigoted zeal of some of the Lodges was not to be suppressed.

"For some," David agreed. "But many of the marchers are simply proud of what Canada stands for; hard work, loyalty and Christian fellowship, rather than the republican anarchy to the south of us."

Jimmy was not to be assuaged. "Is that why the parade is going to march right past our church? The Orange Hall is on O'Connor Street, and the parade should go straight up Bank Street from McLeod's farm. But like I said, they want to rub our noses in it. And if they go past St. Patrick's, we have to defend it, haven't we? We can't just watch."

David wanted to ask why not, but he sensed the futility of the question. He knew the passions of men and of boys who would be men. His brother Liam had been no more willing to ignore a gauntlet than Jimmy was now, and David had seen many heads cracked open for less.

Nonetheless, he tried a feeble rebuttal. "Remember that a war cannot begin if no one shows up for the battle."

"Then they break all the windows in the church or attack some poor old gran as she's heading to confession. They're looking for a fight from somebody, that's what me mates say."

David sat down on the straw bale and fixed a resolute eye on Jimmy. "Jimmy, listen to me. We come to many crossroads in our life, and the paths we choose should be based on where we want to end up and what we believe in our hearts is right. Not what our mates think, or what our uncles and our father believe, but what we ourselves, as one of God's many creatures, believe. Do you really want to square off against a handful of overheated fools, who are equally God's creatures despite their shortcomings? Are a few religious slurs or broken church windows worth the spilling of human blood?"

Jimmy did not reply; he merely picked up his harp and aimlessly plucked a string.

*　　*　　*

Now, ten days later, human blood had been spilled. As David drew near Jimmy's home, he found himself praying it was not the blood of a sensitive youth barely old enough to shoulder the mantle of war.

Before he even reached the house, he sensed the palpable fear on the street. Curtains were drawn, and in response to his knock, a gruff wary voice from within demanded his business. Only once he'd identified himself did the door crack open a few inches. Mr. Donahue's stony gaze met his.

"What do you want, sir?" Polite, but frigid.

David greeted him and asked if Jimmy were there.

The eyes didn't blink. "What do you want with him?"

"Is he injured? I'm afraid he might have been hurt in the fighting at the parade."

He heard a scuffling noise inside as the door jerked wider, and Mrs. Donahue elbowed her husband aside. "Why do you think he might be hurt?"

"The police found his harp broken amid the wreckage. It had blood on it."

Mrs. Donahue's eyes flew wide in horror, but her husband's held a glint of satisfaction. She boxed his ears. "See what you done, Jem!"

Mr. Donahue was less quick to draw conclusions. "But nobody saw him, hurt or otherwise?"

"No, but one man was killed whom they can't identify. What was Jimmy wearing?"

"Brown shirt and cotton britches," she replied, then shot an accusatory glare at her husband. "And your green sash."

David tried to picture the body on the street, but he couldn't distinguish any colours beneath the blood and dust. He didn't recall a sash of either green or orange, however. "He has not yet come home, I presume?"

"No," the mother said before her husband could stop her. She turned on him in fury. "Jem, there's no sense lying! Dr. Browne wants to help, and if something's happened to our Jimmy..."

"I would have heard!" Mr. Donahue retorted. "If Jimmy'd been the one to fall, our lads would have come to tell me."

"What have you heard?" David interjected quickly.

Mr. Donahue's stony look returned.

"You know who it was, don't you."

"I wasn't there."

"No, but I grew up in a neighbourhood like this. Nothing stays a secret very long."

"I can't help you, Doctor. But the neighbourhood is a bit touchy at the moment, so you'd best be off. I'll send word if I get news on Jimmy."

David stood his ground. He looked into the man's defiant eyes, considered the meaning of the silent streets and the drawn curtains. He remembered the constable's theory, and a sinister alternative began to dawn.

"It was an Orangeman who was killed, wasn't it, and you're all afraid they're going to retaliate."

Mr. Donahue said nothing, but Mrs. Donahue boxed his ears again. "Is that so? Don't worry, Doctor, I'll get to the truth of this!" She elbowed her way past him into the street where she shouted at a passing woman. "Bridget, do you know who was killed up at the church?"

Her husband bolted outside to drag her back. "Shut up, woman!"

She wrenched herself free. "Was it a Prod?"

He clamped his hand over her mouth. "Hush up!"

"Who was it, Jem!"

"It were Regan's nephew!" he snapped. "Isn't that bloody grand? The nephew of an Orange Grand Master."

She twisted in his grip. "And who killed him, then?"

"Inside the house, Meg!"

She blanched. "Our Jimmy?"

Mr. Donahue shot David a sharp look. "Don't be talking rubbish—"

She pressed her fist to her lips as if to silence her lament and allowed her husband to steer her back through the door. David shoved his hand against the door to prevent its slamming. He felt sick to his core.

"If Jimmy did it," he said, "or if Regan's boys even suspect he might have—he's in grave danger. They'll track him down, sooner or later."

"You're right about one thing, Doctor," Mr. Donahue said. "It don't matter if Jimmy done it or not, or if he were just protecting hisself. That's why he's gone."

"His best protection is the police."

"The police are full of Orangemen."

"He'll get a fair trial, innocent until proven guilty. And if it was self-defence—"

"Fair trial!" Mr. Donahue grunted with contempt. "The bloody Crown against an Irish Catholic? I'll let Jimmy take his chances on the run."

David's thoughts raced as he weighed his options. On the one hand, civilized society was predicated on a fundamental allegiance to the rule of law. On the other hand, under the cold and relentless scrutiny of the courtroom, a sensitive and impressionable fourteen-year-old boy would be hard pressed to articulate the blind, primitive instinct that overtook him in the chaos and panic of that moment. David took less than a minute to make his choice.

"Then let me help him. He hasn't a chance on his own in the countryside. Let me arrange passage to Montreal, where I have friends who can take him in. Montreal is a big city with plenty of opportunity for an intelligent lad who can read and write."

Mr. Donahue's eyes squinted warily, but Mrs. Donahue had recovered her spunk. "Tell him, Jem! This is not a trap!"

Mr. Donahue stared a long time into the hushed and fearful streets before reaching a decision. "There's a bluff hidden by trees on Major's Hill, where Jimmy likes to sit and write his tales. I'm to meet him there once I have money and a plan."

*   *   *

When David arrived back at the boarding house to pick up supplies for Jimmy's escape, the head groom was nowhere in evidence, and one of the general maids met his carriage instead. Excitement pinked her cheeks and loosened her customary reserve.

"Been a bit of a fuss this afternoon, sir," she bubbled as she grasped Lady's reins. "Mr. Regan's nephew were killed at the parade, so he's gone off to tend to things. The police was here to talk to him just now, showed him a piece of wood from the fight. We could all see right off it were from Jimmy's harp, but Mr. Regan never said a word. Right nice of him to protect Jimmy like that. After that, he saddled up and rode off, to warn Jimmy likely."

David froze in his tracks. "Does he know where Jimmy is?"

"Oh, aye. In his half day off, Jimmy always goes to that bluff above the locks." She pointed east towards Major's Hill. "Sings about it all the time."

David leaped back into his carriage and careened up Sparks Street, scattering street vendors and swirling dust in his wake. Despite the sun, he felt cold with dread. Regan had been a sergeant in the colonial forces during the Fenian wars and was an accomplished cavalryman. He rode a swift, agile mount, and even more chilling, he was reputed to be a crack shot with a pistol.

As David entered the park, the sinking sun cast a shaft of light across the river below, and the spires of Parliament soared darkly against the sky. People milled everywhere, children chased one another in zigzags through the shrubbery, and an ice cream vendor shouted his wares. Up ahead David spotted Mr. Regan's horse tied to a rail, and his heart leaped in his chest. He secured Lady to the rail before proceeding on foot along the bluff, keeping a keen eye out for the head groom. As he ran, he scanned each copse of trees for the frightened boy.

Nothing.

He doubled back, racing against time. Past a pair of clandestine lovers, a family snoozing under a tree. Then a patch of brown caught his eye through the brush. As he drew nearer he recognized Jimmy, crouched low with his eyes rivetted on the crowded lawns. Waiting. Searching for his father's familiar face.

David crashed through the underbrush towards him with relief. The boy spun around, spied him, and to David's astonishment burst panic-stricken from the cover of the bush. He had fled only ten yards across the grass before a shot cracked the air. Women screamed. Jimmy leaped into the air, limbs flailing, then crashed to the ground. Horrified, David whirled around to glimpse Mr. Regan stuffing his pistol back into his waistband as he scurried out of sight down the path.

David raced to Jimmy's side, flung himself down and vainly tried to staunch the blood pouring from his head into the dusty grass. Already Jimmy's eyes were dimming.

"Dr. Browne..."

"Why?" David's throat constricted with despair. "I was coming to help you. Why did you run?"

"Well..." Jimmy's eyes flickered. "You're Orange, aren't you?"

As if that were the sum of it, he slipped away.

Barbara Fradkin's *work as a child psychologist supplies ample inspiration for murder. Her short stories haunt numerous anthologies and magazines, including the four previous Ladies' Killing Circle anthologies, and her detective novels* (Do or Die, Once Upon a Time *and* Mist Walker) *feature the exasperating Inspector Green, whose love of the hunt often interferes with family, friends and police protocol.* Once Upon a Time *was shortlisted for an Arthur Ellis Award in the category of Best Novel in 2002.*

When the Fat Lady Sings

There was an opera singer from Perth
And a critic who made fun of her girth.
"Her notes get flatter
As she gets fatter."
Now he's being spoon-fed by the nurth.

Joy Hewitt Mann

Song Credits

The titles of the stories in this book were taken from existing songs. We have done our best to give proper credit for composition, publishing and copyright.

Knocking on Heaven's Door: by Bob Dylan, Ram's Horn Music, copyright 1973

There's No Business Like Show Business: From the Broadway show *Annie Get Your Gun*, Irving Berlin Music Company, copyright 1946

Don't Cry for Me Argentina: From the musical *Evita*, music by Andrew Lloyd Webber, lyrics by Tim Rice, copyright 1976

When the Red, Red Robin: by Harry Woods, 1926

I'm Forever Blowing Bubbles: Words and music by Jaan Kenbrovin and John William Kellette, Remick Music Corporation, copyright l950

Brian's Song: From *The Hands of Time*, music by Michel Legrand, lyrics by Marilyn & Alan Berman, copyright 1972

Summertime: From the opera *Porgy and Bess* after the novel *Porgy* by DuBose Heyward, music by George Gershwin, libretto by DuBose Heyward and Ira Gershwin, 1935

Rock-a-Bye Baby: Traditional lullaby, author unknown

Let Me Drive: Music and words by Georgette Fry, copyright 2000, Spare Rib Records (SOCAN). Lyrics used by permission.

Them There Eyes: by Maceo Pinkard, William Tracey, Doris Tauber. Published by Bourne Company, copyright 1930

Two Little Girls in Blue: by Charles Graham. Published by Spaulding and Kornder, 1893

When Laura Smiles: Elizabethan madrigal, words by Thomas Campion, 1567-1620, music Philip Rosseter, 1568-1623

Three Coins in the Fountain: Words by Sammy Chan, Music by Jules Styne, Cathy Music Co., copyright 1954

The Night Chicago Died: by Peter Robin Callander and Mitch Murray, published by Dick James Music Ltd. (PRS)/PRI Music Inc. (ASCAP)/Universal Songs of Polygram (BMI), copyright 1974, Intune Lts.

Wake Up Little Suzie: by Boudleaux and Felice Bryant, Acuff-Rose Publications, copyright 1957

From This Wicked Fall: by the abbess Hildegard of Bingen, ll79

Hokey Pokey: Written by Roland Lawrence LaPrise in the late 1940s and recorded by The Ram Trio in 1949. After the Ram Trio disbanded in the 1960s, Roy Acuff's publishing company bought the rights. Copyright 1950, Acuff-Rose Music Inc.

The Minstrel Boy: Thomas Moore from *Irish Melodies, Volume 5*, ca. 1820.

RendezVous Crime
Distinctly Canadian Mysteries

H. Mel Malton
The Polly Deacon Mysteries

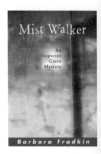

Barbara Fradkin
The Inspector Green Mysteries

Lou Allin
The Belle Palmer Mysteries

Mary Jane Maffini
The Camilla MacPhee and
Fiona Silk series

Jessica Burton
The Jenny Turnbull Mysteries

*Information on these titles and
more at www.rendezvouspress.com*